THE
FALLEN

THE
FALLEN

STEVE BARRATT

Matador
Unit E2 Airfield Business Park,
Harrison Road, Market Harborough,
Leicestershire. LE16 7UL
Tel: 0116 2792299
Email: books@troubador.co.uk
Web: www.troubador.co.uk/matador
Twitter: @matadorbooks

ISBN 978 1803132 976

British Library Cataloguing in Publication Data.
A catalogue record for this book is available from the British Library.

Printed and bound by CPI Group (UK) Ltd, Croydon, CR0 4YY
Typeset in 11pt Adobe Garamond Pro by Troubador Publishing Ltd, Leicester, UK

Matador is an imprint of Troubador Publishing Ltd

It is with all my heart I wish to thank you all, I hope above anything else you enjoy Wicker's story as much as I have done writing it.

Special thanks and love to those who have supported me so much on this journey. Celeste, Tony, Amelia and Jackie without your belief I'd have never reached this point. To my two beautiful children, again this one's for you…

Finally I'd like you all to always believe in the power of a dream. You never know where it will take you…

Steve Barratt

ONE

Morning has always felt a bittersweet gift to me, given thankfully every day to most, strived to reach for others, but in its simple act, greatness ensues.

As the sun rose this day it had a rival; pushing ever forward to reach its rightful place above life itself, the sun's rays struggled to win the battle with the ever-turbulent clouds which were forming. Seemingly a titanic struggle formed above me, warmth fighting chilled summer rain.

Eventually, as with all worthy competitors, a balance was reached; the sun rose high as no mere mortal thing can stop such a wonder, but the rain continued to fall. Like a troubled teenager it refused to relent, carrying on, regardless of logic or need, it just did what it needed to do.

The day continued as the morning had started, clouds continuing to form, at first hazily but rigour gave them form, then power; only to be simply parted by the strength of the sun's summer warmth.

An onlooker might have said it was a battle of the gods themselves, fighting over worlds, over love, over a loss of an irreplaceable artefact, but in truth it was far greater a battle, nature against nature, something even gods avoid.

As the summer rain broke, lightly at first, but gaining confidence in its abilities to succeed, the early morning skies above gave way to a heavier downpour. Slowly gaining power, deciding every living thing under the greying skies should feel its force, it found its way easily to where I was sheltering under the canopy of the trees.

It seemed that it strived harder to reach every dry patch of earth it could find, as if its very future remained destined to forever move forward. By now it seemed that no patch of earth was untouched by the force of the rain; in its battle to succeed it was winning easily, unrelentingly marching onwards to a greater glory only available to know in the mind of the storm itself.

The freshening wind that travelled with it was driving the rain to its goal and, after long hot summer days, I and the surrounding flora and fauna found its moisture pleasant to everyone, everything it touched.

Either knowing it had succeeded in its battle, or pausing for dramatic effect, if a rainstorm could achieve that desire, it seemed to relent its power slightly, allowing the warmth of this once beautiful summer morning to penetrate every nuance of life itself.

In truth both sun and rain contrasted beautifully, forming a perfect moment seldom reached in life, all appeared perfect for a split second and all of life thrived to maintain its beauty, knowing as fast as it appeared that it would soon be gone forever.

~

I had sat that day, as for many days before, underneath the suddenly cloud-filled sky, patiently waiting. Closing my eyes for a second to allow the warm zephyr to brush the stillness from my aching body, I realised I hadn't moved a muscle for an hour or more now, knowing that the slightest movement might give my prey the advantage it needed in avoiding me.

I'd waited, sitting in this very spot, many times all through my young life so far, so knowing eventually prey would venture out into the clearing in front of me. So as soon as the wind intensified and the rain started to become heavier once more, silently shifting my position I crouched back further into cover, continuing my seemingly eternal watch.

Looking at the clearing in front of me was like staring at a favourite object; we all in life have things we cherish, things passed to us by friends or family, things unexplainably linked in to our very worth.

We never realise sometimes how we cherish these things, often placing them on high pedestals in our mind, if not in reality, then away from prying hands or questions.

We link part of ourselves it seems, in memories, whether it allows us to strongly reach for happier times, and fonder thoughts. Like a place to stay in our lives, expanding ourselves sometimes isn't enough, or able to be achieved, so we save moments to hold them safe for us.

How often I'd stood here, a place in time, not a tiny ornament to caress, to hold, had been limitless to myself; too many a time to recall correctly, but memories flooded into me here, every pore filled, drenched even, same as the ground around me. I'd named this place Gold Maple.

Honestly this place was a refuge, sanctuary if you will, from the worries we all succumb to in time, I merely a boy trying to become a man; it seemed I'd travelled many roads already. Not all memories are cherished, literally, some are deceitful, dishonest, but we cherish them anyway, unable to find a way, to place them down without showing a hole in one's own being.

For a young man who held the family's responsibilities, hunting was not only a necessity, but a way of life. This ground, my ground, was merely a patch of worn-away forest, but it allowed both my duties and my sanctuary to merge. My thoughts were my own here, the earth, the very forest around me, accepted me as its own.

This humble patch was approximately fifty square feet, cleared by nature itself, its numerous animal tracks criss-crossed so many times that eventually over the years all the tracks seemed to merge into one expanse of worn-down patchy grass; barren in places, with colours ever-changing with the seasons, or in certain light, encapsulating the entire spectrum of colours in its beautiful extreme. It showed itself in many ways to be the same as any other patch of cleared forest, but holding me in its silent majestic thrall; it was here I'd hidden as a small boy upon the news of my father's death.

This was the place I'd run to, not into the grieving arms of relatives, not the consoling arms of friends; no, it was here I'd cried, till it seemed my very soul leaked out. Maybe that was why I came back to retrieve the unobtainable; myself.

This place still had odd, slightly overgrown patches here and there; someone not knowing the area, just walking past, might mistake it for an old long-gone dwelling, collapsed and ruined in time, long forgotten only to be stumbled upon by chance, whose materials had been cleared away and reused, building another structure, taking its memories with it, to again start a new place in its life.

Or maybe just a shaded part of the flora, unlucky in its placement, never gaining the full share of the sun's warmth or the rain it needed to flourish, so simply weathered away by time.

I placed down a mark in my mind during my hiding here all those years ago, and without knowing, it pulled me back time after time. Sometimes I'd arrive unknowingly, summoned to this place, as not only did I want to be here; the very soil under my feet needed me to be present.

It's hard to explain to oneself why we choose the paths we follow; knowledge helps, it is said, and in that it's correct, but if we always travelled paths others had followed, we would never truly own our identity. Surely we walk where we feel safest most of the time, allowing our adventures into the unknown, anchoring our true selves in familiar places.

The knowledge gained from mistakes is a powerful weapon to all. The owner of the mistake has been given a choice, if they're lucky, sometimes able to erase or change the error; knowledge gained here is worth a great deal more than knowledge passed through words alone. Sometimes the smallest, hardest fought for information is far more valuable than the ornaments we cherish so. In my thoughts, my insecurities, and all my successes I've learnt my anchor was deeply planted in the soul of the earth around me in this place.

Whilst spending many an hour in my solitude here had shown me sanctuary, it had also shown me the worth of patience; fleeting normally in youth, it is a skill highly underestimated by many. Possession of it in fact is a far greater gift, one achievable by all, but obtained by few.

It was with this patience I sat now. Gavriel had been merciful recently, allowing his students to work on their offerings, and carvings, not setting particularly tough challenges this week. I half wondered if something was amiss. Gavriel wasn't normally so lax in his teachings to miss an opportunity to gift us the pleasure of extra work. Being a part of the White Banner held responsibilities; we no longer were looked upon as children, now we were walking our path, our path to manhood. Colony members nodded more solemnly now, I realised as I passed by, they knew the challenges set before us, they knew soon we too would join the brotherhood set to protect them.

Realising my mind had been drifting in thought, I brought my mind fully back into focus, back into the task in front of me, and renewed my efforts to ignore the clenching of muscles in my lower legs folded beneath me.

Focusing allowed the sounds of nature to return to my thoughts; sometimes trying to ignore a sound, tuning out an annoying thought, allowed distraction the doorway it needed, and once in, hard to remove and close the door behind.

Patience had always come easily to me, especially here, and I found it easy to concentrate hard at my studies, often enjoying the praise gained from my mentor.

Gavriel mostly seemed pleased with my achievements in the tasks he'd set out for me, striving to praise, or console if things hadn't worked to the best of my abilities. Always pushing us with a fervour some would see as hard and unyielding, but to me and my fellow White Banner students, a force to learn and grow from.

Gavriel was an honest teacher; as befits an honest man, he was bigger than himself, a strong man, a humble man, someone who the whole colony respected. His place within the colony was unquestionably at the highest pinnacle; our colony had no real structure difference than the next colony along the eastern side of our world, but with Gavriel came an acceptance that we were truly blessed with a powerful leader to guide us.

Often travelling between colonies to assist with disagreements, treaties offered in place of trade routes disrupted, Gavriel's presence was always at the forefront of most aspects of life.

Previous lives often fall within us to stay hidden, it is said, seeking refuge in new facades, walls easily built around them to hide away, forgotten sometimes even by the person within whom they hide. To a point we all hide aspects of our lives, whether to forget or to simply discard without littering the here and now. Gavriel was no different.

His previous lives were not so easily concealed, though; from stories often still told his warrior feats were stories of legend, unrelenting of his prowess in battle. Sometimes, listening as a child growing up, magical in their retelling. If all the tales of Gavriel's past were true, he'd walked many different paths indeed.

He now held the title of warrior priest, a teacher of all young colony men; a man once feared by enemies, now stood proud and true in his quest for peace, a large man of not only physical strength, but mental fortitude which was unbreakable.

Previous tales of his ability as a warrior were legendary to all who gathered around the dark winter night campfires, adding tales they had heard, or had been passed around from village to village, making Gavriel sometimes larger than life itself.

This said I not only respected Gavriel but also looked up to him as a friend and a teacher, often seeking him out to spend time just in his company.

Today's lesson was away from the woodland classroom. This I was pleased about. As the fulfilment ceremonies grew closer I found myself retreating somewhat into myself, barriers set to avert questions of progress or possible failure.

I was actually coping well in all tasks set before me, and the forest was an excellent place to learn, surrounded by nature itself. It led to calm thoughts and becoming at one with yourself, allowing time to process my thoughts into actions. Although I enjoyed the dark rich forest classroom, I always felt more relaxed in self-learning, preferring to be allowed to wander amongst the edges of the forest, which I know like the lines of my hands themselves.

This said, the classroom had its good points, unachievable to a young man alone; even the most cellular of fellows seeks companionship at times. The classroom allowed this companionship, fellowship may I say, all present seeking true self-worth with half an eye on friends' achievements, hopefully mirroring one's own.

This idyllic setting was set so far into the centre of the forest little rain penetrated here, the huge leafy canopy above saw to this; although leading to a darker abode to study in, it also gave sanctuary to the students, making them feel closer together, safe to practise their teachings, without interference, you could say the true home of the White Banner.

~

I sat watching a single raindrop as it worked its way down a leaf it had landed on, once again realisation pinched me back into this reality. Finding my concentration levels wavering I focused in on that tiny raindrop. It moved precariously towards the very tip of the leaf, hesitated as though scared to fall; for an instant it appeared to know it had an existence, sudden realisation that life was precious as an elderly person does fighting for a last breath, then tossing this thought aside like a young man reaching his full acceptance on his fulfilment day leaping off the leaf tip.

Watching it fall ever downwards I was amazed how its shape continued to change from a small blob into a beautiful teardrop, elongating all the time, finally landing in the small puddle which had formed whilst the rain had been falling. Graceful in flight, a minuscule moment of beauty, retraced millions of times in a simple rainstorm but rarely noticed, nature has ways of showing strength in the smallest act.

I wondered when it came to my acceptance on fulfilment day if I could leap and fall as beautifully as that tiny fearless raindrop. Would being upon the edge looking down scare my senses into retreat, would faith desert me when I needed it most. I wondered honestly if I could be accepted.

The alternative I couldn't contemplate, sitting here so peacefully, hoping that I too could easily muster as much courage as one of nature's tiny creations. I must trust my own ability to jump as easily as that little raindrop had.

I continued to watch as the ripples in the small puddle sent perfect ever-expanding circles outwards, shooting, following each other in perfect harmony, only to find the edge of the puddle stemming their freedom from reaching further, till eventually all was still, except the slight nodding of the leaf above the only reminder that the beautiful natural world around me continued to show its grandeur in small acts.

Suddenly hearing a small rustling ahead, I sat back, becoming one with the cover I was hiding in; at the back, on the very edge of the clearing a young leveret ventured forward. Either with the confidence of youth, or the misleading cover of the falling rain, it had decided to push forward towards the cool crisp water forming in the very puddle I'd been watching.

Without a sound, unobtrusively with one fluid motion I removed my light hunter's bow from my lap. Notching an arrow with the quiet grace of a well-travelled hunter I waited, unsure if my prey had heard me. I waited still, scared to breathe.

It occurred to me that it was a young male hare, probably a summer's old, but perfect for my needs.

The young hare sniffed the air. Unsure for a second, it tensed, but again its curiosity or maybe just its thirst made it continue forward; reaching its head to the edge of the puddle it dipped down, taking its first long draught of cool water.

With this the arrow was loose, only the tiniest audible twang of the fortified deer tendon still reverberating in my ear as the arrow made its target. As quickly, it seemed, as the arrow flew, I was seated beside my quarry. The sudden explosive reaction seemed to shatter the beautiful scene laid out in this place, the speed of the change from serenity to bloodshed would seem cruel in its simplicity but this was no simple act, it had been essential for both food, and the successful completion of the task given to me that day.

As I retreated to dry cover out of the rain it seemed once again that the wilderness' peace took over and the surroundings allowed my grace to skin, gut, and prepare the catch for Gavriel's approval.

Working methodically the leveret was skinned, keeping the fur intact and whole; just a single puncture wound where the arrow has impacted cleanly through the skull was evidence that this animal hadn't met a natural passing. The meat was quickly boned and wrapped in leaves to keep moist, the said bones tied together to make a good strong broth or stock later. Mother, I knew, would be pleased, and thanking Rai I continued with packing away my equipment.

Meat luckily wasn't exactly a rarity around the colony. Many game animals surrounded the encampment and the woods were in times abundant in game; foraging, too, was in plenty as the seasons waned.

The most practised of skills amongst the young men of the colony had to be gaining fish from the streams. This was not only a favourite pastime, allowing us precious relaxation, but gained much needed resources our families needed. The young men of the colony often claimed to have nearly caught a behemoth trout and challenged each other in good-hearted competition regularly.

I was becoming quite an adept hunter and loved fishing but Peshy, my friend, was an outstanding fisherman, almost always beating the biggest fish, with an even bigger smile on his face.

As the rain continued to fall steadily, with the clouds showing no signs of relenting their task of shedding their fill, it seemed to the simple onlooker as if the entire sky's colour washed away with the very rain it carried within.

The sky, uniformly grey, tinged only at the edges with a lighter hue, seemed to know its true form; clouds dispersing broke away then reformed in a quest to drench the world below them. I started to tidy away my hunter's butchery tools. These were gifts, simply made by me due to necessity.

I'd always carried a small fine-bladed saw, a gift from my mother in my first year of studies. It was normally for larger game but was very adaptable in its use.

I'd included three sharp knives, of various sizes, a small handmade cleaver, and several clips, again for pinning skin away from meat on larger game. The handles of all my tools, like most tools used by the men of our colony, had become very personal to me; carving small features into the handles gave me self-worth. Simple tools but tools I'd made for me, finished to my want, my liking, things unable to be bought or traded.

Cleaning as I went, these were all placed back carefully in my hunting sack, along with the rolled pelt, and the tied leaves holding the bounty of the hunt carefully within.

Purposefully, I unslung my small hunter's bow, again placed everything into its place into my sack, and I started my journey back home.

The sky had become darker still, but that said I knew my way home enough that being blindfolded wouldn't hinder me, often in fact facing this very journey in the dead of night, with only then the ragged starlight through midnight clouds for occasional fleeting light.

Seeking shelter from the rain under the trees as I went may have added time to my journey, but rather than heading to the easier open ground at least I remained relatively dry.

Stretching as I walked helped to relax my muscles, taut from the day's stillness of waiting, and I thanked Rai again for my luck in catching my bounty, for giving me the knowledge I needed to succeed. Slowly but surely, I ventured onwards towards home, enjoying the crisp clean air given to me during refreshing summer rain.

Entering another small clearing very close to the colony I could start to hear the sounds of daily life, small children playing, sounds of village life flourishing, and turning left through a tiny gap through trees at the edge of the clearing, entered the colony's encampment.

Walking along, several villagers paused their daily tasks, to say hello, nodding their pleasure to Rai, I'd returned safely home. The large group of colony members were mostly a friendly bunch, acknowledging with head nods, smiles or just a wave of their hand.

I'd grown up amongst these people and had no fear to walk among them, being a part of the next generation, Young men such as I were seen as the future, and village life often centred on the young men of the colony.

It was, in truth, a slight relief that this year there were five who were facing their colony's fulfilment day, not just me.

Fulfilment was the highest honour a young man could achieve; it was the day that the village elders and Rai himself granted you the passage from youth to full manhood.

Aged sixteen, I'd planned for this coming year all my life, it seemed. On my seventeenth name day I'd be chosen to step forward and become a man; this itself was nothing special, as many walks of life show pleasure in celebrating years of birth, but in the colony here the fulfilment of manhood took extra responsibilities.

Not only were you passing into manhood, but with Rai's blessing you would be paired to one of your deity's most precious creations, a dragon.

From around the age of ten, the youth of the colony started training for the fulfilment but from birth, in reality, a boy was seemingly pushed ever onwards to glory.

Fulfilment showed not only that had you travelled the path of righteousness, but you had fought hard to become a man, learnt lessons of humility, become a provider for your family and extended colony members. But the most important step taken was your belief in Rai and all he created.

Sighing deeply, air rushing in and out with the worries of a young man facing uncertainty, it seemed to me that I'd thought very little of other things recently. Fulfilment day was only four months away and even nearer for Peshy.

Peshy was oblivious to the worry, it seemed, so making sure that the balance in life stayed correct, I'd taken his worry for him, something I'd not meant to do, but which now lifted couldn't be placed back down.

Peshy and I had grown up together in the colony. Living near each other you could easily suggest that we'd bonded straight away; walking the paths from home to class it had first seemed to me that Peshy was the best at everything we tried to do.

Naturally gifted with a bow, expert at fishing, slightly bigger, slightly stronger, slightly faster, always first into trouble. This annoyed me immensely as we grew; always striving to be the best but coming second, it seemed to me unfair that no matter how hard I tried, how much I'd achieved, Peshy won out the day. It had surfaced one summer's day, not too long after my father's passing; it was either my final shortcomings that gave me no other choice, or the fact that my grieving had turned to anger and hatred, coming to a head in one act I couldn't bear any longer, when Peshy had won a running race in front of our friends, taunting me with second place again.

Annoyance with oneself can be used to push to succeed, making striving for a perfection or goal easier to reach, with added incentive to progress; anger, though, shows only an educated soul it has weaknesses, and can turn the best inward into self-doubt and hatred.

I have angered honestly too many days in life, giving far too much time over to its meaningless flaws; this day was no exception, but one I force myself never to forget.

Why that day above others made me weaker I'll never truly know and the fight between the two us had only been interrupted by Gavriel himself, overhearing the noise created by shouts of encouragement from fellow friends around us.

Acts like these seem to release an inner animal from within us, friends become allies, enemies become tormentors, each baying for success, but all failing to rise above the actions played out to show mercy when it's needed the most. Still today occasionally I rub my chin in deep thought, remembering the memory of the beating I received that day. Now again today old thoughts of going second resurfaced as thoughts of Peshy's fulfilment day coming first seemed to taunt once again.

As if he could hear my very thoughts and memories, Peshy walked around the corner straight into view, instantly grabbing me with a vice-like bear hug, smiling as he spilled out his successful hunting trip tale of the day.

Thoughts again turned back to that fight years ago for me and I wondered how I could have been so jealous of this man I called my best friend today. How could I look back and not see the friendship that had grown from that very day? That final act of sheer malice had changed both our lives forever.

From that day, instead of laying blame for my losses on Peshy, blaming second place to bad luck or chance, Gavriel had shown me the error of my ways.

Gavriel had stopped the fight merely by his presence, with the circling crowd running away to escape the punishment surely about to be handed out. Gavriel just stood and watched.

Both I and Peshy stood still, shaking, afraid, anger still coursing through us, fearing the wrath that would surely follow. Gavriel asked but a simple question that day to both of us as one; "Why waste strength and energy on a task that gains no advantage to either of you?"

"Wicker, you fight because you feel humiliated and wronged, Peshy, you fight to prove you're better, and must win to show face. Neither gains you true worth, but together your strength combined is a powerful ally to your work. You have both been stupid this day, showing that your intelligence had been dulled by emotion; you have shown no faith in your fellow man or Rai himself. Punishment will be a month at each other's side, to show humility to each other, to help each other in your daily lives, to show you Rai's mercy."

Looking back how we had both hated that punishment

at first, glaring at each other, anger and frustration a bubbling furnace, always it seemed just under the surface of our daily activities. Peshy had been the better man in those days; he accepted his punishment with a grace that showed him to be the man he would become.

On the fourth day of our punishment, after a particularly dry, hot day toiling, gathering in the harvest for the colony, Peshy reached over to share his water with me, begrudgingly, but surprised the most, I accepted not as a sign of friendship but from the need to quench a drying thirst that was holding me under its spell. I drank deeply.

It was on that day that we truly spoke to each other, at first about the dry, seemingly never-ending work, but progressing into secret hopes for our studies, the needs of our time, and how much truly we did have in common. Once a barrier is broken down in life sometimes it's harder work to build it back up, something we all do from time to time, but Peshy and I neither had the energy or the hatred anymore to work that hard, so we accepted each other's company in a way not offered by either before.

Since that day friendship had become an unbreakable bond between us, Peshy, still always striding to be the best but welcoming competition, showing himself to be not only strong but a worthy ally.

I, too, had striven to be the best I could be, and had learned to accept my weaknesses, always trying to turn them into strengths.

At the end of the month, in truth it hadn't felt like punishment at all. Seeking each other out to spend the day in each other's company had become a habit, which continued long after we were freed from Gavriel's task.

Today Peshy, too, carried his hunting sack, bulkier than mine and leading thoughts to larger game acquired, also, I knew with a smile, rammed with his tools rather than placed as was his normal way. Peshy seemed always hastening to take the next step before settling his mind in the present, wondering what tomorrow held, not noticing the beauty of the day given. Tomorrow, I have learnt, is not a guarantee, no rich man nor king can command it; tomorrow is best seen as a blessing, but also can be a curse for others, striving towards it, forgetting today is a dangerous goal to set for oneself, something both Peshy and I had debated and disagreed on many a time.

Peshy felt alive in the chase of excitement promised, with tomorrow another chance to succeed in his tasks, in this our biggest difference stood for all to see. Please forgive the innocence of youth in Peshy over this matter; I sometimes wished I, too, could throw the imagined shackles from my mind and plunge headfirst into the current of what will be will be, but as much as I tried to, I always returned to sense.

I wondered if, after my father's passing, a piece of me had travelled that unknown road with Father, forever distant, unknown to the living, whether we reached a place we would all converge again and meet. As Peshy and I walked home in each other's company, both successful in that day's hunt, we agreed, after meat for the home pot had been delivered, to see each other later. Peshy thumped my arm as we parted at the fork in the well-trodden path near our homes, striding on, hurrying to continue tasks which needed completion before it got too late.

TWO

Continuing along, I walked the dirt path, hardened with time after many people had walked this way throughout the years. Climbing the gradient towards home, I started to crest the hill that surrounded our homestead. Trees which looked as if they'd guarded this land for an eternity came into view, as familiar to me as loved ones' faces.

As always happened to be the case, my sister, Acacia, was waiting for me. Either we shared a sixth sense, linking us together that I didn't know about, or her continued patience mixed with sheer luck meant she was always close by on my return, racing downhill fast to meet me at the bottom of our homestead's entrance, as always wearing her roughened clothes, covered in dirt, leaving a dust trail as she ran. Our mother was a proud woman, who made her best of every situation, bringing the two of us up on her own for many a past year, but no matter how she tried to turn my sister into a neat sensible little girl, she would have none of it.

Acacia had a will, a strength, powerful for one so small, but also a love within that showed no boundaries either. If I was the introverted, somewhat shy sibling, Acacia was the opposite, demanding the attention of all present, always joking, in a happy, playful mindset.

Don't think that our mother was trying to change either Acacia or me, she was a stoic individual, full of love, striving, if I look back, maybe to give us more, to try to right the wrong of father's early demise, somehow feeling that it was her fault, or that if we were occupied more we wouldn't see or feel the hurt she still held trying to protect us.

Love definitely wasn't withheld from us, and as children we knew we were loved.

Being older, I remembered my father, remembered the love he also placed inside us, and understood the hurt my mother had taken into her very soul; if not exactly the same, it was a bond we seldom revealed but both knew existed. Acacia, on the other hand, had few memories of Father, being but a mere infant at the time he left us.

Possibly because she lacked a male figure, or maybe due to late-night talks occasionally held between my mother and me, she rarely seemed truly happy unless I was there.

Today, as I tried to walk home, she was circling me like a small puppy wanting attention from its mother to play. She seemed to show unabashed energy, far more than I, after my day's musings.

Although forever staying at more than arm's length away from her, I swatted at her playfully. It's hard for a young man to admit feelings for his sibling but I truly loved my sister, even if most of the time she got in the way; a fact I never let on, but nevertheless still a fact. That said, I hoped she knew in her own way.

Whilst on a circuit running around me, she ventured close enough for me to reach out and grab her, hoisting her high into the air, catching her as she fell, placing her on my shoulders to carry towards home.

Acacia was a small girl, recently celebrating her ninth naming day. Light as a feather but tough as worked leather, she appeared scrawny, some might say, but she had an energy second to none, constantly inquisitive, never shying away from work even at this young age.

Mother had shown her home education at first, mending, cooking, and even at the age of six Acacia could fend easily for herself if need be. The young girls in the village didn't attend the forest classroom in the same way that we did, although in reality they were far better educated than us, most having home-schooling prior to classroom visits.

Maths and English, world history, were taught to all, but only fleetingly basic to the young men. The girls were taught far greater amounts, showing skill in these areas never opened or allowed to us.

As Acacia constantly looked down at me, she asked what I'd caught that day, regarding my every word as honest truth. I contemplated teasing but lacked the energy or want for such a task. Instead, basking in the simple company of family buoyed us both as we walked ever nearer to home.

Mother was standing on the porch waiting for us, keeping out of the rain, trying to not look anxious for our return. I've learnt over the years growing up that, although parents seem to understand we need our freedom to grow and learn, it's very hard to accept that their comforting arms are less needed. This isn't done in a spiteful way, not even in truth done with a thought to malice at all. Just the very act of growing up seems to push your parents into a place they never thought they would occupy, your past.

Coming to the age of nearly seventeen, it's simply put that the mind feels it has reached its pinnacle; I was fortunate enough to have been healthy in my life, I'd learnt well from family and teachers and was a confident if slightly introverted youth. As we grow into full manhood it's very easy to ignore those who try to tell us differently, try to show us there's more to learn; only we ourselves let in the people we want to influence us, sometimes positive sometimes not.

It's a very dangerous time, to feel you can rule the world or complete the puzzle without all the pieces.

Fortunate ones avoid large mistakes, learning as they go, others fail, never to go forward again. A simpler way to consider it would be that if, as individuals, we merely talk, we are only repeating lessons already learnt: it's when we are silent, listening, that we give ourselves room to grow.

Home for us was a simple dwelling, but homely in its setting. Mainly wooden in construction, every nail carefully placed by my father by hand, with Mother helping, years before Acacia and I were born.

A central living area led off to two small bedrooms, on the left mine, on the right the room my mother and Acacia shared.

The bedrooms, though small, suited well enough in their purpose; I held little in the way of possessions, artefacts or ornaments, preferring minimal fuss.

This may seem odd to others, but my solitude and trust fell into the wilderness rather than objects owned. I again didn't collect or own many clothes to call my own, functioning very well with mending when things needed repair. Something I recall from an early age, about Mother always fixing and making for us, had rubbed off in my life today, preferring to properly use and care for the little we owned.

The central living quarters were multi-functional as most small homes dictate. In most it seemed always a place where food took control, whether the preparation or cooking made the area the heart of the home. Seating was in the form of large, filled sacks; into these were placed wheat stems, crushed to soften, alongside several varieties of herbs, lavender mainly.

This gave not only a soft place to rest but permeated the home with beautiful scents, changed regularly with the seasons to freshen anew.

What few books we held we tended to share amongst the whole colony. This was a tradition held with most, as limited knowledge can be dangerous, and withheld knowledge from all is worse still. Most teachings were taught and learnt within the forest school, or at the temple, both places full of history enough for most to learn their fill.

Outside stood the privy, for daily ablutions, holding also a small bowl for clean water, refreshed when needed. Nearby our vegetable patch, currently in summer growth, standing proud, showing the care and attention it always required and received. Several crops always in rotation gave us most of our needed resources. With apple trees planted as saplings or from gathered seed, these encapsulated the vegetable patch, thus allowing comforting shade, and a barrier to the wind.

Most dwellings in our colony followed this pattern, from trial and error most found simplicity the way to a moderate living.

Comfortable but not plush, sustainable and welcoming, but not in abundance, so the dwellings survived year after year. Looking through our colony's history books, reality showed that as people we had taken large strides forward; harsh past winters had not only shown the necessity, but the fortitude of the people to survive.

Whereas smaller groups were more separated in times before, now we gathered in greater numbers, living more openly, more as a colony throughout the year together, not just forced nearer to one another in harsh times. This allowed us as people to share, both resources and knowledge. Growing in numbers we learnt to survive, and in time to flourish.

Setting our ancestors to areas where they laid roots, putting a stop to their wandering, always following the game herds ceased too.

Dwellings now were similar to before, just more permanent.

The main difference back then was that branches of colonies moved to different areas, forming new colonies, within easy reach of each other. These township colonies in the main are still present, forming new larger colonies, thus allowing growth and trade footholds into the future for all.

As I stopped outside the open front door, I removed my hunter's sack. Removing the wrapped, prepared hare meat I handed it to Mother. After the hug we all receive upon returning home she asked if my day had been successful, apart from the obvious fare I gave her now.

I nodded and explained that I'd gained the much-needed hare pelt for my offering and needed to dry it out. She told me to wash and hurried inside to prepare supper. Washing my hands in the rain collector outside, I removed my dirty boots then entered.

Mother had already collected and prepared vegetables, so after again hugging her I went to change my damp clothes.

While supper continued to cook, conversation which I could hear between Mother and Acacia turned to the successful hunt, and whilst delighting in the success of the day's toil I went to the rear porch to prepare the hare skin for my offering, and completion of Gavriel's task.

I'd become more than confident in the preparation of my furs and pelts, and after the initial stretching of the skin onto widened sticks to make it taut, I started to remove the excess tissue left on the fur. Once again using tools from my hunter's sack, I removed my scraper tool. This had been made using the rib bone of a large deer, smooth on the grip, but a roughly sharpened edge to the other, thus allowing meat and sinew to be removed easily with rhythmical downward strokes, starting from the outside, working inwards, careful and methodical work, meaning in no time the skin was ready to be dried. Leaving it on the rear porch to do just that, sheltered from the persistent rain, Mother called that supper was ready, so I ventured back inside to eat.

My mother, a strong woman, still quite young in appearance, always taking pride in the way she cared for us, was dishing up supper with a grace given to her by Rai himself.

Smiling, nodding towards the table, as Acacia and I sat she brought bowls of piping hot stew over to us; with little of the day's bread left we shared what we had between us. Eager as I was to see Peshy, I tried to wolf supper down, but supper, still holding its temperature, took longer to eat than I wanted.

Mother, though occasionally tutting why the rush, didn't mind, with Acacia laughing more than once as I burnt my mouth trying to force it down, full and slightly weary now after eating, and the day's inactivity of waiting seemingly forcing me to rest. I refused to waver, clearing my bowl, and tidied up before leaving.

Acacia wanted to follow me, but Mother nodded her assent for me to go alone, knowing it was important to discuss our offerings. I only slightly regretted the frown Acacia gave me, but out I went, throwing a rain-cheater on as the rain still hadn't relented. Lifting the collar of my coat, I turned to face the rain, and started the short walk to my friend's house.

Walking the short distance allowed my tiredness to vanish somewhat, and as I came around the bend in the path, I saw Peshy waiting for me under the cover of his porch, waving in greeting, then jogging to meet me along the path.

Peshy's homestead was similar to ours, made approximately around the same time, as were most of the colony's homesteads.

His parents, Anselm and Indira, having only Peshy, decided that two bedrooms were needed. Trees, as it seemed at most homesteads, surrounded the rear of the property, giving protection and solitude to those who dwelled there. As we ventured out towards the forest classroom, Indira, Peshy's mother, waved at us, telling us to watch the weather. We agreed we would and, knowing that some of the other young men would already be waiting for us, hastened our step to join them.

The forest classroom wasn't really a room at all; it was a large clearing in the forest, carefully selected and cleared many years ago. Slightly dug into the very soil itself, it somehow kept its warmth even in the deepest winters, seemingly magical, while set so far into the forest centre it sheltered completely those who used it.

Having dense canopy above allowed it to hold even the heaviest rains off the clearing. Large pieces of trunk were placed in a circle, within another circle of ornately carved benches, these having been carved from fallen trees over the years, shaped to be comfortable by the students who used them. These very bench seats had been enveloping when I'd first used them many years ago, both because I was smaller and with the history contained within each bench overwhelming me. Carvings along the back of each seat traced down the arm rests, flowing effortlessly under and through the base of each trunk, placed there by previous White Banner students of Rai, in their offering to be accepted by him.

Each as individual as the next, these carvings aided the magical setting, mostly of forest creatures, with the general flora and fauna which surrounded the colony, and the occasionally forest sprite smiling mischievously around a corner or two. This showed not only great skill in technique, but the patience needed to achieve such an art. Like our offerings, our carvings were all part of teaching us patience and solitude.

Whether a student decided to carve a simple or detailed piece was up to them. The wood itself seemed to want its story to be developed and gazing at the several carved benches already completed you could see our growing colony's history laid out.

On the very outer circle of benches were animals rarely seen in today's carvings.

Over the years bigger predators, such as the Sharbea, a large bear-type creature, had been carved. It was said that a Sharbea could run over vast distances without the need to slow or stop, being much slower than some of the larger predatory cats, like the Oravore, and the ominous Veiled Sinivore or the packs of May Wolfe. The Tusked Mortogg, also a large ground hog, could by itself inflict fatal damage if cornered or injured.

These creatures had been hunted for more than the meagre meat they provided, being driven away to further forests to keep a sense of peace around the homesteads. Many cattle, sheep and pig were lost in those times, history tells us.

So driven away the predatory animals were. That said, very occasionally, normally within particularly harsh periods of weather, packs of May Wolves were seen passing nearby, or the tracks of the Oravore seen in the snow or muddied game tracks near our forest borders. The Oravore was a good hunter, preying on mainly larger game birds whilst they fed on the forest floor.

I was fortunate to encounter an Oravore once, at a safe distance whilst it was stalking prey. I'd been sitting in a tree, just last year, waiting for a flock of geese who were feeding at the outer edge of the forest to come into my hunter's bow range.

Out of the corner of my eye, I sensed movement; holding my bow tighter out of curiosity I held my vision on that fleeting glance. Moving as if time itself wrapped around it, unlike anything I'd ever seen before, came an Oravore into view. A cat of true power, around the size of a large goose itself, its sinuous muscle proving its abilities, showing it a powerful enemy indeed. It's a strange feeling to watch a scene, knowing its outcome, and as a hunter myself I watched its plan come to fruition.

With a burst of power, it launched onto the nearest goose, biting down with immense pressure, instantly killing its victim. Before the geese knew what had happened or where their assailant came from, it had killed another with a deadly bite to the throat. As the geese ran to take off, their wit surrendered to fear as they ran and flew in all directions; this was the Oravore's world, the geese merely players it allowed into its scene.

Finally, as if to show just how easy it was, the Oravore leapt into the air, easily taking a third goose down in flight; the once majestic bird, bloodied and beaten, took its last breath knowing its fate.

With the noise of the hunt that had just taken place, I knew my chances were up, but I didn't in that moment care. I'd seen the abilities of an expert hunter; as if in gratitude, or more likely in contempt of its prey, the Oravore simply returned to the first bird it had captured, enough for its hunger, if not for its blood lust, and simply left, dragging its trophy away, leaving the other two birds to dwell in their deathly forest setting.

I waited a full ten minutes, expecting its return to claim its prize, but to no avail. I dropped from the tree I'd been perched in, thanking Rai for the wonder I'd seen, but also thanking the beautiful Oravore for its grace to leave me a gift.

I often wondered if it knew I was there, leaving its beauty etched on my mind and its meal in my hands. If it did, I am forever grateful; we ate well that evening, all thanks to that striped russet-coloured master of the hunt.

No one I knew had seen the Veiled Sinivore, on the other hand; it was written again in our history that this was a predator above all predators. Accounts varied on the true whereabouts of its territory, let alone any specifics of its prey or habits.

It is widely accepted that to see a Veiled Sinivore brings ill-needed omens on the watcher. Shrouded in mystery it can make you question its very existence, but within the history books, its legendary status reads true. No carvings of the beast have ever been placed on the forest classroom's benches, either in fear of reprisal from Rai, or from the fact that no one in the past who witnessed the animal had ever returned to carve their vision.

My individual carving was nearly complete, but instead of carving a forest-dwelling creature like most of my fellow students, or a legendary fabled beast, I'd decided to carve the only creature I truly felt worthy of my skill, a dragon.

Shaped in flight, it had taken many long hours, but nothing would persuade me to carve anything less.

Fully twisted around a knot in the wood, at the topmost rear of the bench I'd chosen, the dragon had slowly come into a life of its own. Sharpened teeth drew the viewer in as if the carved creature could close its mouth in an instant around prey, or to defend its colony like an unstoppable force. Individual scales somehow shone on the wood's surface, making the light play along its length, carved at slightly different depths to show shadow in contrast.

It had been a constant talking point for years amongst us in the classroom, with even Gavriel pondering its creation; all waited to see its completion, including me.

I had nearly finished, with only the tail left to complete, but to rush now would be in detriment to its true worth in my eye. It would, I knew, be complete by fulfilment day, even if I had to carve the finish at night by candlelight. The other students often pestered me as to why I'd chosen such a complex piece, but there was no other creature in mind when I'd made the choice.

Dragons were a large part of all our lives, from birth, in reality. The colony worshipped dragons, always hearing their guttural roars in the distance, surrounding our land. Past tales wrote that they were given to our race, placed there to protect us, and the land on which we lived.

Rai himself had placed the dragons there to remind his followers, it was stated, to show beauty in creation itself, to show sacrifice, to show worth, but also to warn of not following a righteous path. Accordingly, each month the colony sacrificed animals, and gifts were dropped from fulfilment ledge by people seeking favour, or wanting to show respect to Rai, and our deity's creations. To show that no greater honour we held, than to our protectors.

Tasks set out by Gavriel in this forest classroom were all part of the complex ritual of gaining fulfilment. Whether through your carving or creating your offering was no mere simple task. Every part had to be perfect, a young man's offering to his dragon had to please both beast and Rai himself. Individuality had to show too, simply copying would not do; skill, love, and commitment were integral to each and every offering.

This took not only skill, but time, collecting rarer pieces of shell work for instance; these alone took hikes to get such rarities, many miles travelled by foot were not uncommon, the better to place within your offering.

Hunting, taking care not to damage or ill-prepare furs and pelts which were used to wrap your creation, was paramount, sometimes having to give week upon week of time to gain or work for.

While Peshy and I walked back to the forest classroom we turned our thoughts and conversation back to when we first plucked up enough courage to gaze over the edge of fulfilment ledge. Peshy and I that day were tasked with gaining firewood for some elderly colony members. A simple enough task at first, which turned into a game, if you will, of dare.

We had to collect enough firewood to suffice for several weeks, small and manageable pieces, not the larger logs we were used to fetching for home, or Gavriel.

That made us venture farther out; questing for small but dry fallen trees which hadn't already been plundered like the ones closer to home.

By chance, we realised that we'd ventured very close to the area near fulfilment ledge. This wasn't a place we feared in the everyday, but a holy place, not to be taken lightly, not a playground for youths, nor a place to just hang around.

This place commanded truth, honesty, peace. It was there that day Peshy had started the game, daring me to look down from the edge, daring me to look upon the drop, to see if Rai himself or his precious creations, the dragons, were watching us. Returning the dare to Peshy I teased him, fully expecting him to waver, but his resolve strengthened so, both apprehensive, we slowly walked into that holy arena.

Silent but with the excitement and fear of caution balanced in our bodies so perfectly we dared not stop, in case of either taking control, making us run away or stupidly career off the very edge we walked towards. Carefully we advanced, until eventually we edged ever closer to the drop. Walking seemed to be less of an option as we drew nearer the edge so, dropping onto our stomachs, we inched forward to take a peek.

Looking off that precipice that day gave both Peshy and I a wonder such as we'd never witnessed before, our breath seemed to have to be forced out against the beauty we both witnessed that day. Below us as we crouched, peering off the edge, it seemed hundreds of feet below us a large mass of swirling cloud, stretching as far as we could see in all directions, cloud so unlike any seen before or since that day.

Colours rich and intense, greater than could be counted, seemed to dwell here; coloured hazes appearing also, vanishing to make the viewer ponder if the colours seen below existed or were an elaborate magic, placed there to mystify the mind, or simply imagination given full flight, trying to expand its own horizons in this moment.

It was then, as our minds toyed, playing tricks on us, that we glimpsed our first dragon, suddenly breaking through the cloud, appearing at first as not flying but crawling through the tangible cloud surrounding it.

Limbs thicker than the tallest, oldest trees in the forest, the dragon flew, twisting as it turned, its enormous body breaking free of the binding fog, for mere seconds in my mind holding motionless, its beauty evident in its pure strength. No greater power had we ever seen in our short lives.

For an instant it felt as though we had become frozen in time, absorbing each and every tiny detail of the mystical beast in front of us. Hearts racing in absolute silence, forcing our breath in and out quietly, in case the beauty parted from our unbelieving eyes.

The dragon, mindless to the glamour it created in that singular moment, twisted back into the clutches of the cloud base, leaving tantalising hues of its deep red for our vision to try and follow, clinging to the beauty we'd watched for seconds, but would last within us for ever.

We vowed that day to follow the path needed to achieve fulfilment and promised to always help each other, no matter what. The day the dragon's life and ours combined would someday come and, looking back, I think we both secretly wanted that beautiful scarlet dragon to be our very own risen guardian.

Entering the edge of the forest classroom, we heard voices within, people already present, continuing with their own carvings, or simply enjoying the shelter from the rain amongst friends. We joined the few who were present, sitting near the centre; a few stories were retold of this week's successes or failures in their tasks, but all agreed, this week's task of gaining animal pelts was a simpler one.

In the past, great tasks were often handed to us by Gavriel, sometimes the seemingly impossible, sometimes reached, most likely failed. This often was the task set itself; failure is a powerful weapon, Gavriel once taught, it doesn't mean one has to like failure, it doesn't have to be enjoyed, but a lesson taught can only be learnt if your mind is open enough to allow the knowledge in.

Returning the talk to the week's task showed a wide

variety of animal pelts had been successfully gained; these were, in essence, the outer covering, the main decorative feature of our offerings, keeping the whole safe and intact for its descent to Rai.

Using the forest animals' furs and pelts, we in turn showed our thanks to Rai. Giving us a plentiful bounty meant giving a plentiful offering back.

I knew my hare's pelt, once dried, would be ideal for this task; its small size and colourful texture, added alongside my other skins, meant I nearly had enough to complete the covering in full.

Peshy, on the other hand, had gained his last pelt and was showing it proudly off to the fellow lads at the forest classroom. Mink, jet black in colour. Peshy had mentioned before that he wanted the pelt of the mink to finish his offering and at last, he'd succeeded. Now, once dried and cured, his task would be finally completed.

A slight jealous feeling started to well up in me, but quickly dispersed with worry for my friend. All young men relished fulfilment day; even if apprehension was there, it was skirted to avoid the fear, as not spoken by us was the more sinister thoughts of the fallen.

Occasionally the young men never returned, shunned from existence, it seemed, by the colony, never spoken of in fear of bringing Rai's wrath down on them.

The fallen simply disappeared on fulfilment day. Surrounded by family and friends, young men firstly being dressed in ceremonial robes show their offering to their god. Releasing the offering in thanks to the deities below, showed their commitment to Rai.

Under music, walking to the edge of fulfilment ledge,

leaping off into the void below, faith and commitment to Rai as one. Normally entering the clouds into Rai's domain, fulfilment is then reached. Confirmation is being lifted back to your colony by the dragon destined to be your guardian; the fallen, on the other hand, were not so lucky.

Rumours or whispered secrets were all I or anyone had heard, tales passed from person to person, late into winter nights, stories to reinforce good behaviour, or to scare younger children by older siblings.

Many had been lost; many had fallen over the years, never to return. It was told that the young men hadn't been true to their faith, hadn't prepared well enough; others stated they were dark of heart, not showing Rai their true allegiance.

No one knew for sure except they were never seen again. Families mourned, allowed to grieve, then shunned from the colony, sent to Mortwedge. Losing favour, losing friends, scared away by scandal and fear, a sad tale but always there nevertheless.

THREE

Understanding one's fate is completely different from accepting it. Some people I'd known in the past refused to gain the skills needed to pass into the accepted ranks of the colony. These people preferred to stay on the fringes of society, perhaps even ridiculing the acceptance of Rai.

Challenging the history books, challenging life itself. Over the years the outlanders, as they were known, had swelled in numbers. Their region, Mortwedge, where large colonies had been created over time with numerous homesteads, and small villages of their own.

True numbers were not known by me, and they caused little trouble to our colony, keeping themselves to themselves, occasionally small numbers coming to monthly markets, to trade goods or seeking food unable to be grown in the subsoil of their homes.

Their colonies were further along the land south-east of our colony's lands. A few days' travel but easily accessible for them to travel to markets. It would have been easy for us to travel to their homelands, too, but something that was never done. Outlanders had isolated themselves from society; they preferred it that way, over the mountain ridges away from other colonies.

It was at one such market that I'd bumped into Amia; she was a young woman of similar age to Peshy and me.

Beautiful with a striking appearance, full of the day's warmth, she seemed to glide by us without a care in the world. Not even noticing, it appeared to us, that we were obviously staring at her.

She passed by without a second glance, walking along with her other outlander friends.

We'd set out, Peshy and I, to seek Ivan; he had a small cart always at the monthly Barbarrow market, peddling wares not seen at any other stall. He travelled from colony to colony, he told, selling his wares as best he could. His craft was a rare trade indeed, but one that, over years, he'd honed as sharp as a blade's edge.

He made exquisitely intricate charms, finely decorated with small brightly coloured glass beads, some with tiny bird feathers, hardened with resin to preserve their beauty. Other, more dainty charms held intricate silver work, twisted to form shapes of elegance, or animals Ivan had witnessed, or even dreamt about.

Mystical creatures of legend were worked into some; these were the most delicate of his treasures. The special trick, if it was indeed a trick, was that Ivan not only sold the delicate charms but said he placed magic within the making of them. Most shook their head in disbelief at the old man's tales of magic.

Some openly shunned the man, having little or nothing to do with him. Other tales told of Ivan the old, always being around, stating he'd lived many lives, or at least been in this one for hundreds of years.

Ivan was full of life and mischief whilst at the markets, but never showed himself to be a fool, an intelligent man, keeping his wits about him even at a great age. A man who could talk his way out of any situation, coming and going, no one knew exactly where on his travels, a simple peddler of magic craft, or so it seemed.

To me Ivan was a friend, often I just sat with him as he sold his wares. A true salesman, I'd witnessed, as he charmed the young ladies with tales of true love gained, or how simply his charms would make them impossibly beautiful; convincing the young men that good luck charms would lead to better hunting and guaranteeing acceptance by Rai if his charms were added to an offering.

Never taking either side of other people's thoughts towards Ivan, I simply enjoyed my time spent with him; his delicate intricate work fascinated me, and he allowed me to watch him create sometimes, if business was running slowly.

This day, though, we were both buying; Peshy and I had saved the infrequent coinage we gained through odd chores to purchase a good luck charm for our offerings.

Peshy's acceptance day would fall before Ivan's next visit, but as I had the coin and wanted to see Ivan I went along as well.

We found Ivan in his usual spot, like a small mouse darting here and there around the small group gathered around his stall. He was busy holding small charms up against pretty girls' necks, explaining how the colour brought out their serenity and natural beauty, emboldening them to his charm; showing the purple colour he'd managed to perfect, showing great hunting charms or suggesting that the buyer's every wish could happen by simply buying a lucky charm.

We waited until the fervour ebbed slightly, witnessing truly a master at work; by the time the crowd had departed, much lighter of their coin, Ivan had a large smile, nearly as big as his bulging purse.

He welcomed us both and asked if we'd come for our offering charms; he'd asked at previous meetings if we'd like special charms made for our acceptance day, and finally, after many conversations on colour and shape and size, he'd said he would make us charms as never seen before.

We'd thanked him that day, half wondering if it was just the salesman within him that we'd been been talking to, or the friend we'd gained over our coming to see him every month.

After rummaging through his many boxes of various sizes, Ivan came back to us. Speaking to Peshy first, he produced a charm that seemed to hold the ocean within it. Its dark blue beauty was outstanding, like nothing I'd seen before. The edges seemed to dissipate to a lighter blue, perfectly contrasted with the deeper darker colour housed with the centre.

It looked, once spun, like water being moved, mesmerising serine ripples flowing from edge to edge, all somehow placed within the glass.

Peshy's eyes widened as he noticed the hunting cat design woven in silver holding the blue jewel seemingly in its paws.

Its beauty was beyond compare and, after passing the limited coins he had to Ivan, a sudden sense of realisation passed over Peshy's face that no amount of coin could truly pay for such a beautiful ornate piece.

Whether through that embarrassment realised or the want to hold such a treasure in his own vision alone, Peshy made his excuses with humbled thanks and moved off, still captivated by his wonderful new possession.

Not daring to ask or think how mine could achieve such beauty, I waited as Ivan again rummaged through his boxes. Tutting to himself, shaking his head in muttered responses not meant for me or others to hear, Ivan finally found what he was searching for.

He hesitated slightly, running his hands through his wild uncontrolled hair. Caution filled me with dread; was it something wrong, was there something I'd just done? But as he handed me my charm, all thoughts of fault seemed to be removed from my body.

I can only give an account of my vision from that moment, as the experience of my feelings became overwhelming.

As Ivan placed the charm into my hands I felt a power surge within me, flooding my emotions wholly.

Turning to Ivan, I saw a look I'd never seen on his face before, a cautionary glance, worried perhaps that he'd maybe done a poor job, or a reluctance to give such a piece away.

As I looked at the charm in depth, my eyes focused on the bead of pure red sitting perfectly balanced in the centre.

If Peshy's had held the ocean within, mine surely held the sun in its grasp. Deep red, a swirling firestorm, unrelenting in its power, forced somehow to stay within a glass prison.

It was either my body playing tricks on me, or indeed the magic placed within, but it felt warm to the touch, as if the mere placing in my hand had awoken its power from sleep.

Dragging my vision back from the soul of that colour I noticed its power was clasped in the taloned foot of a dragon in flight, much like the dragon in my carving, traced from the true dragon I'd seen that day from acceptance ledge.

Made of pure silver, I had never held such an ornament of both delicacy and worth in my short life.

As I went to speak, Ivan folded my fingers around the charm, seemingly snapping me back into reality. I faced him.

Ivan, an old man, looked deep within me and, without removing his hands, told me to always wear this charm; he pleaded for me not to remove it, not to place it on my offering and refused all coin I offered.

His pleasure in my friendship had become deeper than I realised.

Hoping that one day I could repay my friend for such a beautiful object, I thanked him with a hug and stumbled away, half in awe and half in wonder at the gift I'd received.

Whilst walking, still my mind focused on the charm I held as tightly in my grasp as a small infant holds its mother's thumb for comfort.

I hadn't noticed that ahead of me a group had formed, including Peshy.

The first I realised that I had been walking blindly was when I walked straight into them. I must have appeared half-witted or just plain rude, as I fought to keep my footing.

The group I'd so rudely interrupted was mainly configured of outlander young women. Peshy was showing off his charm, its beauty captivating the audience who gazed on it; the young women seemed to be as much in awe of Peshy as the charm.

Using his newfound confidence, it was that day that

Peshy and Amia became known to each other as friends.

Being in the Tracouttie colony it was common for other colonies to want to offer tribe alliances, maybe gained through blood marriages.

Young men or women offered to cement truces, or gain favour even, allowing tribes stronger links to one another, yet remaining true to their own tribe in front of Rai's eyes.

This was not seen, though, with outlanders; I'm sure it had been known in the past and although tolerated, not favoured.

It was feared that the outlanders brought separation to families, taking loved ones away, showing a way of life not righteous to Rai, so shunned from their tribes in the past; leading an unholy existence, some said.

Others took a stronger stance, with tales of crimes against fellow man bordering on a hate that was only told in late night tales, between silent hushes and disbelief.

To spend time with an outlander brought suspicion on you and your family, something not wanted by the Tracouttie tribe, something taught to be against its values.

It is a harsh thought, but reality gave us little option as young men in the Tracouttie colony. We were born within it and told how to grow, but most accepted our way of life. I held it no grudge myself, enjoying the life lessons I'd been taught.

Our colony numbers had swelled these days to around five hundred members: each year, more mouths to feed, and more passing into Rai's golden land. Originally years ago, history foretold of the foundation of the Tracouttie people; the tribe back then was in fact two tribes, merged together in times of need.

The Tracoo tribe were fabled hunters, good with bow and spear, they would have been a feared group, a fact I'm sure of.

They would prove also a mighty fighting group. Although smaller in number, successful to almost abundance in gaining meat, this allowed sturdy growth in time of bleakness, a rarity unknown back then.

Constant movements of the game herds meant fast travel for the Tracoo tribe, tracking from place to place, always moving where their food was plentiful.

They were the first documented tribe to use horses for transport, they travelled vast distances, always staying on the edges of the game herds. When the animals moved, they moved, a seemingly symbiotic relationship, heavily favouring the side who anticipated the next move first.

The Tracoo, taking weaker and old herd members, allowed the game herds fleet of foot, often keeping nature's predators at bay too, due to the proximity of man and horse.

Horses had been first caught and used as meat, looked at as another herd to track and utilise.

It was the speed and durability of the horse that showed the Tracoo the possibility of more.

Caught and reared, much like the animals we keep now for food, the relationship then changed. Breeding occurred within the captured stock, and over time a sturdy, solid breed became favourable, not as fast as the first captured animals but the newly bred animals showed fair speed, alongside an endurance to distance.

This subtlety would change the Tracoo's lives forever. Now with the means of faster travel, the ability grew also to carry more equipment. Tented shelters could be taken, with more supplies.

Another resource gained to show an edge over other tribes, each birthing of a new foal gave new advantages, new hope; something the Tracoo would defend with their lives if they must.

The Routtie tribe, however, might have been larger in number, but were more land-based. Food for them did include local game for meat, but mainly resourced around the fertile soil of the valley they chose to frequent their homesteads. These were similar to the start of our dwellings, mainly strong shacks to keep out the harsh winds and driving snow, unmovable, setting roots down here, hoping to make an existence.

Less of a fighting group as they rarely travelled far, their skills became paramount for survival. Expert building techniques were honed, metallurgy discovered and practised, which made them a strong trading alliance, one with resources and weapons to trade. This itself was good for the tribe but started to be noticed by others.

At a time when unrest and tribe attacks were common, it is a dangerous place to sit holding something precious, when all around can only look at you with jealousy, envy, and resentment of your good fortune.

History repeats itself, it is told, nations obsessed with war tend to follow pattern after pattern, whether successful or not. If you ever get the chance to read how a founding nation grew it always tends to lead to a bloodily fought war.

Whether between races of the same people, or a saga of conflict fought through generation after generation of disillusioned factions, it continues until one side declares itself the winner, or another is simply wiped away from existence, like a tear from a child's face.

The foundation of the Tracouttie colony was an actual opposite of this by chance, it seems. The great teachings of our history tell the tale of how the Tracoo and the Routtie tribes first sought shelter within each other's company.

That together they formed an alliance built on sacrifice and grief, so strong, it was allowed to establish a bond that no one could challenge.

The foundations placed down by both sides that day of acceptance became a powerful alliance. Gaining knowledge and governance from each other, alongside the power and weaponry to hold all who dared face them at bay.

It was turning into a very bad winter, and the Tracoo tribe became landlocked upon high ground. Seeking shelter from the driving snow, they cautiously made for the valley floor below.

Managing to trek to the base of the mountains brought them to the edge of the Routtie homesteads. Here instead of hostility they were shown warmth, given shelter and food, the only thing asked of them, to return if ever passing to exchange extra provisions of meat. The winter was harsh, worse than most had seen before.

And the Tracoo were trapped for longer than expected. Passing evenings together under winter skies allowed the sharing of knowledge, sharing food, sharing their cultures. This led to a friendship born of necessity, but grown in kind action, to one another.

Once the hardest snows had left, the Tracoo tribe bid farewell to their hosts. With fond farewells given on both sides, they parted to retrace the fleeting game herds with the promise to return in the spring with fresh meat for the Routtie to replenish their stores.

Winter passed slowly, and having successfully found the herds, once again took up their life following them in pursuit of food. The Tracoo, still following the game herds, in the summertime passed close by the Routtie lands.

A tribe of its word, they turned from the herds to pay their thanks, and to retrace their path northwards, to see their friends the Routtie.

By chance, or by fate lending a hand in the greater scheme, unknown to mere mankind, as the Tracoo visiting horde entered the valley to see their friends, they were met by sounds of battle.

Routtie lands as said were pleasant and fair, the tribe themselves peaceful and forgiving, but enemies can see that for weakness, and waiting for spring to arrive, an enemy had done just that.

Attacking the Routtie people for their precious resources, they met little resistance. Weapons were here to use, but a spear or bow in the hands of the craftsman who made it can be an unforgiving thing, if not used correctly or swiftly on purpose.

A warrior tribe now attacked them; the Arooch, holding little weaponry but the skill to use what they had effectively, became a force that the Routtie people couldn't defend themselves against. Blood was spilled that day. The cost of life thought of as useless, against the value of victory and the spoils of war.

With heavy losses starting to mount, and a sense of doom, the Routtie tribe were being slowly wiped out. Mercifully their past peaceful and friendly hospitality which was causing their downfall would be their saving also, as joining the battle to avenge their friends rode the Tracoo.

Not expecting much resistance, the Arooch had concentrated their attack straight at the Routtie's village.

Little or no thought had been passed between them it seemed, to having a defence, an escape, if you will.

Their confidence overspilling, unable to see an equal in battle. Their first instincts had been correct. Reality that day had decided to take a far larger part, within history it is written clearly to always expect the unexpected.

The Arooch were, if not a completely successful tribe in their own right, known as exceptional at taking from others.

To be an Arooch held little esteem throughout the lands, an untrustworthy tribe, rarely visited, or spoken of without some resentment of their past actions.

Living to the far east side of the more stable tribes' lands, this suited the Arooch, the barren lands there didn't attract many visitors. It was said that tribe members who were shunned from other tribes, those who had taken life without regret, or those simply making an outcast of themselves, gravitated towards the Arooch.

Seeking and finding shelter sometimes gives you enough loyalty to a cause, to agree to help in its sustainability, once accepted, hard to withdraw from, still holding your life before, intact and unstained.

Watching the Routtie tribe go about their daily life from a distance, sitting in the lower reaches of the bordering mountains around the valley, the Arooch had devised their plan.

Awaiting spring gave them the opportunity they craved and running low on supplies gave them the incentive to strike. A calm weathered day, if not slightly blustery, with a crisp air, they started the attack.

The Arooch knew high resource yields and ore in abundance would allow a full year's growth for their tribe.

Setting all other things aside, they planned and started their execution of the Routtie.

Their study and diligence initially paid off with little more than stockaded fences for defence, and limited trained fighters.

Resistance, though, was equivalent to a single sandbag trying to stop a flood. Soon overpowered, its attempt seemed feeble, and panic soon set in amongst the Routtie people.

Having greater numbers of skilled warriors and skirmishers meant an easy victory surely must ensue, and branches of the Arooch attack started fires and ransacking before all the defenders were breached, so strong was their confidence in victory.

In war as in life, one must always prepare for the worst; it doesn't become a part of everyday life, but in the back of one's mind it must be present. The Arooch, so set in their ways, were taken fully by surprise. The history books foretell the tale of that day, and it's taught still to all students of Rai.

Sweeping in on horse, brandishing weaponry in skilled hands, the Tracoo tribe entered the affray.

Used to cornering game herds, with the ability to command knowledge of past victorious battles and showing tactics the Tracoo knew to be flawless, they rode on, flanking both left and right with their mounted warriors, cleaving the unsuspecting Arooch. Turning and trying to flee, with warrior horses on two sides, defending villagers on another, gave the Arooch but one option. As once confidence had filled them, hysteria now took its place, forcing them into the only clear path away from the burning village.

As the remaining Arooch ran through the smoking embers into, as they thought, the clear path back towards the safety of the mountain reaches, they faced the armed foot soldiers of the Tracoo.

Blinded with fear, and unable to turn in any direction, swamped with the enormity of their plight, they fought with the little strength they held onto.

An enemy who has faith, a man who fears death, a warrior unrelenting can be a very dangerous animal to face.

Once you beat a man, pain is something that drives them on, avoidance of that pain being their motive to succeed. If you beat a man too much, so he hastens death; he no longer feels the fear of failure, he accepts it, that is a truly beaten foe indeed.

The Arooch were swept from the battlefield that day, as given to the history books, forever to tell their stories as lessons against greed and their ultimate failure.

The battle, hard fought on both the Tracoo and Routtie sides, was a mere horrendous section of that day. Battles are always bloody in every aspect of life, whether beast against beast, or man against man. Can in fact we still call a man a man, whilst he forfeits all sanity and strikes a man whom he doesn't want to rise again?

Death can be a brutal truth but beyond the actual act of having to take another's life, there always seems left a trace on your soul of the deed done. After the initial bloodshed had ceased, action turned to saving the encampment itself, wrought with fire, the tribeswomen and children who themselves had been fighting for life, were the first who turned attention to their homes after the Tracoo intervened to help them.

Now all hands tried to save what could be salvaged, time sanctioning the reality of the forced actions faced into a falsehood, whilst busily fighting again for homes and shelter.

This gave time to section thoughts into bite-size pieces of truth, easier to swallow.

After many hours it seemed the fire simply became bored, or after consuming all it needed, felt sated and disappeared, leaving the smouldering remains of homes, artefacts and people, once standing relatively moments before.

A somewhat muted silence took hold of everyone that day, with occasional murmurs and muttering of life and possessions lost, drifting eerily on the wind. The Routtie, a once-proud, flourishing tribe, sat on its knees, years of hope crushed in an act of pure hatred, but even sitting there in the dirt, most realised that without the Tracoo, they would not be sitting there at all. Adversity can do one of two things; it can break your will, remove your courage and seem overbearing, giving no hope, or it can galvanise one's spirit, grabbing certainty back, giving faith and strength in the most unlikely scenario.

The day that the Routtie tribe fell, they proudly stood up again; bolstered by the friendship of the Tracoo, they decided fate had hit them hard, but not defeated them. No braver action is written in our history, of the people who founded the next chapter in that book.

After many days of treating the wounded, removing the dead, mixed literally upon the enemy themselves, the grieving process continued. The Tracoo were luckier in this, their dead or injured counting small, but being a smaller tribe than most, still impacted on their size; many horses, severely injured, had to be taken away to be dispatched, as mercy decreed.

This led to a sharing of a greater need in both tribes, each seeking companionship, shelter and food, together side by side sharing grief, a stronger bond than love, it is said.

As one eventually can hopefully learn to love again, grief stays with us always. It is said that time heals all, but in grief I feel that statement doesn't do justice to the act. Grief reminds us daily of its existence within us, makes us remember loved ones' faces, maybe places visited, recall fond memories there. These once cherished, now somehow appear tainted with darker thoughts.

Therefore, time doesn't heal; it simply allows us to formulate how we think, what we do in fact, changing us forever. The hard part is if we give in to grief for too long, allowing it to change us for the worse, never again lifting our spirits in thanks, it overpowers us.

We then, rather than forever holding onto the past, scared of trying again, have to rise and forgive, often ourselves as we seek to find reasoning in the act of death itself.

One of the hardest paths to walk in life is the one set in front of you to take, especially if you feel alone. Tiny steps can be taken, slow if necessary, but continuing to move forward. It helps one so. Therefore, time doesn't actually heal you but allows you to travel further away from the point of loss; you actually heal yourself, with time.

After the pyres of both the Routtie and Tracoo tribes had long burnt away, the ashes dispersed in ceremonies held dear to those left behind, the pile of Arooch were buried. Returning them to the ground showed respect, but no ceremonies were held that day, just simply a job that needed doing.

Placing a large pile of stones over that mass grave, it was left for nature to cover and remember.

The exact time both tribes joined has not been documented in the passages of history, but general thought leads us to assume that not long after that terrible battle the Tracouttie tribe was born.

Moving away to the next valley west of their original homesteads, the now larger colony set new roots down, upholding new traditions together. This over time became the biggest tribe in the whole Astohar region, growing steadily over time, setting new roots, new trade alliances, alongside continued expert hunting.

Making a powerful ally to hold for other tribes within the region, their battle prowess never taken lightly, they grew to become a powerful colony, still widely regarded as the forefathers of life today. But little did everyone know that peace among the founding tribes would be short-lived. All this before the breaking of the world, from which Rai himself rose up to show mercy, to save his people from extinction.

FOUR

Fulfilment day looming, talk in the forest classroom turned back to everyone's thoughts. Five of us this year were hoping to become accepted, with two planned to go over the next month. Rogan then Vinn would be first; Peshy would be the third, myself fourth and Clay fifth.

The week leading up to acceptance day was always steeped in tradition. For the individual, the week was a time of nerves, mixed with frustration. Being so close to the biggest event we'd faced by far, we seldom got a second to ourselves, it seemed.

For we young men, getting accepted was everything; the final week before held special meals, normally spent not only praising Rai, but spending time in celebration with the people closest to you. The people who'd helped you get to your special day. Gifts were often given at this time, ranging from new weapons, to jewellery, often given to wear on the special day itself.

Gifts of food to your family from neighbours, everyone celebrated the coming events. Acceptance meant a great deal to the whole colony, allowing everyone a time to rejoice in the colony's growth.

Visits from family and friends who lived in other tribes held special meaning too. All coming to see your leap of faith, but mostly craving the viewing of your paired dragon, for no matter how many times you'd seen a dragon, their sheer magnificence outshone every other beauty held within your mind.

With little private time to yourself that week, all moments taken up with ceremonies, spending time with Gavriel in the temple allowed an escape as such, a time to reflect and to pray, which seemed to hold more prominence at this time of life.

Gavriel lived not far from the forest classroom, about equal distance in fact from both acceptance ledge and the forest itself. Always slightly disassociated with colony life due to his standing, it must have been hard for Gavriel.

He was a friendly man, a man we all as younger colony members looked up to. Knowing his presence was to feel greatness, we were fortunate indeed to have such a skilled teacher.

Gavriel himself often reflected about his past, sometimes with us present but mostly in solitude. He walked the same paths we walked now, breathed the same air, holding his own hopes and dreams for his students to pass into the ranks of the accepted.

He often in his teachings looked into the past, but this was hard for a man whose reputation was so revered.

History tells of deeds accomplished, often glossing over facts to show interest in the subjects spoken of within. Tales of Gavriel's past were legendary, and most were in fact truly told. It's strange to talk or read about history when the person teaching or telling is part of the fabric of the story.

But this Gavriel did. Whether to try to lessen his worth, staying humble as a religious man tries to be, or whether trying to paint a less savage past, he always played down his part.

Stories were written of Gavriel the warrior, growing from the young man he was in the Tracouttie tribe back then to how, in the battle of the breaking of the world, he alone stood in defence of his beliefs, willing to give his life for his god. Looking at the man, teacher, friend I knew, it was hard to look plainly at the living piece of history in front of us.

His home was different from most of the colony structures around. Built of stone, Gavriel lived within the hallowed walls of the temple itself. After the war had ended, chaos subsiding, Gavriel built his home, his temple to Rai. Unaided at first but as word grew of the story played out that final day, others offered penitence to Rai.

Helping Gavriel create a home for worship, a place of solitude, a peaceful place, much needed after the violence of the past, over time realising that from now on, a much-needed peace was needed, a time to grow, a time to rest, the forest classroom was founded.

Gavriel himself, not only teaching the will of Rai, but also teaching the young men of the colony, the need to walk a path of enlightenment; self-worth in life cannot be given, you must earn the right to use it.

You can walk tall, pretending to be something you're not; for a time, that works. But within yourself you cannot hide. Remember this as, when you face Rai, your actions will be there to see. Rai will look, it is said, but you will understand, if you walk holding your life in a lie, it will be disrespectful; not to Rai but to yourself, in reality the one true soul that counts.

Over time with people connecting to their god, Rai himself returned our favour with a gift beyond compare, our protectors, the dragons. The creatures placed between the breaking of our earth to prevent enemy facing enemy again. Man versus man can claim poor judgement, at best it is said a fool can be talked into action if words are placed sweetly on the ear.

Man versus creature, however, has little poetic sympathy. When creature wants it takes, man cannot stop its will by words alone, but strong actions can sometimes turn events. The breaking of the world kept man and creature apart, Rai mercifully saving us from obliteration that day.

Solitude and reasoning were all the teachings young men faced that final week, before their acceptance. Rogan and Vinn were young men within our tribe, as with most our age, we knew them well, having grown with them over the years. All together we were a select group, all understanding years before that our acceptance days would fall close together.

Acceptance was always on the young man's seventeenth name day. History had decreed that on acceptance you reached full manhood.

If Gavriel and Rai deemed you were worthy, you took your place among the elite of your tribe. Seen as a true valued member of your colony, it gave you and your family honour and pride, able to fully commit to Rai.

As darkness started to fall, back at the forest classroom, with talk drifting away, failing light meaning people unable to continue with the carvings they were idly trying, as a group we decided to meet again on the new teaching day tomorrow. Saying our goodbyes, we all moved as one out of the classroom.

Peshy and I wandered silently along towards home, pleased the rain had eased. The summer rain had fallen most of the day, and the surrounding world looked fresher for it.

The evening's fireflies had started to appear, swarming, circling, chasing each other in the coming darkness of a beautiful summer evening. Though damp, the floor was firm underfoot, and as the day's heat awoke from the soil, rising to be free, a low mist started to show.

Reaching higher as we walked, the mist weaved around us, creating a mystical setting. The beauty of nature cannot be replicated; the greatest artists have tried many times, people try with words or sonnets, but to stand in nature and become one with it has no equal.

We parted company that night, Peshy and I, with a simple nod, knowing that morning would soon be upon us. Climbing towards home, I glimpsed the lights of home, strange, eerily even, shining through the rising mist.

Tiredness started to dull my weary thoughts. I would be glad once lying in my bed tonight.

Mother was still awake, tidying as usual, a quick hug and checking I was all right, she allowed my tiredness to take me away to my room. Washing the day's toil from my hands and face in the basin of cool water in my room, I quickly dropped my clothes and climbed into bed.

A habit of mine since I'd received my charm from Ivan was to gaze into its wonder whilst trying to sleep. A calming influence was always assured when looking into its deep red-coloured heart.

Spinning the charm with my index finger seemed to somehow move the colour inside the glass bead, and no matter how tired I was, it had become a routine, an obsession, a ritual I had to complete. Calmness walked with me whilst in its company, a feeling of pure peace never held by me before.

Occasionally I could have sworn that deep within the red colour, something drew me in towards it. Like a moth, trying to fly too close to flame, I couldn't resist. Something called me, teased with a delight I secretly yearned for, not known to me.

It could have just been the act of falling asleep, or maybe a trick of the light, an active imagination, or tired from simply being, expelling energy still inside from the day, I couldn't tell you. But that night, as I held my charm in front of me, I could see perfect scales sweeping through the glass bead; forever twisting, moving fluidly. Gracefully, in a tight regular formation, the form ever fleeting appeared and disappeared as soon as it came.

Looking closer at the silver twisting form of the dragon's foot, its intricate design amazed me. Fine silver thread had been worked, moulded together to somehow form the edge of fine scales, so evenly matched.

It being carved from one ornate piece of silver, with decorative markings showing along its leg, made it seem lifelike in appearance. How Ivan had moulded such a piece, I'd never know, but my appreciation towards him, and its beauty, were limitless.

As it held its deep red treasure, neatly grasped between its perfectly formed talons, it filled me with eternal hope. That soon, so soon, my acceptance would be here. Nothing in my life bar caring for my family meant more to me. Making them proud, making my friends happy, and showing respect to my father who sat at Rai's side. Wishing he could have been here, to see me try for acceptance.

Before I realised, I must have slipped into a dreamlike state. Dreaming with details so real, it was as though I had closed my eyes and opened them seconds later in another place.

I often had dreams; I suppose like any other. Dreams of success, dreams of another lifestyle, holding wealth or being popular. Dreams of other times, being other people, being different.

The people who say they understand one's dreamscape differ with their tale telling, often saying dreams are variable; some good dreams can mean the opposite, we're told. Foretelling futures lost, or simply showing you a new path to follow. Some dreams having omens, both good and bad, but who can honestly tell?

A person dreams things the mind is trying to focus on, I feel. Trying to form a solution of a problem gained. Maximising time allowed to ponder on subjects difficult to explain. Sometimes we dream of people lost to us, family and friends who are far away, maybe.

The one thing I can truly add here, is to never underestimate what shows itself to you in a dream; you never know where it will lead.

My dreams at that time were somehow different. I'd asked Peshy a few days previously whether since he'd received his charm he'd experienced anything strange. I didn't want him to think that I was acting weirdly, so didn't divulge the exact dreams I was thinking about, straight away.

Peshy looked at me, saying he hadn't really noticed daily changes but stating he slept more peacefully holding his charm, saying the beauty within helped his nerves. These were naturally growing, nearer to his leap off acceptance ledge. I asked if he'd dreamt more, finding greater solace in his sleeping thoughts. He nervously looked about us, checking for anybody listening to our conversation. He twitched slightly, wondering if he was telling a secret, one so special that even a friend shouldn't share.

He explained he'd dreamt not only more often, but with a vivid dreamscape never witnessed to him before. He explained he awoke in a section of forest unknown to him.

After trying to assess his bearings he started walking, or should he say stalking; he appeared to be either inside, or was, a predatory catlike creature. Powerful, at one with the night, he couldn't find words to describe to me the power he felt within that dream.

He hunted that evening, successful beyond his normal abilities. Cornering prey that didn't have a chance, his skills so adept it was unfair in its simplicity for him. Colours and smells of the scene so extraordinarily rich, that when he awoke, for a few minutes he still had the sensation of feeling he had sated his hunger, still could feel the cool forest floor under his hands and feet. Or did he mean paws?

Several other dreams he recalled were all similar, either hunting or trekking vast distances. In forest always but sometimes up in the canopy, looking down, assessing the best route of travel. He nervously raised his eyes to meet mine, assuming I would laugh or joke about him and his dreams. Peshy didn't know that my dreams. although completely different, were as vivid as his, as vivid as if I lived them myself.

I found it hard to explain my dreams that day to Peshy, as I honestly found it strange myself to accept, and to place into valid thought. But as Peshy had been honest with me, I reached into my secrets to tell him.

It was the night I'd received my exquisite charm, full of its wonder still gripping me. I held it close as I attempted to sleep. Most nights since then I'd held it too, in truth. I seemed to drift to sleep in a peace, contented with life, at one with my very soul, it seemed.

In thought it appeared only seconds had passed by, then on opening my eyes, I lived and breathed a different reality.

The first time I'd felt as though I'd awoken fully, jerked back into existence. I was lying on the forest floor, slight dampness under my back as I rested, lying down in a clearing.

I could smell the forest around me, I could somehow even sense the very air surrounding my body. A stillness, not cold, but air that's lost the day's warmth, perpetually frozen in time and space.

No movement surrounded my being, as if I was locked in place. Not feeling scared, but with an unnatural feeling of calm, a belief that all was right with the world I'd been placed in, like a blanket wrapped around me, making me feel safe. I ventured to move and found that I could easily shift my position, though not changing my calmness at all.

I focused on my surroundings and realised I was home, not in my bedroom, or even our shelter with my family, but my patch of forest. My sanctuary, my inner place to run, the one place I loved.

Wondering how I'd ventured here, seemingly asleep, a part of me realised that I was actually still in bed, somehow a part of me transported to this magical place. As I took deeper breaths, I noticed I wasn't alone. Sitting across from me at the edge of the clearing was a dragon, huge in size, and apparently asleep. I watched the beast with an awe that shocked me to the spot. If Rai himself had painted this dragon, no finer brush strokes could have ever matched it. Its size was taking up most of the clearing, and being curled up, much like a cat at rest curled on a pillow asleep, I realised its true size would be larger again, if the beast raised its head and stretched.

I hesitated in case moving woke the beast; not scared as such, but longing to gaze whilst it slept so close to me. If it wasn't the dragon Peshy and I had seen that day off acceptance edge, it must have been a sibling, as its colour matched perfectly so.

For me to say colour underestimates the sheer beauty I looked upon. The scarlet deep red, swirled with anger through each and every scale, with the perception that they would be hot to touch, their colour forever changing as the beast took long ragged breaths in and out.

Its body moved with the beat of its giant heart, slowly but surely, rhythmically even, enchanting me, the watcher, to fall deep into the vision, unable to believe or remove myself from the glorious sight.

The moonlight shone its dappled light through the canopy above, edging each and every scale with a silvery tinge. Placing a tiny wall around the fiery scales, seemed to highlight their depth, contrasting light against shadow, peace against war but somehow balancing beauty between them.

Its tail, powerful and long, wrapped around its body, ending near the beast's face, scaled and horned to somehow shield and protect an already armoured, immense and impenetrable fortress of a body. Every scale perfect in placement, with the inner fire forged to never relinquish.

Trying to let every aspect of the dragon's beauty soak into my soul I longed to place my hand on the creature. Would it burn to the touch? Daring not to risk, for fear of its wrath more than its burn. Or would it awake, removing itself from my vision? I sat and stared with a love never before felt within me.

Its head, with a stature of pure power, had a translucent quality, gleaming with tendrils of fine wispy smoke escaping from its nostrils, reaching ever upwards towards the canopy sheltering the beast, until vanishing into the clear skies above.

I had always loved the dragons, and since that day of first witnessing one, had longed to be paired with mine. Sitting here in my sanctuary with a dragon curled near me, I had everything I had always wanted or needed. A strange bonding occurred that night, as though I'd been here before; or this was my true being calling to me?

I'd never felt more secure, and the happiness I'd craved since my father's passing filled me again. I shed quiet tears that night, both of sadness and relief that I again could feel that way. Something I thought forever lost to me, never to recall or replace.

It is said that dragons seep glamour, a magic released from within them at will, so that all other beings do the dragon's bidding. Already fully tightly wrapped up in the moment, if glamour was present, I sent it no ill will.

Something else drew me here, drew the dragon too, a togetherness shared somehow. It was then, whilst I sat in reverence, with elation and sorrow mixed, that the dragon awoke. Whilst my vision reached for every detail of the dragon, somehow trying to imprint its exact form into memory, to hold forever within me, I suddenly noticed movement. As I glanced back the dragon opened its eyes.

I've never felt particularly small in life, true, still a growing man, that said, but at that moment I felt very small and insignificant indeed.

Staring into the depths of a thousand lives lived, liquid gold pooling and reforming to show clarity in its thoughts, it slowly moved its head nearer to me. Unable to move, or just fearing to, I froze, unsure even if I continued to breathe. That moment shall stay with me until I pass on to Rai.

The dragon raised its mighty head, and with a mere thought nodded slowly at me in respect. Raising itself to its full height, a beast of incredible size stood in front of me, far larger than even I could have guessed, its head reaching far over the tops of the tallest trees around us.

It yawned, huge teeth, the biggest I'd ever seen, pure white as settled snow. Each one serrated on all sides, showing the sheer sharpness of each pure bladed weapon it held in its jaw. Row upon row, like soldiers ready to battle.

As if unsure whether it would curl up again, to sleep for longer, or to stay upright to try to catch the far-off rising sun, it hesitated. Then, realising its wants, it raised its wings and with a single jump launched its mass into the air. The wave of power raised in that one action was beyond my control.

It sheared branches from the biggest trees, sent animals, before unseen to me, to flight for cover, forcing my eyes closed to prevent damage from debris, and making me hold onto the nearest tree, stopping myself from being blown into further danger.

As the calmness returned, chaos leaving its mark behind, as it always does, I suddenly sat up, back in bed, back to reality the next morning.

Peshy, holding his breath as I spoke, stood still, I would say unbelieving at first, but recognising that, as his friend, I wouldn't lie to him like this.

We tried to make a sense of our dreams; whether random or not, we felt they had meaning that we shouldn't ignore. Vowing to seek Ivan's wisdom on the next visit he made, we held secure our secrets till that time.

Shaking the visions from my head, with the very sleep that had given me them, I felt a pang of regret for leaving that clearing behind in my dreams again. My dreams always took me back to the same place, but never again did the dragon return to me there. Like a lost soul, I yearned for his company, both awake, and within my dreams.

At other times I appeared to be searching the clearing and surrounding forest, trying to hunt him out, as if he were hiding behind mere foliage. Wanting to hold something which is not real can lead a person to madness. But following a dream, trying to make it into reality, I so hoped I could achieve. Unsure if signs placed in my dreams held relevance to my waking life, I tried to focus on the tasks ahead.

I jumped out of bed, accepting another day's teaching to make that dream hopefully come ever nearer.

After breaking fast that morning, then after washing and changing, I made my way along the path leading to the forest classroom. Another beautiful day had awoken, the early sun's summer warmth burning away the night's cool mist.

Being one of the first there that morning, I relished the relative quiet of the setting. More friends and classmates arrived, and eventually, with everyone present, Gavriel walked into the forest's classroom. Explaining that Rogan and Vinn would be studying in solitude together this week, back at the temple, he stated that as usual he would make himself available to their every need, as their acceptance was at the coming week's end.

He told us to study well, to continue carving, and make sure our offerings were making progress. Another easier week, we all agreed, as he returned to the temple to assist our friends.

Adding detail to my carving, I half listened to the conversations around me, people mostly talking about the forthcoming acceptance day, with Rogan and Vinn's offerings complete, already in place within the temple.

Placed there for all to see and Rai to shine down on, their carvings again fully done, lessons well learnt, this week would seem an endless one of procession for them. Late night prayers, mixed with family meals, all part of the final week before their big day.

As I carved my dragon thoughts turned to my acceptance day. I couldn't escape the thought of it. It seemed always there, like a buzzing insect, annoyingly close, but too far away to deal with. I felt I lived in a perpetual circle; of work, deeds wanting attention, and family needs.

None of which I regretted, but it made me long for the solitude of my walking dreams.

It was then that I heard a familiar sound, but in an unfamiliar setting; turning my head to look straight at Peshy, he stared straight back at me, realising we both had heard Ivan's cart wheels trundling along. Normally Ivan only travelled in these parts upon market days, sometimes coming a day early to allow him time to set up, or finish works he was doing.

But today the noise of his unmistakable cart filled the edges of my thoughts.

Making a feeble excuse, Peshy and I made haste to catch up with the old peddler.

Finding him wasn't hard; we started walking along the path that led to the market, following the slightly grooved tracks that he left in the dirt road's surface. Seeing though, after a time, that his cart tracks deviated from their normal route, we followed them, finding our friend under an aged apple tree, wiping the road dust off his face with a finely woven cloth. We waved as we approached.

Ivan was an older man than he appeared, long miles often travelled had aged him. As he sat on his cart's edge, he pondered us walking towards him. Since he'd given us both his charms, we'd not seen him, and with a caution I'd never felt in his presence before, I walked towards my friend.

His first words stunned us, stopping us in our tracks, apparently reading our questions before being told.

"Your charms are working, well I see," he said with a smile on his wizened face. Seeing the shocked look on our faces, our silence to his words spoken, he continued to talk.

"Many people take me for a fool," he stated, "others never give me a second glance, but I have travelled this great land of ours many times, over many years. Things can be found, and lost, but knowledge gained should be cherished so. My charms are but a mere token to some, and in truth the ones I sell each month from my little stall, often are simply that. Charms to make people believe what they want, or need to believe, this remains up to them.

"The charms they buy are trinkets, things to store away, or to wear to feel better. Gifts for loved ones, gifts to yourself to pick you up when feeling low.

"Charms to place things they put faith into, love, peace, serenity, they're worth no more than that. But they believe they work, so sometimes they do. Faith in one's abilities can waver, either through doubt or self-belief. Having good luck, or something close to you that gives belief, gives you that luck. This can be worth more than the price paid to gain such a thing."

"Other charms have different qualities," he said, smiling, looking us in the eye. "Some hold great powers within, that I find need allies to show their true form. Only when the power is placed into its sanctuary, and the holder knows their true destiny, will the true greatness of that power rise, and do great things.

"All power can't be treated as great, though, and bad omens exist, showing dark power is alive and can't be trusted. As powerful as true greatness is, a darkness lurks within this land too.

"If you ask for explanation of these things, I can give you none, for it is not my lesson to teach. I merely see the elemental powers in places I visit, assisting them to find the true ally they need. They call to me, shall we say.

"If it's the knowledge of how I combine these gifts you seek from me, leading me to tell tales of what you both truly hold, I again will disappoint you.

"If my creations told me their tales of want, told me the lives they've lived, I'd be a powerful man indeed, but before you is a simple peddler, trinkets of worth for sale, my skill in the making, handed down to me by Rai himself.

"My only voice in this matter is that if you hold such a gift, it is yours alone. Given for a reason I cannot explain. Know only that you hold a power that you deserve to hold.

"One day whilst following history, you must make a decision to continue as always, or turn to write your own path in the history written from that day on. That choice, my friends, will be yours to decide; no other makes a man's path. Some try to influence you, turn you to places you wouldn't have visited or considered, but in the end the true path can only be taken by you. Remember, no man can make you do a task that you truly don't want to do; every one of us faces choices.

"How you choose writes your destiny. Make sure if you ever get the chance to read your past that regret isn't the biggest player in the game. Try to listen to your values, seek knowledge from the past without trying to rewrite it. The power of the past should be exactly that, left in the past."

Confused, and with so many questions still whirling around my head, I stared blankly at Ivan, Peshy to my side wearing the same glazed look in his eyes.

It was at that moment that Ivan chose to follow his path, his own destiny spoken of in that conversation.

Turning around, not saying another word, he walked to the front of his small cart. Placing his hands on the weathered wooden board next to the front of the cart, he lifted himself up onto the small rickety seat. With a flick of his wrists holding the reins, he waved goodbye to us, his pony begrudgingly trotting off. It never once lifted its vision, keeping its head down towards the floor. Turning to regard us once more, I think understanding our held questions within not answered, he smiled. "Understand again," he shouted over the noise of the cart trundling along the dirt track towards the market. "You already have the answer to all your thoughts, you just need to work out what the true questions are."

Leaving Peshy and me standing there, Ivan and his little cart continued along the road, eventually dropping from sight as the dirt track twisted left, behind the forest we'd walked from. Bewildered and assuming we must be somehow wiser, without a question asked or in honesty answered, we shrugged and vowed to share our dreams more; maybe together we could work out what they meant.

FIVE

Confusion still hung in the air around Peshy and me; trying to focus on things we knew we could understand, we decided to go hunting that day.

Much needed food was always welcome at home, supplying our share for this week's festivities would show us in good faith. Food given as a gift would always be accepted amongst the tribe, this week adding further pressure to those families of the accepted. We understood that feeding many more mouths than normal would be tough. Very soon we hoped that, as we prayed in that final week, our friends would be doing the same for us. So with hope within us, we walked home to get our hunter's sacks.

We preferred to hunt alone, Peshy and I, so today we parted company.

Peshy always liked to hunt more northern territories, pitting his wits with the fast small deer on the open plain. The fleet-footed Uppula were always found in fair-sized groups;

cautious of feeding in too high grassland they preferred to stay to the edges nearer the shorter grass, keeping away from possible ambush.

Blending in, camouflaged with their habitat, they were both fast and elusive. Light stripes on a mostly umber-coloured pelt made their form seem to change at a distance. This suited the Uppula well, their numbers steadily rose around the colonies in the Ibothiel region, of Pohalith. Uppula were hunted by most colonies I knew and, as all game herds were, constantly harassed by the region's predators.

Packs of May Wolfe, mostly roaming at night, took the occasional Uppula, working in their pack mentality to seek out the smaller or frail elderly deer. Attacking at night whilst the Uppula tried to rest gave another advantage to the May Wolfe packs.

The wolves, though not as fast as the deer, succeeded as their stamina remained unmatched. So the inevitable happened, more often than not. The real threat to the Uppula, apart from man, were the predatory cats. Oravore could take an infant calf easily, or maybe a weakened elderly doe or buck.

But the Veiled Sinivore were capable of taking even the strongest Uppula, a sight I'd never seen, but only in the aftermath of the bloodied scene left behind.

Peshy, after leaving his home with his hunter's bow and sack firmly in place on his back, started his journey through the forest. After walking for nearly an hour he rested, thankful for the summer's heat but refreshed more in that moment standing within the cooling shade of the trees.

Planning his next move, taking on board water and some

jerky, he decided that day to set animal traps in the game trails he often walked and knew well.

He hoped that if he wasn't successful with his bow, that day on the plains, he might catch unsuspecting prey in his traps. These, though, would have to wait for him to return later, on his way home; always a risk placed here, as nature being nature takes opportunity when it sees it. Small hunting cats often stole trapped animals, merely leaving evidence of a successful gain, suddenly lost once again. Sweating in the now mid-morning heat of that summer day, Peshy started his journey once more, from the forest edge to the foothills about an hour away.

After gathering the equipment which I knew I'd need, with, as always, my hunter's bow, I started out towards my hunting grounds.

The totally opposite direction to Peshy, I headed south, to my sanctuary.

The light breeze of the summer's day was perfect, cooling to the bare skin of my arms as I walked along. The heat of the mid-morning promised to continue, to eventually become an overpowering sensation of heat.

Detouring slightly to pass near a small stream, I ran a cloth handkerchief in its cool slow-moving water. I soaked my neck and head, relieved by the trickling drops of cold water running down my back. It only took me a short time to reach my hunting grounds, but the relief to get out of the direct sun was tangible.

How wise I'd been by deviating to that stream; it had cooled me down immensely, as I drank some of its cold water I'd taken with me. I rested, waiting for my entrance to the forest clearing to disappear and be forgotten by the prey who heard or saw me.

At peace, slightly drifting to the edges of sleep I sat still, wedged into a tree trunk I used frequently.

To state how long I'd sat there that day would have been impossible to say, minutes had merged into hours, it felt. Soon after I'd arrived, I'd taken three rabbits; swift shots with my bow had felled all three animals a small blanket's distance apart, none knowing or sensing the fall of their kin.

Sitting in the dappled shade on this glorious summer's day, I watched nature; truly gifting me with a beautiful sight, watching the long yellow-stemmed grass wave backwards and forwards rhythmically. It danced in the breeze, its flowing patterns seamlessly changed its form, creating pockets of deep shade, where elsewhere the colour seemed to flow like liquid bronze, freed to escape into the soil itself.

Dragonflies flew, darting backward and forwards, bright blue azure wonders each and every one, occasionally interspaced with vivid green, which highlighted a translucent wing edge here and there.

Whilst captivated in nature's beauty, feeling at one with the place where I sat, it happened.

I looked, but at first didn't truly see the creature that entered the beautiful scene in front of me. A large male Tusked Mortogg crashed through the undergrowth, skidding to a stop in the clearing. The characters of the play I'd been observing dispersed, dragonflies one minute dancing on the breeze, simply turned a wing and took flight to play their scene elsewhere.

The liquid bronzed grass merely parted as the strongest opposite blackness of the creature's fur took precedence now, every sense occupied by its strength.

In appeared to stare straight at me without seeing, as if it had wanted to join in the beauty once there, but shocked now as if wondering where it had gone.

It turned, pointing its snout upwards, sniffing the air for predator or maybe food, I know not which.

Thinking it was safe, not noticing me or not concerned either way, it stood still, gazing at its surroundings. It appeared to be contemplating its next thought, as I slowly notched an arrow into my hunter's bow.

I focused on its presence. This was a large beast, dangerous if cornered; a fight at close quarters would indeed see harm to each of us. Even though I carried knives for meat preparation and small cleavers and my bow, the sheer size, muscle and sharpened tusks gave the Mortogg advantages I couldn't claim. For a split second I hesitated; this much meat could feed my family, giving much meat for the upcoming ceremonies too. So a truer shot would never be needed more. As I lifted my hunter's bow and aimed, I couldn't help but notice the tough black fur of the beast, sticking up in small tufts along its back. Its size was about the same as mine, tusks appearing longer than my forearms; sharpened edges, with each end worn away to a rounded point, used to dig up ground fruits and for defence. This would be a challenge indeed and, though scared, I prayed to Rai for an honest kill, so took my aim.

Aiming at the side of the beast, just behind the front legs, I hoped as with most animals that I could penetrate there to pierce the animal's heart. The slight shake to my arms gave me concern but, holding a breath then releasing it and my arrow at the same time, I watched.

The Tusked Mortogg sensed the threat at the same time

as the arrow found its mark; jerking as if shocked it took a step forward then fell face first to the floor.

The arrow's shaft, sticking halfway into the Mortogg's body, told me its strength was indeed great. Normally a shot from that distance would pass through a small deer or rabbit easily. I'd taken large birds before, and arrows could easily kill from that range without a problem. Noting the distance of the shot to memory for future encounters, giving thanks for my true aim to Rai, I started to unpack my butchery tools.

Suddenly the forest around me became spooked, birds took flight and a silence, once there, was replaced with running, crashing sounds, I was aware of something rushing towards me. Fear gripped as I thought possibly another Mortogg approached, angered maybe by my taking of its kin's life.

Looking for shelter I dropped my tools and grabbed my bow. Quickly retreating to the safety of my hollowed tree trunk, I waited there for the threat to show, arrow notched ready. It was with relief that I saw Peshy leap into the clearing, but fear soon took over, as I looked at him, covered in blood.

He dropped to his knees in front of me; fearing he was desperately injured I rushed to his side. He looked at me, fear in his eyes, and mentioned simply a word… Sinivore.

Peshy, although out of breath, and covered with large scratches, was otherwise not seriously hurt. His arms apparently had suffered the worst injuries, so whilst Peshy tried to calm his thoughts and breathing, I ripped sections from my shirt, starting to bandage the worst of his wounds.

After time, his breathing returned to normal so that, although shocked, he could now speak. I asked him to tell me what had happened.

Peshy had been hunting like me, watching the game herds stretched out across the plains from his hiding place. He'd soon realised that they were too far out to reach and wouldn't travel to his location that day. Knowing he couldn't get closer without them seeing or hearing him, he'd waited, hoping they would venture nearer, but gave up as they didn't give any indication they were coming closer.

The Uppula had drifted further into the plains, staying in their groups out of harm's way, so Peshy decided to retrace his way home, checking his traps.

It was then, while checking his earlier set trap lines, that he first heard the noise. Crossing through a small copse of trees before entering under the forest canopy he sneaked a look over the edge of a small rock formation; at the bottom of the rocks within an easy drop away from Peshy, caught in one of his stronger big game traps sat a Veiled Sinivore.

Peshy watched it struggle, trying to rip the very metal itself from its leg; its rear left foot ensnared within the twisted wire, frantically shaking its entire body trying to escape, but this only achieving the opposite effect, simply tightening the wire.

Peshy, in awe of the beast, was also greatly saddened. Its power having legendary status, somehow, now though captured like this, showing it to be vulnerable too. He knew he had to act quickly, so dropping into the Sinivore's view, climbing down the left side of the rocks he sat on, Peshy considered his options.

I watched Peshy explain as he told me he tried to free the beast; it appeared to be cowering away from him, he said. Thinking he could simply, quickly, untwist the trap, releasing the Sinivore, he tried.

Speaking in broken sentences I understood that the events of the day had truly shocked him, as he continued to tell his tale.

At first the Sinivore tried running, pulling away, anything to allow escape, but either never meeting man before, or not knowing Peshy's intentions, its threats then turned towards Peshy, thrusting its large paws in his direction, batting at him as if he sat there as a small mouse, letting Peshy know that its claws were real by extending them fully.

Then with its options restricted, only knowing attack, cornered and afraid, it struck.

Raking its huge claws down Peshy's arms, then the side of his face, backing away slightly only to leap again, trying to both flee and save its life. Peshy had fought it off with just his bare hands, these covered in scratches deep into his flesh like his arms, large wounds that needed cleaning properly to stem infection.

Peshy sitting in front of me, looking both hurt and scared, said, "It's still there. I couldn't help it, so I ran. I knew you'd help, and I'd knew you'd be here. We have to get back there."

Several things started to run through my mind. Noticing firstly that Peshy had lost lots of blood and spirit I helped him to his feet. It sounds harsh, looking back, but I couldn't just leave my kill lying there either. I tied a section of rope around the Tusked Mortogg's rear feet and, once I'd hastily packed my tools and bow away, tied the remainder of the rope around my waist and went to help Peshy walk. His legs had escaped the Sinivore's attack, but he'd scratched them running through the forest's undergrowth trying to reach me.

His left ankle was swollen, too, from turning it over in

the rush back to find me. This was getting worse, but he could walk. I couldn't move fast either in truth. Dragging a Mortogg, half carrying my friend, I allowed Peshy to hold onto my shoulder and we started the walk back to the colony.

On a normal day the walk back could be done even lazily within the half hour mark; today dragging my kill and helping Peshy it took just over an hour, gladness filling me as we got back home. Acacia saw us first and ran down to us, wondering what had happened, I lay Peshy on the ground near my home and ran as fast as I could, dragging the Mortogg. Leaving Acacia with Peshy I shouted for my mother to come quickly.

She leaned out of the doorway with a surprised look and saw me running towards her. Dropping whatever she worked on she ran out to meet me. I told her of Peshy's injuries and some of the story, dropping the Mortogg off near home. She came with me to Peshy and we both helped him up to our home, where mother started to wash Peshy's hands and arms.

Acacia was sent to ask Gavriel for assistance; even though he had an important week ahead, both Mother and I felt he was the best to help us, so Acacia set off to find him at the temple.

Once the painstaking job of cleaning deep into Peshy wounds was done, the water in the bowl, tepid and heavily stained with blood, was a chill reminder of how dangerous this could have been. Whether through rest or just time to compose himself Peshy seemed better all round. Smiling but still shocked he was worried that he'd left the Sinivore in trouble. As we each stood to start our journey back, Gavriel knocked upon the door, accompanied by both of Peshy's parents.

Gavriel sat, one hand holding his jaw in contemplation, motionless as Peshy described the events that had occurred that day. Mother, Acacia, Anselm and Indira sat quietly too, wrapped up in the tale. Occasional gasps of breath from my little sister. Gavriel agreed that we needed to go back and see if the beast was still there or had freed itself from its prison. Even though Peshy was weaker than his normal buoyant self, Gavriel agreed he was best to come. We needed the exact location without wasting precious daylight as the day was drawing closer to an end. It would be a fair way to travel, so without hesitating we set off at a slower pace, with Peshy doing his best not to be left too far behind.

Managing the distance if not at speed Peshy persevered with the journey, never complaining about his wounds or his ankle. We rested occasionally when we could to refocus and go over details Peshy had told us, and soon came near to the spot we searched for, unnervingly quiet.

We walked around the small, jagged rock formation sticking out of the floor in the wooded copse, and here I sighted my first ever Veiled Sinivore.

Resting against the rock face, hunched down, trying to make itself fit into the very cracks in the rock, it stared straight at us, its left rear leg at an obtuse angle, obviously broken, the thick wire seen leading to its leg having been driven deep into its flesh, binding the beast tight. Blood surrounded the scene, and I wondered if all was Peshy's or had the beast fought so hard to escape it had ripped its own skin and flesh in its attempts.

Cautious, we stayed back; whilst the Sinivore was calm we talked about how to release it. Gavriel, deep in thought, listened to our claims of victory; with either a kindness to our youth or allowing him longer to think, he indulged our thought out, but naive conceived plans.

Gavriel then spoke. "The Sinivore is a much beloved beast; stories about its legendary status travel places you have not yet encountered. It's rarely seen and when is it's stated a bad omen.

"No one goes out to trap or knowingly kill a Sinivore, that would not be easily done normally, but here we are. In reality the Sinivore in front of us isn't the only thing in a trap. Seeing it here in its weakened and damaged state prevents us giving it back its natural course of life. How can we remove the trap without its injuries becoming much worse? The likelihood of getting injured, or possibly getting killed ourselves, is great. That leaves us few options. If we believe the bad omens are true, then killing an animal of this status brings us ill tidings. We can only leave it here, so that it starves itself to death.

"Pain from its injuries will eventually take its fight away and lead it to death, but these will not be quick things, with the truth sitting here in front of us being different from all the tales I've heard."

We sat watching the animal, its beautiful grey fur, dappled with shadowing, showed its toned muscles off perfectly. Its face broad and strong, with large disc-shaped eyes, black but with a light of strength even now in its situation of torture.

Long sleek legs, powerful for both running and climbing, couldn't help it with either now, and, as it sat looking straight back at us, we were only truly left with one humane option.

As we all agreed as to what needed to be done, Gavriel said that Rai would understand; even bad things are not always done on purpose. None of us liked the fact that the Sinivore suffered so.

Peshy stepped forward; as he had trapped the beast he would kill it, he wanted to end its suffering and felt responsible. I didn't say so, but I didn't want the job, even though it needed doing, and was much relieved when Gavriel said he agreed. Notching an arrow in Gavriel's bow, Peshy stepped forward.

All three of us had killed many animals before, but to kill the first Sinivore I'd seen not only seemed unfair but saddened me to their plight. These creatures might have been mythical in stories told at late night campfires, but they were rare in our world, and it seemed poor luck indeed that this was how we'd encountered our first one.

The beast itself never faltered in its contempt towards Peshy. As he walked forward to secure a better aim, it launched once again towards him, throwing clawed paws in all directions, its fight humbled by its predicament but not lost, and until the arrow was firmly bedded into its flesh it still shook with an anger that I'd never seen.

To be sitting in a storm of hatred, energy battering you from all sides, crashing noise and violence to suddenly calm and peace is a strange place to be, but that's where we were; the deed done, we all walked over to the body of the beast.

Removing the wire trap from its foot was nigh on impossible. Only with severe strength did Gavriel loosen the noose and remove it. It had nearly eaten its way completely through the foot and left behind the destruction of that story.

If the beast had got out it would have been crippled from that day on, unable to hunt for food, and would have possibly suffered unmentionably in the time it took for death to raise its sickle.

Gathering small rocks from nearby we hollowed out a small basin of soil using branches from the trees, placing the body of this beautiful creature within. Covering it with collected rocks and stones we paid our last respects and left its grave to the falling darkness.

Gathering our thoughts and helping Peshy we returned homeward. As we walked, hearing the May Wolves howl their prayers to the moon, we sent our prayers to Rai, hoping this indeed was enough to keep at bay possibilities of ill omens.

Upon returning we entered the forest classroom. The moon was riding high, the hour later than we had initially thought, but weariness had dulled all our senses.

Gavriel nodded he would see us tomorrow and ventured out towards the temple. A solemn look featured on his face, both concern and regret, something we all felt that night, and for many nights to come.

Helping Peshy stumble home we worked our way through the forest's edge, tracing the moonlit path laid out in front of us. It seemed Rai was still showing favour by leading the way; we slowly but easily made way towards home.

As we approached Peshy's homestead he suddenly stopped, the moonlight showing a seriousness to his features.

Peshy stretched out his arm towards me, opening his fingers, I looked and struggled to see what he held, hardly making out the two small objects, sitting perfectly in the centre of his palm.

Moving closer I could see they were two sharp teeth, glinting white. Meeting Peshy's eyes with mine, the question I thought must have travelled between us as he answered without me speaking. The teeth, they were on the floor near the trap, they must be from the Sinivore.

Peshy seemed to hesitate as he closed his hand around the teeth; unsure as to what I would say, he turned away.

Asking him why he'd picked them up, he couldn't reply to me, simply saying that he'd just seen them and didn't want them to go to waste, thought he would use them on his offering.

I shook my head in disbelief at the day's events; worrying still about ill omens, I shared my concerns with Peshy, feeling bad about his opinion on the teeth. He started his slow walk along the path to his house, turning just the once to look at me, smiling as he went. I again shook my head, turning towards my home, letting the moonlight guide my path once more.

SIX

Reaching my bed was all that mattered to me, and although only feet in front of me, it felt miles away. I staggered forward, slumping fully dressed onto my mattress, still covered in the day's blood and dirt, but as soon as my head found my pillow these thoughts simply drifted away, as I quickly fell deep into a fitful, restless sleep.

Deep within the exhaustion of the troubled day I had fought through, strange visitations troubled me. These seemed to penetrate the serene sleep I longed myself to find. A scene both unsteady and frightening to my struggling conscious played out. I found myself walking in my dreams, not resting, which I craved, as if my dreams were prolonging my tiredness.

In my dream, surrounding me, distant ominous noises threatened; they engulfed me, noises guttural, animal-like, but of no creature I'd ever encountered. Deep, so very deep; they shook the core of my very being, to sudden pitches so high in nature you had to cover your ears, trying to block the noise somehow, before it must pierce your very soul.

Strange again were the actual surroundings; dark, dank, with life itself seemingly void here, this place wasn't somewhere I knew. As with most dreams I had, this foreign land was void of everything, senseless in both colour and most feelings, except fear, and hopelessness. These feelings owned this place, they controlled this space, a space I didn't want to be in.

The fact I was here felt wrong, felt as if the dream itself didn't want me here, as if it grew angry, resentful of the fact that I existed in its space, pulsating even, pushing me away, not forcefully, not physically, as nothing stood in front of me to do such a thing but more of a mental thought, a threat to hurt, a threat to violate, to harm above all else, to leave and leave quickly like a presence always hanging in the air, chasing me.

Then with that final thought controlling me, I turned, my head telling me to run, a shadow then eclipsed my entire body, sending me flying backwards through the air, falling, falling.

Suddenly I awoke with a start, sitting up in bed, breathing heavily, soaked to the skin in sweat, still in yesterday's clothes.

I often had dreams, visions even, about hunting, animals caught, my father, normally good dreams. Dreams about my acceptance day, and my readiness to do well in my trials, but this was darker than anything I had ever experienced before. Concerned that it was linked to last night's happenings and worried whether Peshy was still okay I slowly rose out of bed.

Quickly washing last night's limited sleep from my eyes, alongside the dirt, sweat and blood off my body, I changed my clothes.

I noticed the first greying tinges to the sky outside; it was still obviously the early hours of the morning, so quietly I walked into the living area of our home.

A chill breeze was the first clue something wasn't right; had I in my thirst for rest, my bed, been in such a rush to not close the door to our humble home?

The door to my mother's and Acacia's bedroom was slightly open too; this being normally closed I ventured over to sneak a look. Acacia wasn't in her bed, and she wasn't obviously in her room, I looked around our house and couldn't find her inside or outside on the porch either.

I checked back into Mother's room to see if she had climbed into my mother's bed in the night, maybe suffering from a bad night's sleep like I had, but again no sign. Worried, as Acacia never left our home without permission, I woke my mother to see if she knew if Acacia was okay, and where she was.

Acacia was missing; as I ran around the colony looking for her, word began to spread, but so did my panic. Acacia had never and would never run away like this. I tried to distance yesterday's events, added to last night's bad dream to the situation, but the more I thought of the dream the more I feared an ill omen had indeed struck me for my actions with the Sinivore.

By now Mother and I had searched the surrounding woods near our home, calling out for Acacia, not even a footprint being visible of a possible route of where she'd gone. Hoping that she'd simply slipped out early to gather wood or water we checked all the normal places, but again found no signs she had been there recently.

I'd woken Peshy, and although still in pain from last night's injuries he helped search. People all around were calling Acacia's name, but to no avail. I headed to Gavriel's, whilst the skies above released their darkness into first light, allowing here and there the occasional tiny patch of lightening grey colour.

Whilst walking through the forest, closing in on the boundary to the forest classroom, towards Rai's temple, I became aware I wasn't alone. Whether my hunter's senses were already switched on searching for Acacia, or somewhere inside they naturally always helped me, that early morning they gave me a second's warning, probably saving my life.

The force of the blow caught me square on the left shoulder. If I hadn't ducked as I had it would have hit me clean on the back of the head, but even this stunned me, knocked me to the ground. The power seemed immense, somehow pushing me metres across the ground into the base of a huge tree, winding me further.

I had been in a few fights as a young man, mostly with Peshy before we were friends, but I'd never been hit with a force so powerful as to physically make me surrender my entire body instantly. The pain was awful, but more than that, it remained unbearable. It felt as though my whole torso had been crushed; breathing shallow breaths was nearly impossible, but these were the only ones manageable. Gross movements too painful to consider, and whilst I lay on the floor against the tree base, before even getting a chance to refocus my attention on what, or who was attacking me, it started.

A sudden overpowering sensation of grief, loss, anguish even, a mental pain forced itself into every part of my body, somehow, if possible, adding to the excruciating pain my body was already suffering, barely holding onto my consciousness, not truly knowing how I did at this point.

I could somehow sense people around me, in the near distance, but as weak as a rodent in the paws of a hunting Oravore, I couldn't have moved if my life depended on it, and at this moment I felt it surely did.

A rough, hessian cloth, warm, musty and damp, smelling putrid, rotting with the smell of decay, was placed, wrapped around my face. Not tightly, I could have easily taken large breaths if capable, but still racked with physical pain, shallow rasps were all I could manage freely.

My vision was being affected twofold now; the coarse material, hard to see through in the darkness anyway, added to the strange overpowering sensation that held my body somehow still and powerless. I somehow knew what was happening, but it was as though I looked on from the sidelines, as if it occurred to another being, not myself.

I was helpless, senses muted, dumbed with pain, terror and someone's control over me, physical and mental. I couldn't call for aid, my voice failed me. No words came from within, my inner voice was mine alone. Scared and silent my own brain tried to comprehend, and it couldn't do that now. I couldn't move to help myself, pain alone stopped me but added to this was a strange force seemingly holding me still. Even though my thoughts were my own, my fears overwhelmed me and all I could do now was feel a tear roll down my left cheek.

Ropes were tied to my legs, binding my feet together. It felt as though I'd also been tied to someone else too. They didn't bother to tie my hands, they were left free, but they were not in my control to use anyhow, so it seemed a hollow gesture. I noticed them now only as heavy limbs lying prone to my side.

Once they started dragging us across the forest floor I wished they had tied my arms together; maybe then the pain would have been less, as now they chafed and rubbed against the detritus of the rough ground, flailing around, hitting rocks, branches, and the bases of trees as I was pulled past. I couldn't move them, but I could feel the pain, this hollow gesture was understood not to be a thankful one.

It seemed an eternity we were being dragged, the only break in silence was the scraping of our bodies on the forest floor. No voices were heard during that time, only the wailing I made internally; I continued to try and remember that I was still awake, somehow not trapped in a bizarre dream, the pulsating pain a constant reminder that I was indeed awake, and very much still alive.

The footsteps of my attackers as they walked crunched forward, onward to a purpose only they knew. I was amazed how strong they seemed, never resting, never stopping, purposeful in their motion.

Swift in travel, and after travelling a distance unmeasurable to myself, we came to a stop. If I told you now that I lost consciousness more than once during this time, and I shed many a hopeless tear, please forgive my weakness, but hope was all I had and with every step my attackers took my hope diminished.

I would like to say I'd become used to the strange sensation I was experiencing, but honestly, I'd just learnt to cope better with it whilst we moved; once we'd stopped the sensation seemed to intensify.

Nausea, a swirling sensation, threatened to make me lose consciousness again and maybe I even did whilst stationary for a while once more. A soul-destroying sense of depravity, loss, hopelessness, pulled me somehow as if the ground was rising and I sinking deeper into it. Hoping the ground might take the morose monotony away I wished I could sink further, deeper within to safety, a freedom from this pain, both of the mind and body.

We all experience pain in some form in life, whether physical, emotional, torment, a broken soul, or even a simple passing of a loved one, it's something that each one of us knows we will meet one day. Mostly we continue with help, perseverance of character, belief in Rai's guidance.

But these things were beyond my help right now, my mind imploded with horror, visions of torture wove themselves into my thoughts. My body became more overpowered as though each muscle was trying to burst from the very fabric of my skeleton, tightening to the maximum it could reach, causing unbelievable pain. I was screaming inside my head, but still no sound left my mouth.

And as my body twisted into its strange contortions on the forest floor, I realised that whichever magical power had me in its grasp, I was totally helpless. It was then that the bones in my left arm shattered under the arching stress and strain my own body made; although very hard to say for anybody, I wished it would just finish me, make the pain stop, it had won, I had no more left inside me to give.

It was then the sudden piercing light seemed to burst from within my chest outwards. Unnatural screams filled the air around me, a noise of which I'd never heard or want to hear again, like a creature had been suddenly set on fire, or mortally wounded next to me. Yet above the noise, above the terror and horror I'd felt, was the instant relief of the pressure I'd been feeling, the sensation within my head had ceased. Although the air around us felt somehow dark, unnatural even, I could think, I could move, that meant I could try and fight to escape.

Or at least my mind thought I could; fumbling for the cloth around my face with my left hand, I realised as the pain returned that I could no longer use that arm. Trying to loosen the rough cloth by shaking my head, though, gave me some vision back with the lightening skies.

It was then I realised that I held my charm tightly with my right hand and it felt as though it was pulsating, warm to the touch. It had a heartbeat of its own, even. Light emanated from within, or shall I say retreating to within, making me realise that this had been the source of the piercing bright light a few moments before.

Gaining my surroundings more as my head started to clear, I found indeed that I was tied to another person. Lying still, no motion at all. I prayed it to be Acacia, that she was all right. But I knew as I unwrapped the cloth from the girl's head that it wasn't my sister. Although of a similar age, she wasn't someone familiar to me, someone I hadn't seen from our tribe even; covered in grazes and with a large lump to her head she lay unconscious but breathing, still alive.

It was then that I saw the first of the hooded figures stand, just a few metres away, raising themselves from the floor, as if they themselves were part of the very dirt. Slowly, methodically standing into a scooped stance, slightly bent forward, arched, almost about to pounce like a hunting cat; but this was no cat, this was something else.

I wanted to think human, as it must be, but the stench that came from the creature was surely too much to handle for a mere human to stomach. For as the smell only slightly reached closer to me I retched, then vomited my limited stomach contents.

Arms and legs shorter, but not overly more than mine, concealed under a blackened robe, a hood hiding the creature's face totally, it turned towards my position on the forest floor.

As it turned and made its first movement towards me, that's when I heard, faintly at first, voices in the distance, either attracted to the bright light or the creature's piteous screaming but human voices, coming this way. With all my strength I shouted, screamed even, at the top of my lungs.

Trying to sound an alarm but not sound terrified is very hard to achieve and I'm not entirely sure which part of me called harder but I called and called.

The creature hesitated only for a moment, then, grabbing another body from the floor, which I hadn't seen, disappeared with two fellow hooded creatures, running at an incredible speed towards the temple. Either exhaustion, fear or sheer relief using up my final energy at that point I collapsed into unconsciousness once more; as it took a grip of my body my final thought was of Acacia.

My memories of the next few days are interspersed with moments of vivid reality set in between the foggy sleep of a recovering body, waking occasionally to have a bitter liquid forced down into me for the pain. This only made me nauseous then tired, and I battled these feelings now in the small periods I was awake.

Finally, when it felt like an eternity, which actually was

only three days, had passed, they let me sit up and stay awake a while longer.

I found myself resting on a large bed in a simple room, one of those set aside in a large building the colony used as a temple of healing. This was on the west side of the complex of outbuildings that surrounded the greater temple of Rai.

Its placement was both peaceful and sheltered to allow shade from the sun's midday heat, protection from the winter's harsh winds, and a sanctuary to get away from all others. Only if you had the will of Gavriel could you visit someone, or if you were attending the patients. The maidens of the temple were the law here, and they were very strict who they allowed in.

Desperate for news of Acacia, either my constant questioning every day or my pleas eventually falling on the right ears, Gavriel walked into my room as I sat in bed looking through the window, glimpsing shadows play on the surface of the branches of the trees at the edge of the surrounding forest.

Stern features met my gaze, which were probably just as stern, as he perched on the edge of my bed.

He placed a single hand on my leg, it seemed to me to steady himself, more than anything else; this act alone shocked me, as the strongest man I'd ever known, or legends written about, told of his strength in every situation.

When he spoke, his voice seemed more timid then I'd ever heard it; like a father speaking to his newborn child, a warrior speaking his last breath to a loved one, and the message he told tore through my soul.

"Acacia hasn't been found," he said. The words seemed to enter my head; I heard them, I understood them, but

I couldn't fathom what that meant. So many questions jumbled my thought processes at once. *Why? Where have you searched? Any clues? Any witnesses? Who looked?* Many more mixed in, too, and in the next hour or so Gavriel tried to appease my incessant pleas with answers he didn't have.

Members of the colony who had been out searching for Acacia had found my near lifeless body lying on the floor where I'd collapsed. They had indeed seen the bright light that emanated from my dragon medallion, the guttural screams from the animal beasts that had captured me, then my screams for help. Carrying my body to Gavriel, thinking I was beyond saving, they had, with the rest of the colony, continued searching, were continuing to look for my sister. Gavriel had brought me here to the temple of healing and now was with me again.

This time the questions were all Gavriel's, but realising I needed more time to deal with the shock and recover he stood to leave. With the slightest nod he turned and left me. The tears still burned my cheeks with the warm path they traced on my skin. I again drifted off to sleep, thinking of Acacia.

Acacia's voice woke me; or I at least thought it had, but it was my dream.

I found myself walking through the forest once again near the classroom; a place so familiar to me that, if you had asked, I could have taken you there blindfolded.

A place where I had spent many hours practising my lessons, days carving my dragon onto the tree bench, but this time it was silent. Darkness all around me. At first, I started to panic, started to think that this was going to turn into the dream, or shall I say nightmare, where my senses were overwhelmed before, but soon realising I was clasping tightly to my medallion already. A calmness seemed to ooze from it to me; pulsating with a reddish glow, it even pushed a sense of calmness into the general sounding area. The glow seemed to be fighting back the darkness; fighting to show its light, its true power. Regardless I held on tightly, walking forward. It was then I noticed the movement out of the corner of my eye. Slight at first but growing as I looked further into the darkness, a large object, mass if you will, was in front of me, hidden by the thickest canopy of the trees' foliage. As if some will had summoned it, or simply my wishing it was lighter had caused it, the medallion around my neck began to glow with more intensity, giving even more light through my fingers, and several metres away from me, sitting down on its back legs, like the biggest May Wolfe you'd ever seen, was a dragon.

I would say the beast was bigger than anything I'd seen, but this was no beast. It was, in fact, magnificent. The colour of red fluctuated as the muscles moved in its limbs, throwing the light from the medallion into cascades over the reflective scales covering its body. I thought before red was red, but I could see different shades of red, I can't start to explain in mere words.

The texture broke the individual hues apart, then rejoined them into sheets of liquid material. Every tiny movement from the creature merely breathing caused ripples, the minuscule scales on the limbs gave shadow, defining each muscle perfectly. The body of the dragon, so immense, powerful, seemed to lure me in. Without realising it I had walked close enough to be in danger, suddenly remembering or hoping this in fact was a dream.

The dragon lowered its head, so that its elliptical eye stared straight at me, then it spoke. "Wicker, you are in grave danger. Remember, together we are stronger, apart we are weak, we need each other, more than you realise, but forces move against us. Grow strong and find me. I'll help you when it's time."

With this the dragon raised his mighty head and moved slowly backwards into the darkened forest. Wanting to gaze more, wanting to question his words, I tried to speak but before my words left me, the dragon had simply disappeared. The glow of the medallion started to diminish and the next thing I recall was waking in my bed in the temple, still holding tightly to my medallion, whilst inside it the red colours swirled and flew to the hidden currents it rode.

Thinking to myself that, as soon as I was better, I needed to try to speak with Ivan again about the powerful charm he'd given me, I vowed that until then I'd hold my dreams secret to myself. Somehow, I needed to see if Peshy had been experiencing anything strange again, too. For now, though, I just needed to get out of here.

It seemed my pleas to leave went unheard, or just ignored. The maidens of the temple never spoke unless it was telling me to take my medicine, or to bathe my cuts and sores, but I knew they were looking after me.

My mother came to see me and after crying and holding me too tightly she explained that they were searching everywhere for Acacia. I felt useless as I couldn't help, but she insisted I rest. I told her some details of what had happened to me, trying to avoid the pain I could see I caused her in the telling of the story. I left out how much it had hurt as she seemed so old and fragile at this moment, something my mother had never looked. I asked if Peshy was all right and could visit. She said that he was good and was currently away with a group searching the outlanders' territory for Acacia.

The outlanders had been helping too, apparently, with members of their colony mysteriously missing too. This had started a new friendship between the two colonies, and as soon as he was back Mother promised she would tell Peshy I was on the mend. She promised she would be back soon too; I didn't have the heart to tell her that she looked so tired that I wanted her to rest. I just smiled and nodded that I would rest and see her soon.

Over the next week I started to regain my strength. My arm was still broken, obviously, but had been straightened and placed in a wooden device to keep it straight. I could wiggle my fingers out the end and had seen people have them on before, even on their legs, making them have to hop, so I hoped it would be all right. Gavriel visited me every day and made me retell my story slowly from the time Peshy and I had left him after dealing with the Veiled Sinivore. He stopped me occasionally, pondering things I'd said, or to take notes, even asking me to repeat my description of the beasts that had attacked me in the forest to the elder Rai priests.

Gavriel too seemed fascinated by my medallion charm, and even took a closer look, but agreed that it was mine to hold and would not take it away from me.

I felt guilty not saying anything about my dreams, but I wanted to keep this part secret to me, for now. I wasn't sure if I was just going crazy, or was just being cautious, but for now I held it close to myself.

A week passed by with frequent visits from Gavriel, always with questions about the fateful night of my attack. Books were brought to me to continue my training but little or no effort went into this from me. I slept, mostly, longing for visits from Mother with news of Acacia, but although the visits came, the good news didn't follow. No sign had been found, not even a trace, and now I learnt the search was being scaled down. I had to get out of here, my arm was improving, I gained strength every day, I had to help.

Temple maidens said another two weeks, but with Gavriel's help I managed to get that to one more week, then I would be allowed home to continue my recovery. During that final week, they removed the wooden form from my arm, replacing it with a strong, stiff bandage, woven from flattened root stems.

It was a relief to finally get the larger wooden frame off, even if movement was still limited; the weight difference was hugely better. At least I could lift my arm again. The pain within was more of a dull ache, and the temple maidens said my arm was healing well; it was straight and would eventually be strong again.

It was while I was gathering my things together to leave on the last day that I had a surprise visitor. A small knock on my door, which I nearly missed, but only seeing the person standing there as I turned around to move some clothes alerted me to their presence.

There she stood; the young girl I'd been tied to that night in the forest. Still covered in grazes, although now nearly fully healed ones, a bandage obviously lighter in construction than on my arm but made of the same material wrapped around her head. She stood still, either not wanting to enter or scared to, but I beckoned her in.

We didn't know each other; she, as far as I was aware, had never seen me before, and the only time I'd seen her was when I'd removed that foul-smelling cloth from my face to find her unconscious, tied to me.

I asked her to sit. She was a young girl, I'd guessed right, about the same age as Acacia, six years my junior. She told me her name was Yamilla, shy, quiet, telling me she lived amongst the outlanders. Her older brother, Trian, had become one of the fallen many years ago. She had been born away from our colony after their family had been shunned as tradition stated must happen.

She hung her head, ashamed to admit this, and if I'm honest a part of me wanted to make her feel ashamed; history taught us that the fallen and their families weren't worthy, but here in front of me stood a tiny girl. She had never done any wrong that I knew of and had come to see me now, wondering if I was well, thanking me for saving her.

Her shame was not justified; mine now was.

SEVEN

Finally came the day I was allowed home.

Gavriel came to walk with me and steadily we left the temple. I'd spent the rest of the day after Yamilla left saying goodbye to the maidens, thanking them for all they had done, vowing to them and myself to take food back in offer of goodwill. A small gesture for all they had done, but honestly all I could summon in my current state; hopefully still seen as a welcome one.

It was a refreshing feeling to have the wind blow through my hair again, to feel the sunlight warm my back. We walked along, but it was with trepidation that I glanced around, still unsure of who or what lurked about. An uneasiness I'd never felt in life seemed to follow me now. Either because of warnings received in my dreams, or still trying to get over my attack, I grew wearier from worry these days.

Gavriel and the warrior priests had spent many days hunting the creatures, the catlike creatures I'd tried to describe, but like my poor sister Acacia, no trace of them had been found. We tried to talk of lighter times, of Peshy's upcoming acceptance day, but in the back of my mind was an uneasiness that wouldn't leave me to rest.

Mother nearly ran when she saw us crest the small hill as the path split towards home; she'd been waiting obviously for a long time and again with more than a tinge of sadness I wished Acacia was here with her normal boundless energy to greet me.

Gavriel said his goodbyes and promised to call in soon and left us to finish the last bit of the journey home. I could already smell the home-cooked bread and soup, and I realised then and there I was finally home.

I was home, but the normal sights and sounds, although filling my every sense with comfort, and strength again, also seemed dulled by Acacia's absence. Mother, on the outside, tried to remain strong, but it was obvious to me that she was overcome with grief. Not only had she lost her daughter to Rai only knows where, but I realised she must have thought I'd been lost too, for a time. Being home at least meant I could help her and look for my sister, but for now we simply rested in each other's company.

I came to sitting in the long chair in the living room, a blanket placed around me, with the glowing embers of the fire still shining, giving more than enough light to show off the features of the room.

Mother was asleep in the old rocking chair, and I think she had probably taken to sleeping there since we'd both been gone. In between the long blinks of the restlessness of waking in the hours of darkness, there always seems a time to contemplate your thoughts, your actions, and as I lay, warm and safe, I drifted into the night's events of the attack.

I wanted to explain to myself the details, the slight moment of things occurring, that are simply overlooked in recalling a story.

I wanted to see, thinking again of the smaller things if something could be remembered, retraced, reclaimed.

The nightmare hadn't been specific, Acacia wasn't in danger, but it had woken me; was that a sign, had I been meant to be awake? To be there for her, to be the one instead of her to be missing? That feeling I felt prior to the attack, saving my life by a split second, allowing me to duck, avoiding a catastrophic head injury. The power the creatures displayed over us, holding us in a state of alertness to feel the pain they handed out, incapable of movement, held somehow magically bound.

Then the creatures themselves: were they simply men, dressed to scare, to terrorise with masks, disguising their appearance, or in fact were they indeed creatures unwitnessed before?

And as a hunting colony, how could we find no trace of them? Not a footprint, not a broken track of their distance travelled. And finally, Acacia, where was she? After this many weeks, if she was safe, if she was free, she would've returned.

As the fire's last embers died away, and the sun's early rays made the dust mites illuminate the air, seeming to fill the room with hundreds of tiny bright flying dancers, Mother started to stir. Grief still in her eyes but smiling to hide the pain, she came and held me. And while she started breakfast, I went to get some fresh water from the water barrel outside.

Sunny but still holding the night's chill, I stretched and could feel my left arm feeling much stronger. Hopefully soon I could have the protective casing removed and it would be all right again. I needed to get back to hunting, and searching, which I planned to do later that day, once I'd found Peshy.

Breakfast had passed, and after I promised not to do too much, I walked to Peshy's home, not far a walk from our homestead. Indira greeted me with a smile and a hug at my arrival, and with a heavy heart told me of her sorrow about Acacia. It was becoming obvious that everyone thought she was gone for good, a fact I couldn't think of as a reality, even if the truth meant it was so.

Peshy, she said, was not at home; and I was told he was out, she thought, at the forest classroom, so at a slow walk I meandered through the colony.

A simple walk normally, today took longer both because my strength was weak, and everyone I saw stopped me to give their good intentions, some asking for the tale of the evening, others asking to pass on their prayers to me and Mother.

So, after a while, a blur of faces and people rushing by talking became not only tedious but troublesome.

Excuses of tiredness, if not wholly accurate, allowed me to pass the majority of the crowd and I managed to slip my way through the market place, towards the forest classroom.

Once there, a slight reminder tickled the back of my senses and I halted in my tracks, my awareness seemingly on overdrive, as this was the first occasion I'd entered the area since that night. Up ahead I could hear the voices of my friends, so with an effort to push aside the fear I held, I continued to the wooden benches, and the sanctuary of our forest dwelling.

Rogen, Vinn, Clay and several others met me with a small cheer and came over to welcome me back and to rib me about my arm. Being back with familiar faces, albeit being the one they joked about, took the tension from the air, and I felt more relaxed as they asked about what happened.

Peshy wasn't there, and I found out that during the searches for Acacia, Peshy had been spending more and more time searching around the outlanders' territory with Amia, the outlander girl we had seen at the Barbarrow market the day Ivan gave us our charms.

Many laughs, and rumours were already circulating about Peshy, but I held my judgement. Colony members and outlanders weren't normally seen together, everyone knew that.

After hearing about the recent searches and generally listening to the latest colony stories, I started to make my way back home.

Taking the longer route home, trying to avoid the crowds in the centre of the colony's busier areas, I decided to skirt the edges of the Ibothiel hunting grounds; a wide berth for someone not up to their best, but allowing me time to contemplate my next actions.

I watched the far-distant herds of Uppula throw dust into the air, their numbers too fast and too great to count from here as they ran across the plains, being chased by a predator or simply to cross the distances needed in their search for the tender green shoots they craved.

Here I noticed, on a large rock near the side of the path set slightly back just in the shadow of the overhanging tree, a strange dark mark, approximately a metre above my head. At first glance I simply mistook it for an insect and nearly didn't give it a second glance, but as the shadow fluctuated across the face of the rock, the branches swaying and undulating in the breeze of the day, the mark showed as the sun's light shone on it, revealing a silver-grey tone against the rust-coloured features of the stone it sat on.

I had to climb around the back of the rock, being very careful, as the side the mark was on had no real handholds as such, and even though the mark's position wasn't very high from the ground, the best position to view it from was above, so with caution and an injured arm I slowly made my way down, around the edge to finally sit beside the mark.

If beauty could be achieved by carving alone, the three minuscule silver fingerprints which had been placed into the rock face itself, had somehow been perfected. The delicate nature, the form, the craftwork was unnatural, unbelievable. The marks were, as stated, three perfectly placed fingerprints, about a third of the size of each one of mine, the total area covering the total size of around the span of my thumb, formed intricately, precisely, each line individual. Placed a hair's breadth away from its neighbour, the semi-circles in perfect alignment showed they had come from the same hand, if a real hand could have made such a piece of wonder.

On closer inspection, the silver colour seemed to somehow shift with the ever-changing light, deeper tones set along the ridges allowing light to show off the glory of the whole piece. Someone had burnt their mark into this place as a reminder that they had been here or that this was a place of great significance. I had never seen such a mark before and with the strange goings on recently I knew instantly that Gavriel must see this. Brushing them lightly with my own fingers to remind me and to thrust their beauty into my mind forever I jumped the few feet down to the ground and made my way to see Gavriel.

Gavriel stared at the marks, initially absorbed in their beauty, too, I think. He'd ordered the monks to bring several wooden boards, and hastily they had been constructed to form a rudimentary platform, allowing two people to stand easily side by side next to each other, next to the fingerprint marks.

Drawings and rubbings were made, and again warrior monks were sent forth to ponder the marks' origins, the significance of their location and their meaning. Nothing like this had been seen before, and word soon spread of their location; the colony all took their turn of having a look.

Peshy soon came into that company too; after nearly taking me off my feet by way of greeting, he studied the marks himself.

Talking as he walked me back home, it was as though we had only seen each other the day before, as if nothing had changed. We hadn't spoken for weeks but in reality life had changed much in that time.

Agreeing to meet first thing in the morning, Peshy said his goodbye and walked home, as I used my last vestiges of energy to get to the homestead.

Peshy, as promised, arrived first thing in the morning and as I had my morning wash, I could just overhear the conversation between him and Mother over the rattling of the breakfast pots being washed.

As I entered the living area, Peshy was helping put the final plates away. We walked from the homestead on our normal path towards the colony centre, generally chatting about the night events before, the fingerprints I'd found and their meaning, but mostly starting our conversation on the areas covered in the search for Acacia.

Peshy stated that he and a group of the other young men had started covering the normal places we visited, when they weren't practising prayers, or our teachings. They had covered, Peshy said, the local watering hole where we dived on particularly hot days and hung around in the pleasant warm autumn nights. He'd even started to venture further out alone, he told me; that's when he'd bumped into Amia.

Amia had been walking on her own, picking flowers in the hour before dusk fell, not far from the outlanders' Mortwedge territory but far enough away to be noticed by Peshy. Peshy had ventured further than he originally thought that night, trying to scour the area for any signs that Acacia had been this way. He'd heard a noise and quickly hidden, only to see Amia wander past. Amia, worlds away, singing a haunting melody to herself as she singled out wildflowers into a ragged bunch she held loosely in her hand. Peshy watched her and noticed how her hair, so fine, travelled fluidly on the slight breeze, flowing like tumbling water over pebbles in a babbling brook, little realising as he leant forward that he was about to lose his footing on the rock where he perched.

The noise he made cut through the night's peaceful reverie like a stone hurled at glass. Nearby birds took to flight, Amia stopped singing, and as Peshy lay face-first on the dirt Amia walked over to him with a stern look on her face. He could only mutter, "Hello."

Peshy told me how, after she helped him up, they had laughed about his humiliation of falling, and then they had started to see each other more.

Amia even helped to search for Acacia, telling him that recently several children from the outlanders had also gone missing. The mistrust between our colonies still hung very deep, with communication very limited, each colony having a general dislike of the other. But nothing of this the other knew. The younger generations of the outlanders were seemingly raised differently, Peshy told me. He shocked me with his next words. The small girl I'd been tied to, Yamilla, was Amia's younger sister. Amia was so grateful that she wanted to help search, so they both gave their time, their friendship and now, I think, maybe more into the search for Acacia together.

Qeraviel and Mortwedge were some distance apart, but the first outlanders to be pushed aside from the main colony hadn't wanted to travel too far.

Teaching told us that, shunned from the community, they took their belongings and gave up all their beliefs for the good of the colony, starting again in a new place, away from the eyes of Rai. Becoming a family member of the fallen was to fall yourself, the exception being a father already a warrior priest, whose son wasn't returned on his acceptance day. The warrior priest must, and always chose to, serve the colony over his family; being the first in line to turn his back on his previous life as they walked away.

I had observed the outlanders from afar, often seeing them in small hunting parties while I was out hunting myself. They always seemed together, never alone. Assuming safety in a group was natural to them, I thought it strange at first as I always hunted alone, but after recent events, maybe they knew something I didn't.

Although living apart, they were often at Barbarrow's market place, purchasing goods, selling vegetables they had grown, and a few had become regular to the eye, almost familiar if not accepted. Most often again in groups, keeping themselves to themselves on the edges of the crowds, outlanders mainly keep quiet going about their daily needs, very rarely making eye contact. In our teachings we were taught much about them, mostly how to avoid becoming one of them, as if they were inferior. Our teachings taught us that, learning to please Rai, sacrificing your needs for the benefit of all, for Rai, as a colony we were strong, apart we fall.

To fall was shameful, bringing sorrow to your family, hardship because of your lack of faith, inability to be accepted by your god as a true warrior amongst your people. If Rai rejected you, the colony rejected you; it was written, it was obeyed that way.

Mortwedge had been born much the same, a very similar colony indeed to Qeraviel sprang up where they settled. Smaller in size, and magnitude, some may say, but over the years it had expanded and evolved, as had our colony. Slightly lower ground than ours, a gradual downwards gradient from Qeraviel took you eventually to their lands, showing our colony on the very distant horizon on a clear day. Shining on a sunny day to be like a beacon of hope above them, always above them, as if to emphasise that fact.

Although on lower ground, it was more sheltered, so in wintertime more sustainable winter crops could be grown. Root vegetables took a firmer hold in their lands, and they soon grew crops far beyond our capabilities. This had been advantageous to the outlanders, for it had led to the open marketplace for all. Before this no outlanders ever mixed with the colony, as trust was nonexistent before then, even now tolerated at best.

Separate lives, merely a few miles apart, had existed for many years, with only the occasional friction causing concern; normally outlanders stealing food, or trying to return to a familiar place or person for assistance. These were quickly punished and stamped out, no justice, no remorse for the fallen.

No temples adorned their territory, no holy grounds, as they had become shunned by Rai, so no effort had been placed into their worth there.

Low-level buildings were raised in Mortwedge, blending seamlessly into the surrounding forest, crescent-shaped on three sides, allowing the colony to disappear into the surroundings, to be forgotten, it seemed, by themselves too.

Further shelter if needed came from the elevation change. Soon after the colony's main encampment finished, the ground started to incline, allowing further protection, the forest rising over the ground, undulating to form a large swathe of green, snaking for many a mile, circling from this point south of Mortwedge edging onto the vast open plains of Ibothiel. If the outlanders' territory had sat at the left-hand curve of a circle, ours would occupy the right side, with the plains encompassing the majority of the inner space. A vast expanse of land that few had travelled in its entirety, due to both distance, terrain and extremes of temperature in every season.

Within the very centre, the Great Lake. I'd visited once, that was all, but its beauty would never leave me. Appearing like a mirage, an expanse of water, large and deep, blue so intense in colour, lightening at the edges, where the banks now dry and dusty once grew grass and held life in its hands, history showing its existence long before our colony formed. Fish lived within its waters still, and remnants of the earlier civilisations who settled here remained on the banks of the southern side of the lake, ruins of a time past, a time when the climate was less hostile than now.

In our lessons with Gavriel we had travelled and stayed nights on the plains, often catching food, setting traps, hearing stories whilst staring at the lights held in the sky above our heads; watching, as it seemed, Rai himself pulled the darkness across the skies, shifting the ever-changing dots of light from place to place. Gavriel taught us the names of some of these lights, named after famous warriors of the past; myths and legends all. Maybe one day he even joked he might be up there too; we never doubted that for a second.

These plains were extensive and large herds of Uppula easily roamed and lived here, constantly travelling to find the best grazing sites. The larger males, showing off their twisted horns, often locked in combat with other males in glory for the win to be in charge of all they surveyed.

Alongside, predators followed the herds. Like the Oravore, the elusive Veiled Sinivore, the packs of May Wolves, and occasionally the rare Shaebea were seen moving along the edges of the plains. Large black creatures holding huge claws on their paws, muscular with thick fur, too hard to penetrate even with the sharpest of arrows. No point in shooting at a Shaebea, the stories went; you can't hurt one and you can't outrun one, best to just keep out the way.

Shaebea, thankfully, in the main kept themselves to the far reaches of the forest edges to the very far side of the plains. Rumours of large numbers of the beasts had been told and retold over the years, but I had only seen them in solitude or a mother with cubs.

The very far reaches I'd seen only on maps or been told of in tales. Here lay a wasteland of sorts, a jagged mountainous region of rock, strewn as if thrown away by Rai himself in the making of the land, jutting up in pinnacles, obtuse angles crossing over one another, broken fingers of malfunctioning hands sticking through the soil. A hostile place by all accounts; few travelled here, and if frequented, not welcomed so stayed briefly, or never to return.

As Peshy and I walked, discussing the outlanders, around the next corner stood Amia. The look of expectancy on her face showed me that Peshy knew she was going to be there. Peshy himself glanced at me and walked to Amia; with the slight touch of his hand on hers I saw their friendship had indeed progressed much further than even Peshy had admitted in his words. With a slight twinge of jealousy and annoyance at my friend I felt myself blush. Amia must have sensed my change of mood, or noticed my look towards her, as she steered the conversation sharply back to a subject she knew I couldn't argue about, Acacia.

As we walked, I took my place slightly behind the two of them, as they engaged in a conversation trying to include me, which I tried to avoid, but the subject I couldn't avoid; my sister.

We came to a shadowed patch of grass, not a place I was familiar with, but both my companions were and as we sat, Amia uncovered a small basket hidden there in a thicket of dense brush. A small selection of hand breads, seeded, hand-baked over a simple fire. Oils to dip in added to the flavour, simple but wholesome. Flavoured water with local picked berries in stoppered bottles sat in the basket too, and Amia didn't hesitate to offer me some, even after my rude approach to her initial presence.

I hadn't realised but in simply sharing food and listening to her speak I found myself enraptured in her company too. I didn't see her as Peshy saw her, but her smile and laugh made easy conversation and soon I wondered why I had questioned her nature at all in the first place.

As a group we talked about my sister and Peshy described how he and Amia had searched many areas, places unused both by our colony and the outlanders, places held in both eyes as territory in between, unused.

Amia started to tell of recent similar tales of people going missing from her colony, sometimes in broad daylight, young children sent to fetch water never returning. Mostly the pattern had been painfully the same, disappearances in the night, people found missing from their beds, doors open, never to be seen again.

No attackers had ever been seen, though, and definitely no hooded creatures; the outlanders believed it was just bad omens.

Amia had searched the morning after the attack for her sister. Like I had she had awoken to find the door to her home ajar and Yamilla missing. Frantic with worry, little did she know that by then Yamilla was actually safe in the temple of healing. It was only when Peshy and a group from our colony arrived later that day to inform the outlanders that she discovered her sister was safe and well. They promised her return once healed. Amia and her mother travelled back with our group that day, visited and stayed a few days among the rooms in the temple, only returning once they had had a chance to speak with Yamilla; this act a sheer kindness by Gavriel and the temple sisters.

That's how an agreement had been reached to allow a search of the outlanders' territory by a few of our colony members, accompanied by a group of the outlanders to look for Acacia.

Since the attack, some mistrusted more with the understanding between the colonies, thinking maybe even the outlanders had something to do with the attack in the first place.

Others chose to disregard it as something that just needed to be done, with more simply ignoring the fact, believing in the word of Rai. For myself, honestly, I was starting to change my thoughts and feelings, the more I learnt about the outlanders, feeling that anything I could use to help me find Acacia would greatly increase the chances.

After talking for a while, we made plans to meet again the following day. The three of us decided to search some of the plains; we would get a small period of time before Rogan's acceptance leap tomorrow. These plains had already been covered, Peshy thought, by the warrior priests, but decided to take a closer look anyway. I made my excuses after a few hours, leaving the two of them together, slowly making my way back towards home, savouring the thought of the extra help of another friend.

EIGHT

Mixed emotions filled me that morning, Acacia seemed always at the forefront of my mind, but strange feelings of elation today entered too. My fellow White Banner student and friend, Rogan, had his acceptance leap today. Nothing in a young man's life could matter more, and I knew that very soon I would be experiencing the nausea Rogan would be feeling right now.

As Mother and I sat having a light breakfast, as the day's activities would be surrounded by food, I thought of my friend sitting in the temple with Gavriel, his prayer rituals, being started at first light, lasting all morning before his parade through the colony to show his path to manhood had begun.

After making my excuses to Mother, promising to meet her in time at the festivities later in the day, I made my way out to find Peshy and Amia, as promised, the colony not really noticing my wandering amongst the already party atmosphere starting to manifest itself. People were already setting up tables and chairs in small groups, preparing food ready for the later events.

We met where I'd left them the previous day, both Peshy and Amia already waiting, busy in each other's company. So off we set, trepidation in our minds, mixed with conversation of the coming day's events. Peshy was having to explain to Amia the day's activities. As an outlander, born in her colony, she hadn't witnessed them, and wasn't allowed to attend the acceptance day event.

I felt a strange pang that this somehow felt wrong. Amia was helping me and had become a friend. It seemed unfair that society had taught us that they were different, were beneath us. Outlanders were decent people who, from what I'd recently learnt, were struggling with the same things we were, their colony members missing too, the same hard-fought battles daily of tasks needing doing. They were the same as us. This questioned my teachings, questioned my thoughts, even, you could say with recent events, questioned my god.

We slowly walked onwards to the plains, stopping first at the rock where I'd found the three silver fingerprints. Still glistening in the morning sun, we studied them awhile. Gaining no further knowledge or clue, we decided to trudge on. The plains were exactly as they sounded. As earlier stated, the Uppula ranged freely here, large herds moving freely across the area, and most of the region's beasts were found here in various numbers.

Caution always paramount, we started our search, making sure we stayed in sight of each other all the time, just in case.

The evidence of the breaking of the world could be seen here more clearly too, even though the plains were mostly flat, for as far as you could see.

To the side of the plains, where the forests edged the scene, you could see, if closely observed, the ground undulated slightly, this being caused, we were taught, when Rai himself broke the very ground we stood upon, to save our races from each other, causing earthquakes which scarred the earth in all regions still evident today.

It was this day that I noticed for the first time a large group, digging a square section in the distance around one of these slightly raised sections.

Amia told me that they were outlanders, and recently they had started to excavate these areas after finding precious stones. As a group we started to head that way, continuing our search.

The plains where we stood were mainly dry currently, shortened dry, yellow, hardened grass stems jutting out of the ground we travelled, already eaten long ago by the game herds and being nearer the edges, long since abandoned for any nutrients by the animals. They had moved further into the plain reserves for the sweeter, richer grass still fresh, viable with health. The rains even here fell regularly, so this place maintained itself well.

As we gained ground on the working group of outlanders, I noticed Ivan skirting the edges of the holes being dug, his beady eyes bright with excitement, not really noticing our approach. Only after several calls did he lift his head and hand in acknowledgement, skipping over, belying his years as he always seemed to, excited to show us the finds he'd uncovered that morning. He held a small tray in his hands, in which sat several small brightly coloured stones, various colours all. Ground colours most, brown, yellow, a vibrant green, and a pale blue, similar to a hazy spring sky, but one was a bright purple, unbelievable to have just been plucked from the ground. It had obviously been cleaned by Ivan, but impressive to think that only hours ago this sat hidden to the human eye.

The outlanders were working with simple picks and shovels, and even though a large group, they were very organised. They seemed quiet and didn't look up at our approach. I wasn't sure if that was because they were unsure of us just as much as we were of them, or should I say I was; Ivan knew them all by name and he jostled amongst them as a friend would. Stopping here and there to inspect a new stone, or a potential treasure found, he seemed in his element. I realised this must have been going on for a while and wondered if indeed this was how my amulet stone had been found.

Ivan asked of our travels, not perturbed by the fact Amia was with us. Ivan was himself with the outlanders, and it appeared he didn't hold sway with the colony's thoughts over such things.

People are people, he once told me at the market, and coin is coin. I wondered in fact if he felt more strongly than this mere statement.

We'd barely searched that morning by the time we met Ivan, scarcely covering plainly visible open ground. Acacia wasn't here, I knew this, but Peshy and Amia were more than happy to humour me in my searching, this area already having been covered weeks ago by warrior priests.

Peshy suggested we cover the area where the plains started to change into forestry areas, along the edges of where we stood; this also had been covered but I think he wanted to search as much as I.

As we started to move, discussing our plans, we asked Ivan if he was to be seen later at Rogan's acceptance leap. He asked for a moment alone with Amia. Ivan stated he would be there, and as Peshy and I wandered off, Amia stayed talking with Ivan, our plan to circumvent the plains along the south side, following our initial approach in, giving us time to get back and be ready in place for Gavriel's instructions for the day.

Our efforts that day were fruitless, nothing ventured, nothing found. No new signs of footmarks in the dirt, no new silver prints, and our conversation often turned to how or why they'd been left behind, their meaning, and why placed where they were.

Having no real luck, and building energy turning to the coming day's events, we followed our path back towards the colony. Rarely were there two acceptance days one after another like this, but after my attack, the colony had been busy. Searching for Acacia and protection had been paramount, but acceptance couldn't be delayed anymore.

Rogan's day had arrived, Vinn's tomorrow, so the colony had pulled out all the stops in preparation.

I'd had little to do with it in reality, still not fully recovered, my stamina still weakened but improving daily. Mother had been helping though, with baking and cooking of the many dishes required for two acceptance leaps so close to each other. This would be a much-needed reminder for the colony that Rai was still with us, especially after recent events. Peshy and I realised that before long, we would be the ones sitting in the temple, reciting our prayers, ready to jump. My thoughts turned to Rogan, secretly wishing my friend luck, hoping he'd come back to us.

Parting, we knew briefly for washing, we agreed to meet again to walk to the temple for the ceremony start.

~

Simple instruments which we'd made over the years were currently in the hands of colony members who'd learnt to make and play them. Their skills were now illustrated, as beautiful music filled the air, a light high-noted song, promising hope, if such a thing can be promised in music. A fitting accompaniment to the scene in front of me.

Acceptance ledge was indeed that, a large rocky ledge, seemingly set in place by man, but a natural structure adapted for use by the colony, approximately thirty foot in length, extending out into the ether around the same width as its length. The ledge was mostly flat, sitting slightly to the right of dragon rock, in truth an expanse of smaller rocks, huddled together, making at first glance one large protuberance, sticking out of the ground, flattened on the top, thus allowing dragons to easily perch, hence its name rose into our existence.

It was written Shenash himself created this rock, a seat to survey all he protected.

Both dragon rock and acceptance ledge sat to the side of a larger open expanse. This, also a natural formation, took the form of an elongated circle, teardrop-shaped, if you will, sided both to the left and right with raised long wooden benches, rows upon rows, slightly higher towards the back, having been expanded over the years, allowing more and more colony members a better view. The central arena was open, allowing space for colony rituals, and giving all party members an adequate space, plus a large area for the dragons to land and take off without colliding with the colony members seated at the edges.

The final piece was towards the rear of the area. The lengthened section of the circle lent itself to be the perfect walkway, long enough to show the individual in all their glory approaching their destiny, to show the true meaning of this day's greatness, acceptance.

As a member of the White Banner we had been stationed along this pathway, lined either side, interspersed with senior warrior priests, fully dressed in formal dress. Warrior priests carrying ceremonial swords, wearing headdresses, making them stand even taller than they presented themselves normally. After initially gathering at the temple, Gavriel had run through our rituals briefly. This was something taught to us often and all knew exactly what to do. The warrior priests were always present to take lead from if things needed to change.

Rogan's father, a well-known warrior priest, had been stationed near the front of the inner circle, close to dragon rock, easily in distance so he would have a perfect view of his son's big day.

Most seats were filled, colony members always arriving early, with several still standing, waiting for the events to officially start.

Even with all the seats, it was common to see colony members standing to all the edges of the acceptance area, longing to see from where they stood.

Everyone loved acceptance day leaps; no matter how many you'd witnessed over the years, the chance to see a dragon again drove everyone here. Anticipation, already risen, was becoming palpable currently in the air.

As the music continued to permeate over the general muttering of the crowd, all White Banner and warrior priests in place, standing as guards of honour, the distant but steady sound of approaching ceremonial drums started to be heard. As more of the crowd either heard the drums, or as they got nearer, the crowd's noises ceased to be noticeable. We, as honour guards, held position, standing tall, forward as we had been taught, unmovable in our duties. Sideways glances showed the approach of Gavriel, Rogan and his priest acceptance party.

Soon, with the ceremonial drums marking their arrival, somehow giving strength to the music being already played, Rogan made his first steps into acceptance.

Dressed fully in gown, headdress and ceremonial shoes, carrying his offering, he seemed both older and more serious than I'd ever imagined. I'd grown up my whole life with Rogan, and we were good friends. A quick glance seemed to be all he gave across the entire scene being played out in front of him. Whether nerves or willingness to start overtook him, he simply stood where placed by Gavriel.

These rituals over the years focused on positivity, speeches first by Gavriel praising Rogan's strengths, his compassion to the colony and Rai, with focus on his studies.

This allowed everyone present to gain a presence of the young man they saw standing in front of them today. Rogan's father, albeit a warrior priest, stood close by, beaming with pride, trying very hard, in vain, to hide his obvious smile. A very proud moment indeed for both, one which I often realised I'd never feel.

Rogan's offering came next; walking onto acceptance ledge, glancing down, Rogan started his own speech.

Blessing Rai, his creation of the world and thanking him for the opportunity of this day, asking for strength, perseverance and the glory of becoming a warrior priest. Extended arms, stretched out in front, dropping his offering from the ledge into the waiting clouds below with a simple motion.

Turning now to give a simple bow to his father, then Gavriel, listening once more to the crowd applaud his speech, and the thanks to Rai, Rogan again outstretched his arms, this time to his sides, and taking a step forward, leapt from the edge. A hardly audible gasp rose from the watching crowd as Rogan disappeared from view. If Rogan's father wanted to react, he didn't. Standing stoically, he held his ground, his eyes not even looking towards the ledge's edge. His smile no longer evident, he simply stared forward, waiting, listening as we all were, for the noise we all wanted to hear.

Anticipation wavering, the crowd tensed as the minutes passed. Then suddenly all heard the roar we all needed to hear, flinching as the huge shadow bathed everyone standing on acceptance ledge, the downforce of the wind making all stagger slightly where they stood, eyes forced to bear the differential sunlight edging the dark form it encompassed.

The dragon continued to rise, high above all of us, showing its true form and beauty.

Cheering erupting from the crowd all around us, the warrior priests alongside us, the White Banner students held firm. Swirling downwards now, wings spread wide to control the speed to a slower decent, the dragon's colours now started to take over from the initial shadow seen against the sun.

A deep raw copper, glorious shades of rich orange, mixed with darker brown hues, gave the dragon a sense of impenetrability. Colours mixed to show a darker underbelly with lighter tones, highlighted across the wings and flanks. Although a large beast, significantly smaller than the red dragon I'd met in the forest, this beautiful creature, stockier in appearance, seemed more powerful, muscular even, every sinew working hard in flight controlling its path.

Landing heavily, but still gracefully, the dragon swirled its eyes, taking control of the scene it placed itself in, everyone thankful it had brought Rogan back with it.

Rogan himself, looking awestruck, sat clinging to the back of his dragon. Disbelief replaced with relief he'd accomplished his day. Gratitude and glamour in his eyes as he looked down at the dragon he sat on.

Climbing down, legs shaking, he fronted the dragon, falling to his knees, holding his hands up, placing them on the snout of the dragon's face. The dragon leant forward, allowing its face to contact Rogan's hand, nudging Rogan slightly to obviously stand. Face to face now, a moment of acknowledgement seemed to pass between them, bowing to each other. They were one; paired in battle if the need arose.

Kneeling once more, Rogan in respect and awaiting the downforce, once more held his place as the dragon powered into the sky in front of us.

More than one of us lost our footing with the power displayed here, unable to stay still in the wings of a hurricane force.

Rising high above, showing strength, beauty and, honestly, magnificent power, it twisted away, dropping into the depths below, leaving all behind with a guttural roar, deafening all witnesses present.

Rogan was still kneeling after the cacophony of both noise and action ceased. Gavriel approached the silent man, raising him up to his feet with a gesture of his hand. Hugging him, announced him to the colony as a warrior priest. Rogan's father, eyes tear-filled, moved forward to hug his son too, as the whole colony joined into another joyous cheer.

And as a group we followed Rogan, Gavriel and his father out of acceptance ledge towards the colony's centre, where the party celebrations would be held.

The party continued long into the night, all colony members eventually getting time with Rogan. White Banner students gave him our own congratulations, asking many questions about his leap. Rogan answered, still dazed by the long day's events, but still he remained himself, enjoying the day although tired.

Mother and I retired later that night, after eating more food than I could remember in a long time. Leaving Peshy with his parents, we all agreed tomorrow would be great if the same events repeated themselves.

Vinn had left much earlier, as he had a very early start in the morning; his day being next, it must have been hard for him to both enjoy Rogan's success and deal with his own nerves. But that was tomorrow. For now rest was needed, so a slow walk home beckoned and thoughts on well wishes for Vinn.

NINE

The screams of fire awoke most that night; like many, I had been asleep. If I had been dreaming it was unreachable now. Hastily grabbing my clothes, I put them on, not sure as to the correct order in which I picked them up from the floor. A look out of the homestead window revealed that it was still the early hours of the morning, darkness still holding onto the secrets of the night. In the distance, though, an unnatural glow filled the sky, an eerie orange glow, changing shape as it manifested itself into otherworldly forms, guided by the cool winds of the morning.

Mother and I ran towards the fire, my stamina better but not up to my best. We could tell even from this distance, and we were on the other side of the colony, that the fire was large, apparently centred around the temple. As we reached the centre of the colony people had already formed long human chains, busily working in the blind panic of water-carrying, a line of people streaming like insects passing pots, vessels, anything that could hold water, steadily down the line towards the temple. The distance from the nearest well was considerable with some people having to run small distances to cover the gaps in the line. These holes slowly filled as more and more people awoke and joined the chaos.

I needed to see for myself what was going on; part of being in the year of my acceptance meant that if any attacks were made on the colony we had to report to the temple itself, to assist the warrior monks in any way they saw fit. Sometimes that could mean to fight alongside them, under guidance, or simply carry the wounded away from battle. The line of colony members snaked all the way to the edge of the forest classroom, and from this distance I could already see the damage the fire had done and was still doing.

Buckets of water thrown from a distance were merely stopping the roots of the giant trees catching alight. The canopies of several large oaks were fully ablaze. The magnitude of the fire's heat made it almost impossible to get much further into the forest without injury.

The sound of that night was immense; something so destructive sounding so alive, noises thrown from the belly of the fire, wood splintering, hurled through force, bursting alive with heated sap exploding in all directions, the hissing and crackling of the leaves as they fell burning from above our heads to the floor, to become ash underfoot.

The forest, part of our sanctuary was burning, and I could see no way to stop it. I think everyone present felt the same as raised voices, competing to be heard, hoped for divine assistance.

As I circled the fire, taking me to the rear of the great temple, I noticed Ivan; he and Gavriel were together with several warrior monks. Ivan seemed to be in some form of trance, speaking incantations, silent, mouthing the words, eyes fully open, seeing but not really looking; something I had read of, but never seen.

Warrior monks surrounded him, protecting him, with Gavriel in the lead. It was at that moment that Gavriel noticed me and held his hand up to make me stay still, so I simply watched as somehow the flames, that had set fire to the great oaks of the forest classroom, themselves started to change colour. As I watched, I suddenly realised the flames had also somehow attached themselves to the very stone of the temple, burning the trails of ivy that clung to the old stones like tentacles of a sea monster, leaving dark black lines, tracing up the walls. The flames here took on a blue colour, again an unnatural thing to see, and I wasn't sure on this night if the events here played tricks on me, but right now, I could see Ivan was putting the fire out.

As Ivan muttered his incantation, the flames seemed to hiss, somehow alive, even, as if they weren't just flame as I knew it, but they somehow had a job to do and were angry that they hadn't achieved it. They fought, clinging to the edges of the stone building, and I could see after a while that Ivan was physically flinching as the flame battled him also somehow mentally, as if challenging him back.

The warrior priests stood firm, awaiting an attack, all senior guards, weapons drawn, poised, capable of striking in an instant.

Realising that other students of the White Banner had now gathered around me, we all stood watching as Ivan battled the flame in a mental game of tug of war.

Suddenly a scream from the complex behind the temple

broke through the noise of the fire and surrounding fight to control it. Gavriel motioned to us to go and seek its source; this with a mere point and look. Without hesitation we moved as one group around the warrior priests, leaving them in their battle, to find one of our own.

After taking a wide berth around the burning temple, stomping out two small fires on the way, we found ourselves in the complex of buildings which sat in the larger temple grounds. The temple of healing sat to our immediate left, alongside smaller stables and livery barns. Animal housing occupied this site, mostly to the right of us on the east side, with the north of the complex given over to the ancient burial grounds, the stone tombs of our forefathers, where only the great of the colony were buried.

It was here that we found where the screaming had come from. In the distance we could see temple maidens trying to put out fire that had started to take a hold on the healing temple. As around the great temple, a blueish unnatural flame burned here, not all-consuming as on the other buildings, more of a distraction, if you will, time-consuming, to somehow keep people busy, as if the flame had a purpose somehow.

Beyond this, though, the scream came again. Two temple maidens were being dragged away, and as I stared through the smoke, hazily in my vision I saw the same hooded figures that had haunted my dreams since the night of my attack.

Whether I froze, or just stood staring, I realised I probably was one of the last to run towards them to help the maidens.

It was only the noise, as our group charged forward, snapping me out of my reverie, that made my feet move.

The distance between us shortened and with blue and orange flame around us on most sides, our group fanned out to show its greater numbers.

At the time I didn't count but knew around a dozen of us stood against their two.

Hooded figures, shorter than all of us, bent forward, but fluid in their form. Their movements, rapid, somehow more in tune with being closer to the ground, gave them a stockier appearance. I grabbed a simple branch of wood as I approached a figure from the side, as it halted and merely stood still, not really looking at our approach.

The other figure had also heard our approach and had stopped dragging the maiden away and joined his counterpart by standing still, an arm's length away from each other. Others of our group had small swords, or like me pieces of wood, or similar objects picked up from the floor, impact weapons, useful in these situations.

We were not fully trained in the art of war, but in our final acceptance year, we were all good hunters. All adept and trained to a level of fighting, a dozen of us together would be no easy task for two to take on, and with an air of confidence we closed the gap towards the hooded duo.

The audible gasp as the first hooded figure dropped his mask was heard over the surrounding noise of the still-burning fire. The creature in front of us was indeed catlike in appearance, its face scarred and pitted. Sharpened yellow teeth provided an evil appearance through the split upper lip it displayed.

Eyes pierced through me as it flicked them from one of us to the other, like a small Oravore, toying with a downed bird for fun before the kill.

The face wasn't covered in fur; it was of human skin tone, but marked, as if coloured a different way. The blue and orange nature of the ever-changing firelight around us gave their features an even more unworldly trait, and it was this vision and hesitation that allowed them the first move.

The second figure, realising the trick had worked, moved with lightning speed. Leaping to a height unimaginable to me, clearly three times higher than I'd seen a human jump, further again by far in distance covered, suddenly he was behind us out of the approaching circle.

Stooping lower than his stature he swept forward, taking two of our group by surprise. Instant screams of pain awoke the senses as they fell to the floor, blood covered the ground as I noticed the foot had been completely severed from the leg of one of them. The next few moments were chaos, and at times I was the most scared I'd been in my short life. We'd stood confidently as a group, but from thinking we'd take on these two figures and succeed in our goal to protect and find out who they were, we were now fighting for our lives.

The hooded figures sent forth quick reactions with powerful blows; on more than one occasion I saw people thrown from the combat by several feet, and I too was knocked over by blows so powerful I was amazed to stand again after.

We were not winning; we were managing to survive, just. The figures had removed five of us to my count, to what level I couldn't tell, but the bodies lay still on the floor. No assistance could be rendered now as we all circled each other in the process of trying to stay upright. We had learnt from our early mistake and tried to stay together. The blows when they came were fast but could be dealt with in a group; by protecting each other we could defend and attack as a pack.

This merely had the effect of moving them deeper into the forest, away from the complex of buildings. The trouble was this suited them better, as the fire wasn't illuminating the area around us as much.

The darkness played into their hands. The trees were closer together and our strategy of staying as a close group meant we couldn't stand together here; these options now counted against us.

As they retreated further into the forest, we decided to stand our ground and watched them back away into the shadows, their eyes the last thing to disappear into the darkness. Slowly retracing our steps, we made it back to the complex, and started to try and deal with the carnage.

Two of us remained on guard just in case the attackers came back. Rogan and I were the two that took watch first that night. Darkness still hung in the air, and I knew not what the time was.

The maidens who weren't injured themselves in the struggle helped the fallen in the fighting, and news soon came to us that three Banner men had lost the fight forever that night.

The flames were being beaten back; and before too long the larger fires around the complex buildings had been put out. Now began the easier but more laborious task of damping down the smouldering embers, just in case the fire resurfaced to claim its foothold once more.

After an hour the guard duty was swapped, and I started to help with the burden of moving water.

Stopping very briefly to pay passing respect to my friends' bodies, which lay covered with large blankets in the vestibule of the temple of healing, I dare not peek under the covers at that moment in time, scared to know the truth of who lay there. I had to focus on the duties needed now, mourning could be done later, in the cold light of day, if we got through this crazy night.

With the ground now being saturated, it started to give off steam, adding to the already growing smoky haze, filling the skies around us. We started adding our strength, or what was left of it, to the rest of the colony's efforts. Ivan, still battling the main force of fire centred on the great temple, had seemed to age years, beads of sweat running down his face; more concentration I'd never seen on an individual as he showed then and there.

But he was winning in his efforts. Alongside the constant tireless efforts of the whole colony the fire was weakening. Smaller and smaller it became, with the very ground surrounding the fire holding on becoming more waterlogged, stopping not only the spread of fire, but starving it of a fuel source to grow, burning its intensity out.

The next couple of hours seemed to be a constant blur of fetching and carrying, orders heard on the wind from one group of people to another, but in the chaos it worked. Finally, as a group we prevailed, with the last residue of fire clinging to the great temple, holding on to the stone itself, finally giving way under the relentless pressure Ivan had placed on it for hours. As the last flames dissipated, Ivan himself collapsed into the waiting arms of Gavriel, who swiftly picked him up, and took him towards the temple maidens who had gathered nearby.

As that morning's sun started to rise above the treetops, showing the first hint of another warm summer's day, the scene it shone upon allowed the colony to see the horror of the night's events in their entirety.

The fires being now totally extinguished, stupidly I thought that had ended our work for the night, or should I now say that morning.

But in reality, it had only just begun. People stood still, staring in disbelief rather than face the reality of the night's visions swirling in the front of their minds.

Several colony members had burns that needed treating; some severe, where clothes had been engulfed in the blue flame. Unable to simply be put out, it had consumed all it touched. This had been no normal flame we had witnessed.

Others, with minor wounds and burns, scratches or twisted ankles and the like from the constant back and forth in haste fetching water, were also taken to the healing temple to be seen by the maidens.

The maidens were themselves overwhelmed, with exhaustion, grief and the sheer amount of people needing their assistance. The colony, in shock, looked for leaders in this time of need. And Gavriel, once again, didn't turn them away.

He managed the temple maidens into small groups, supporting them to care for the colony, giving the White Banner students roles to play in assisting where we could with this.

Warrior priests were split into fighting groups, reconnaissance groups and a recovery section, guarding, protecting and supporting on all sides. Gavriel was making sure we wouldn't be assaulted as easily again. Whoever did this had walked among us and started havoc, not simply to be done again, Gavriel vowed that day.

The colony's water reserve was also dangerously low as the wells had taken a huge amount of damage over the night's work, bricks taken from the edges, removed to gain quicker access, the boarding to keep them safe discarded in the panic, and this needed to be replaced before anybody fell into the deep chambers below ground.

Water flowed into the wells from the underground springs, and as long as normal colony use was monitored, these never ran dry. They naturally replenished themselves quickly with clean fresh water, but this was a slower process than we needed right now. Water would have to be fetched from the Great Lake to fill the painfully low wells around the colony, so work groups were already being set up to repair the wells and fetch the water that would have to be sought that very day.

The smoke still hung in the air, with the bitter taste of burnt undergrowth, bark, and all the debris that had perished in the flames. That taste couldn't be washed away even by drinking that morning. It clung to the clothes, the hair of everyone. With not enough water to bathe the smell away we knew it was going to be a constant reminder for the rest of the day's work ahead.

The remaining White Banner students and warrior priests were tasked with the moving and burial of the lost that day. We had lost three of us in the fight with the creatures, and it wasn't until we went to move the bodies of our friends that we also found two more downed warrior priests. The maidens had cleaned and dressed the bodies of our friends, placing them into clean white shrouds, as was our way. Placed upon their bodies was a simple garland of forest flowers, marking the offering to Rai, an acceptance to stand by his side, to join him in the afterlife, to continue the teaching he had given us, an oath we all accepted.

It was as we took the bodies from the temple, laying them near the holy burial grounds, that we saw the downed warrior priests, slumped nearby. Rushing over, it was clear they had each died sometime in the night, but the look on their faces painted a haunting picture, which none present, I feared, would ever forget.

Each face was painfully, horribly contorted, a deep anguish written into every nuance and line of their haunting expression. Something you couldn't entirely think possible, frozen in sheer terror, fear being their last thought. If it was indeed possible to be frightened to death, this had been that outcome, their finale.

Weapons not drawn in fight, or even anger, their arms simply raised to protect their eyes from the horror they faced.

Warrior priests were strong, fearless men, who had learnt well and been accepted by Rai himself to be the colony's protectors. These men were accepted to be great warriors, leaders among our people. As we stood over their bodies that morning, we all wondered what, or who, could have made them cower like this.

Each had faced many battles; toughness wasn't questioned, but to see them in this state made the heart beat faster, to contemplate what had scared them so. Then we noticed something else.

The great tomb seated in the middle of the holy burial grounds, behind the fallen priests' bodies, was a sacred place. Rai himself had touched these grounds, blessing them centuries ago, it was told. Only Gavriel with the senior warrior priests could enter.

We could accompany Gavriel if asked, or on burial duty, but today a greater need called us to enter onto this holy land.

A runner was sent immediately to Gavriel as we slowly spread out to surround the great tomb. From this small distance it first appeared like a hesitant smoke, still surrounding the tomb from the night's fire, but as we stepped further towards it, it dissipated inwards, moving of its own free will, to the right side of the tomb hidden by the tree line.

The large wooden door to the tomb had warped, not burnt; no marks appeared on it at all, and it somehow still hung from the large iron hinges holding it in place. Several large splits obvious to the eye, but mainly structurally intact, they held firm, as if some force had grabbed them and physically twisted them in two directions at the same time, trying to tear them from the walls they protected. Gaps at the bottom of the doors meant a person could lie on their stomach and crawl through, and we wondered if someone had breached our holy place.

As a group we circled the building, with our main focus on finding the source of the strange smoke on the right of the structure. As we rounded the corner, we all witnessed something that we couldn't believe, or understand how it could have happened. Large statues, built into the tomb on each corner, these of great past leaders, warriors all, grand masters of the colony over the centuries, placed on the building to celebrate their lives and their honour in Rai's eyes, had been deformed.

These statues stood approximately twenty foot tall, carved from solid stone, part of the building's structure, the corner strength of the building, the design of each warrior an exact match to the once living man. They were dressed in their warrior dress, holding various weapons of war, always on guard to defend Rai in the afterlife, showing that in death they continued to worship and defend our god as they did in life itself.

The uniform on each statue, the stone weapons, had all originally been hand carved; hundreds of hours of painstaking work had created perfection, each one from a single carved solid piece of stone.

So now, how could the statues on the right of the building show contorted, twisted faces? Horror appeared to seep from the eyes of carved stone, hands raised, fingers individually set apart trying to block the view from the stone eyes looking out.

The warriors' clothes had been ripped from the bodies, somehow lying on the floor near our feet, pieces of perfectly carved uniform, their carved swords, with bows and short knives discarded as if trying to rip themselves from the fabric of the building. Each large piece of stone, once carved into a large solid object, lifetimes ago, now lay somehow individually, tossed away, in an attempt to get away from the horror they witnessed.

Impossible is a word I used to use; things thought hard to do, or too complex to fathom. Now impossible isn't a word I believe in; anything can happen, to anything, after this day.

The once solid wall of the tomb now stood rent, a gaping hole showing in between two of the once glorified stone warrior figures, ripping into the great tomb, laying bear the contents to the world, smoke billowing back into the hole. We stood in disbelief as Gavriel ran over to where we stood.

Not hesitating, he ran over to the bodies of his warriors, saying a few silent words to each, his hand placed on their foreheads as he bent down, kneeling at their side. He then stood with a look upon his face of hatred, an anger I hadn't witnessed in this man. A glimmer of the warrior within, once feared and talked of by his enemies, rose again.

"To me," was all he said, as he drew his sword, striding forward towards the great tomb.

As a group we entered the swirling smoke of the building; whatever had rent a hole in the side of this great building had been no mere man. Large stone pieces were simply cast aside, torn from the building itself, as if mere pebbles had been dropped from a child's hand whilst playing. We climbed over and around these now discarded parts of our heritage. Our history lay around us, and as each was passed, we felt Gavriel's fury rise. Placed on several of the larger pieces of the stone were tiny silver fingerprints, picked out by the rays of sunlight coming through the opening in the wall behind us, eerily similar to the ones I'd found on the rock whilst looking for Acacia, but singular.

Placed as if on purpose, individually, as a sign for us to notice them, leading us forward somehow through the smoke.

If Gavriel had noticed the first footprints he didn't mention them. He couldn't have missed them, as he had walked clean over them. Not hesitating for even a moment, he continued forward, so we followed too. The footprints were human-shaped but large, as the fingerprints were small. The two extremes seemed confusing, but as if it mattered somehow, both bright silver, each showing every ridge, line and crevice, each detail of the marker who had left it, as if had been there for eternity, carved into the stone floor centuries ago. Although this was my first ever venture into the great tomb, I knew that these footprints, like the fingerprints, were a new addition from something unwelcome here.

As we walked further, the smoke's haze dissipated, showing me the great tomb's inner walls for the first time. I'd thought in the past that this would be a highly decorated place, with gleaming colours, vibrant use of paintings maybe, showing Rai's creation of life through brightly textured fabrics, but this really wasn't the case. The building, now crushed somehow, showed that even in its regal stance before this last night's torrent of abuse, it had been a simple structure.

A place of simple worship, a place of honour, trust, a resting place for the spirit of the warriors past. Coloured glazed windows, high up on every side, allowed dappled light to criss-cross the space; several different colours traced from the glass onto the light itself showed a simple beauty, adding to the serenity of this holy ground.

A large stone display area, set aside to the rear of a large, raised plinth, held large books; some I'd seen in our forest classroom before. Gavriel had often read from them, and I'd wondered where they were kept. Scrolls and amulets, again of various sizes and colours, sat upon parchment laid out on the shelves, either marking specific paragraphs of text, or highlighting a phrase to recall.

The only thing I could see that looked even slightly elevated out of normal place was a golden goblet perched high on a plinth sitting at the feet of a statue of Rai himself. I wondered if this was the goblet of tears that Rai himself had handed to our forefathers, a cup which held great belief in our teachings; a cup that Rai had caught his own tears in, after he cried when breaking the world to save us from a devastating war.

The other item out of place was a wooden box at the foot of the goblet's plinth, wrapped around the edges with a single gold band; solid-looking from where I stood. Heavy but moveable, carved, it seemed, from a single piece of wood. As I looked, I realised that what held my gaze was the box which held the ashes of Rai's dragon, Shenash, the guardian of the colony, protector still even in death, left here to watch over us at all times.

I didn't realise that I sank to my knees, holding my charm tightly once more in my hand, the charred dressing of the bandages cracking and failing under the strain I placed on them. It was then that I noticed Gavriel calling my name; at first as if in a dream, distant, far away even, a voice somewhere not meaning to break my reverie but so annoying to the ear you can't ignore it.

Then suddenly my name again; Wicker. Gavriel touched my arm. "Wicker," he said once more, half a plea in his voice as I looked at him. Then I noticed the charm was admitting a bright light, illuminating the whole tomb chamber in bright vivid red tones, painfully honest in its intensity, but as soon as I relinquished my grip the light started to fade.

As the others stared at me and I regained my focus on the surroundings, I heard the cry of the voice to the left of the tomb. As we all turned in that direction, in the darkened room after the blinding light I saw a table, huge in its construction, again made of solid stone, simply carved, more functional than ornate, and lying on the top was a shape, a form, which looked like a rolled-up piece of fabric.

A warrior priest stood next to the table as Gavriel approached followed by the rest of us. As I gained ground, I heard others say that it was a body. When I reached the table Gavriel tried to stop me but was too late. Here and in this holy place, slumped, wrapped in a piece of tattered old fabric, was Acacia.

Her small frail body lay motionless, resting otherworldly in its form from the normality I knew of my sister, usually so full of boundless energy and life. I had to glance away from the sombre scene in front of me. Acacia lay straight, somehow awkwardly placed that way, as if the events that caused her death didn't matter anymore, her expression placid, not grimacing in fear as the stone guardians of the temple outside had been; small mercy made me thank Rai for that fact at least.

Her skin was so pale, tinged on her extremities with the faintest blue, making her seem cold. All I wanted to do was scoop her into my arms, hoping that doing so would bring warmth, bring life back into Acacia. No one tried to stop me reaching forward but I wish they had, as the realisation of how cold she actually was shocked me to remember that scene for eternity.

Although she appeared calm, her body showed itself to be heavily bruised. No obvious large wounds were visible, although honestly, I didn't look that closely. She seemed smaller lying on this cold table, raised in front of us, with her body drained of life, drained of colour, drained of hope. She'd been missing barely a month; even if it felt longer, a part of me wished I was still searching for her, instead of wrestling the truth lying in front of me today. I wondered how someone could have changed so much in that time, her body obviously wasted away. But I knew not what she'd experienced recently. I longed to know that she hadn't suffered, daren't even hope that she hadn't been scared, but a part of me knew she had been both of those things, without me to protect her. I felt useless, afraid, pitiful even.

Sensing my grief had become too much, I noticed Gavriel step into my view, shielding my vision from Acacia just for a moment. Here my world came back to reality; my emotions tore from within with a scream, I know not where from. Bright red light once more emitted from my dragon-stone necklace, highlighting dust particles floating around the temple in a beautiful but haunting vision.

Surrounded by my fellow students, Gavriel helped me out of the temple, guards placed around Acacia waiting for temple maidens to be free to take her to the chapel's resting place. Would I ever really know what happened to my little sister was a question no one here could answer.

TEN

The students of the White Banner had taken me home. I remembered too much of that long walk; silently trudging, barely managing to place one foot in front of another. I remember the smells, the broken remains of the fallen trees, still smouldering, giving every breath I took in a sense of blackness, a feeling of autumnal weather closing in on us, albeit on a summer's morning. The ground underfoot I recall, blackened by the fire, trampled by the traffic of everyone running back and forth with water in the previous night's panic, the birds occasionally bursting into their morning verses, unaware of the intensity of the night's burdens faced by all, and the sorrow I felt deep into my very bones.

Whilst walking I closed my eyes. All I could visualise was poor Acacia, lying on that cold hard stone table, her tiny frame, seemingly so frail, so lifeless for someone who always shone so brightly every day. Eyes jerking open, hoping it was some horrid nightmare, the reality didn't make the pain or the vision cease, just the slow thud, thud, thud of footsteps allowed my mind to block out the picture for a few seconds.

Warrior priests were already at the homestead, when as a group we crested the small hillock on the path home. I could hear the crying from a distance, but I was already empty, my tears had fallen. The numbness I currently felt had no sadness left. Mother lay at the feet of a maiden of healing, surrounded by warrior priests, heads all bowed in respect of the news just passed to her.

Emptiness, true emptiness, is a strange feeling, I'd been saddened before, tears I'd cried before, but this was different. I think you could have stuck me with several arrows, I could have reached for Rai's blessing then and there and not felt any readier or felt any more pain within. I was done, wanted to somehow leave myself.

Don't get me wrong, I hadn't physically given up; it was more that the pain inside had somehow won, defeating me from the inside, grief overpowering rational thought, until the only feeling I had left was the acceptance inside of knowing this was reality now. Life always continues, life finds its way whether you fall to the side or not. Sometimes we need to remember that if we fall, life strides on. We may not want it to but it does and it's unstoppable, until the day Rai calls us to stand before him. We either stay on the side of the path, or we simply stand and carry on, forever changed. That day I stood and carried on, never to be the person I was before I held my sister's cold body in my arms.

Mother had to be helped that evening, inconsolable in grief. Temple maidens gave her medicine in a drink form to help her sleep, she stayed in the temple of healing for the next few days.

Gavriel offered me a sleeping pallet in the temple too. He was currently staying there as the colony cleaned what remained of the grand temple of Rai after the fire, but I wanted my solitude; my thoughts were dark and best left to themselves right now, I felt.

Peshy and I spoke several times over those days, mostly of my not being able to save Acacia, my fear and worry I'd let her down, but mostly of how stupid I felt, how scared I was of losing someone I loved.

Acacia wasn't the first person to leave my life; father left one day on a mission when I was very young, never to return. My memories over time had either faded, or I had invented a truth about the situation. I needed to accept, to get over the loss of him, which allowed me to move forward on the path in life.

This, however, felt different, whether because I was older, whether I knew my sister better, for longer, or because of the guilt I held, making me feel somehow responsible. If I'd been there, been able to help her, to fight for her, I could have stopped this.

Questions seemed to fester around and around in my head, over and over again, as I sat against a tree, overlooking the clearing in my patch of forest in Gold Maple.

The patch where I grieved over my father, I found myself sitting in once more.

As day turned to night, night to day, realisation dawned.

I needed to find out who had done this, if those creatures that had attacked me were involved, and why they were taking people from the colony, to what end.

I had to stop this, somehow and some way; Peshy would help I knew he would.

Making my way to see Peshy, I somehow regained a piece of myself. Grief takes us apart, spreads us thinly, but having the strength to say to yourself, no more, is a hard thing to do. Anger, vengeance and pain drove me right now; if that's what I needed to find who did this then I'd use every bit of it to succeed.

As always seemed to be the case recently, Peshy was found in the company of Amia. They were simply seated near to one another, talking quietly, on an outcrop of rocks overlooking the game herds. A quiet spot, off the beaten track, not hidden, but far enough away from passing people to be discreet.

Recently I'd heard lots of colony members talking about the outlander girl among the colony all the time; knowing it was Amia I'd not become involved. She had become a friend, more so to Peshy, I could see that.

Well, everyone could see that, and I wondered if Gavriel had noticed and said anything to Peshy. Outlanders and colony members, even though recently they had searched together for Acacia, still were mistrustful and eyed each other suspiciously.

Initially pride made me hesitate in walking straight up to them both, not wanting to show the hurt I so obviously displayed still, but the anger and resentment within me rose to overpower this and made me stride onwards. After, it seemed, a few hours of talking, Peshy and Amia agreed to help me try and find out if anything more could be found out about Acacia's death. We all knew that it wasn't going to be easy or painless for us. Knowing things might be dangerous too, we agreed to talk to Gavriel.

Amia said she would talk to the elders from her village to see if any information from the missing children had been found there, explaining what had happened in full at our colony. We agreed that any help and information we could muster now could only help to protect all the people we cared for in both colonies.

Over the next few days limited information was gained, due to the workload needing to be done in the colony. Not only did we still have to repair the temple, nearly in its entirety, but the wells still needed more water. Trees needed to be felled which were damaged in the great fire, unsafe to be left standing. And the funerals of all our dead.

All this alongside Vinn's acceptance day, which was fast approaching; it couldn't be delayed any more. Also the colony needed more warrior priests now more than ever; his time was here, he needed to prove his place in our society.

~

Funerals were simple occasions within the colony, and we had too many to arrange over the next few days.

Warrior priests' bodies were returned to the holy ground of the burial site within the temple grounds, simple words spoken by Gavriel as the warriors were buried with their swords, to help them guard Rai in the next life. No families were present, only fellow members of the priesthood, alongside the white banner students. We were the only family recognised by Rai here.

White Banner students were treated similarly but slightly differently; we hadn't become accepted yet, but it was known that our lives were Rai's. We, too, were buried, but with no weapon, as we hadn't gained this right yet.

Rai's knowledge and trust was with us, so burial of the White Banner meant we too sat at Rai's side in the afterlife.

Colony funerals were different altogether; a pyre was erected close to acceptance ledge, a higher outcrop just to the right of the entrance, its size around thirty large paces in either direction. A perfect spot to gaze upon the territory all around. This place had been used over the centuries as a burning plaza for our dead; the smoke could be seen for miles on a clear day, rising high on the currents of wind that frequented here.

A beautiful spot, not insignificant in either its beauty or power. It held a high place in all our minds.

Simple ceremonies are often the most powerful, allowing your own mind to remember the ones who have been lost. The temple maidens brought Mother to the ceremony, dressed all in black, held up at times, her legs not seeming to hold the weight she now carried with her. Acacia had been wrapped as custom dictated, a small woven reed gown covered her, wrapped as if she wore a green jacket somehow.

Face covered, just a shape now where her head was wrapped. A white cloth visible from under the reeds.

Warrior priests placed my sister on top of the pyre and, with Mother sobbing into the arms of the temple maidens, Gavriel nodded to me to step forward. Shaking, not knowing if my legs would make the short distance from where I stood to the pyre, I seemed to stumble, but managed to get to Gavriel's side.

Taking up the torch, I simply looked around; faces all around me looking down at their feet, some skyward as if praying or trying to stop the tears from falling by keeping their heads upwards. And Peshy openly shedding tears with no thought but grief in his mind and soul. Acacia had been like his sister too, and I wished I could cry like that to release this pain, but nothing was left.

Turning away from everyone's grief I whispered a silent prayer to Rai to protect my sister. And a part of me wished I was going with her as I touched the torch to the dry grasses wedged in between the stacked logs of the pyre in several places.

I think I was the only person left sitting there as the darkness rolled in that night, watching the embers of the pyre as they continued to glow after burning for hours, just the occasional shadow crossing overhead as if Rai had sent his dragons to collect Acacia for him.

I felt I couldn't leave until she had, and as the darkened clouds moved through the night sky, I said my last goodbye and headed not for home but for my safety, my sanity, my tiny patch of forest, Gold Maple.

Solitude makes us contemplate ourselves in strange ways, not often truthfully, it must be told. Recently I had questioned every part of my life, it seemed, after my attack. It had only gone from bad to worse and I wondered if I was being punished for something, somehow not fulfilling a promise I'd made. A young man stood here, holding the memories of an old one. Life torn apart from the normality of others. I felt broken, damaged, unworthy of the life I awoke to every morning, empty inside. It's hard to admit feeling empty, for what does it truly mean?

Some people pray for another day that never comes, some plead for life as it slips away from them. Others cling onto it with their very will of force, living each second as if it's their last. I awoke each day longing to sleep, to shut down, to hide away, to not exist. Please don't think

I wanted pity, I wanted nothing, that was the point, nothing.

I survived for many days at Gold Maple; I couldn't explain how, or how long in reality, but survive I did, and only Peshy's efforts of just sitting in the clearing, not leaving, made me surface to face him.

We didn't talk at first, sitting in his company, no words passing between us, just time. Eventually one day whilst watching him fail miserably at skinning a rabbit properly, we talked. No words could sooth the pain I'd grown to accept; added to the pile of my father's death, and my attack, Acacia's death now scarred my history, a part of me, always to be carried to wherever my future lay. I wasn't a man of the colony until my acceptance leap, but no childhood remained for me, I was neither, in limbo.

I wished manhood would allow my thoughts to pass, to forget, but I knew that none of these things would vent my feelings back to the past. But focus I must, the reason why, I would work on.

Peshy stayed many days and nights with me at this time, each of us putting other things to the back of our minds. Gavriel occasionally visited, news of Mother not coping well didn't surprise me. And I often wished Gavriel would shout at me, tell me to pull myself together, tell me to think of her, even. But he never did. The simple act of bringing food and sitting with Peshy and me in the clearing, watching the insects peacefully live their days in silence, appeared to be a necessity for him, too, these days. We talked about acceptance.

Broaching bigger conversations was still difficult but together we talked more and more, often into the early hours of the morning, Shenash's bright lights in the sky way above us, more often than not. Slowly I regained a piece of me, not that it was theirs to give me; it wasn't even hiding in Gold Maple. Time allowed me to section my thoughts, to realise I'd sat down too long.

I needed to move now, different from before, always to be changed, but forward thinking was needed, and acceptance was my way forward. I couldn't let Peshy forget his honour, either; he had delayed his leap, too, for both me and him. Acacia's loss cut deep within him too.

'I did my best' is a simple sentence; I threw myself into the tasks given out to me, firstly felling trees. This allowed my anger to manifest itself into usefulness. I still occasionally sobbed uncontrollably and perfectly chopping damaged trees down before they fell gave me the solitude to work and be alone.

The branches, once removed, were taken to be chopped smaller for firewood, the trunks taken by warrior priests to shore up the breaches in the temple. This would have to make do until more stone could be sculpted to repair the once great building. After several days of chopping logs, I proved one thing to myself; I was getting stronger. My arm, although aching most days, now worked. I'd grown both in size and in stature, muscles starting to show, more adept than before.

Gavriel had told us that we needed to hunt soon; Vinn's acceptance day was looming, after being set aside for the colony to heal. Preparation for this needed attending to, so a group of the White Banner students, including me, set off the next morning. We agreed to skirt the eastern plains first, eventually venturing into the northern forests of the plains. Here we hoped to catch both Uppula and other roaming beasts, as well as a smaller party of us, once there, to dig up and sledge back to the colony some larger stone pieces to start to fix the well edges.

These had been removed. as the water in the wells had become lower the night of the fire. Although some remained undamaged, some of the older stone pieces had crumbled away and needed replacing. These smaller sections we could collect; the bigger pieces needed for the temple would have to be mined by larger groups, and this was left to the warrior priests to carry out. Working on the temple was a religious job. I heard Rogan had been tasked to help complete this; seeing him now as part of the warrior priests made us all smile, hoping that soon we would be by his side.

Hunting went well, and we all succeeded in gaining much-needed meat, both for the upcoming ceremony and for the colony's stores. The pieces of stone needed for the well repairs were also gained relatively easily. A hardworking group, we managed to get more stone than we thought we'd need, packing it on the bottom of the sledges, meat placed around and on top. We started the sledges homeward, tired; we were glad the journey had been uneventful.

Our minds often wandered, while sitting at night around the fire, or on longer uphill sections home, where we had to work in teams to move the heavy loads onward, to who had attacked the colony. I'd opened up about my attack, too, and as a group we all pondered now on why they had attacked.

During this time, we prepared the daily catches, Uppula mainly. The spring's newborn were beginning to be more adventurous now slightly older, often breaking away from the main herd, seeking out the fresher green shoots they preferred towards the plain's edges, making them easily within the predators' reach. This also allowed us better chances of taking them with a bow strike from range, quickly and more efficiently, sometimes felling two or more before the herd realised and sounded its warning calls for the rest to run. We ambushed the main herd for two days like this, until our sledges were bursting with the bounty we'd hunted. Thankful as always to Rai, we ate well on our trip, giving us much-needed energy for the stones' heavy retrieval, although as mentioned earlier, easy to get, harder to move. Sitting around the fires at night, we skinned and jointed the meat into smaller more manageable pieces. We wrapped these in soft linen cloths, making sure to keep them out of the sun, covered always, allowing us a couple of extra days to return the meat still fresh.

The colony had been so busy recently, trying to repair the damage done to our temple, our wells and surrounding territory, that hunting had taken a downturn. The nearby animals moving deeper into the surrounding forests also meant we had to venture further out for our hunting needs. The fact this allowed us some time to join forces in our hunting, alongside time to discuss recent events, became cathartic to me.

Realising others hurt too, over recent troubles, recognising that I wasn't alone in my fears, somehow helped.

If you're on a journey, especially a troublesome one, knowing you have fellows around you strengthens your resolve to completion. The end of that journey isn't always a happy venture but sometimes just getting to the end of something, alive, means you become more self-reliant, and after all, what more can anyone of us ask for, than that.

Within three days of travelling we had returned, only having to stop once to repair a sledge's running track on the return journey due to the weight of stone. The colony, as always, welcomed our return; this time I think more than normal, whether it was grateful for the extra hands to continue the repairs, or just with relief we had all returned safe and well.

Vinn waited for us, too, and told us that in just two days he would take his step forward into acceptance ledge. And manhood.

So the next day, while Vinn worked on his offering, and prayers in the temple, the rest of the White Banner students cleaned, and readied acceptance ledge.

The fire, thankfully, had merely brushed the outer edges of the flora here, easily removed, or disguised to show no signs of damage at all. The seats all remained solidly in place from Rogan's leap, and simple enough work by us all made the arena ready once more for use. Guards were still in place around the colony, upon Gavriel's instructions, and this still seemed slightly strange, as we'd lived in peace for years.

The warrior priests all knew us and allowed the White Banner to areas currently being protected; everywhere was allowed except the temple. Gavriel had himself given orders that unless it was for acceptance day prayers, the temple was off limits to all the colony. Repairs continued here; large tree trunks being shaped to fit the holes made in the assault on the building.

Stonemasons had already been sent to locate larger pieces of stone that would be required in the perfection of the task ahead. And Ivan went with them, saying that he knew where the larger pieces could be acquired. This area ran parallel to the home colonies of the outlanders, and with trust currently low, a band of warrior priests accompanied the masons, just in case of further attack. The guards among the colony often whispered they thought the attacks had been started by the outlanders.

But we knew strange magic had been involved that night, so having the guards close by was currently a good idea. Until we knew exactly what, or who had attacked us, we had to remain vigilant.

So, while the colony members started to prepare the meals needed for Vinn's special day, I returned home to clean the roads' dirt off, with thoughts of tomorrow's celebration rushing into my head.

The day went off without a hitch; Vinn started his day early as was needed, prepared speeches, and prayers read to him and by him in the temple, as was our way, how we'd been taught.

The White Banner students lined the path into acceptance ledge, the warrior priests in place, with throngs of spectators watching the ceremony from the seated areas around us all. Vinn gave his speech, dropping his acceptance offering gift, the roar greeting him from below so loud that it seemed mere feet below us, instead of the hundreds of metres we knew it was below.

Turning to say his final prayers and thanks to Rai and the colony, Vinn leapt from the edge, dressed in his ceremonial splendour.

It always seemed a long time to wait with a suddenly silenced crowd, all waiting to hear the incredible noise from gigantic dragon wings being driven upwards. Faintly then audibly stronger we all heard that noise; the crowd jostled into life again in anticipation of the first glimpse of Vinn's return with his dragon.

Dragons show both force and beauty, sheer mass and power belittle all around them, and Vinn's dragon pushed all its strengths to the forefront.

It suddenly shot into view; with the speed it twisted upwards I wondered how Vinn actually held on.

Climbing higher than ever before, it seemed, it suddenly folded its wings and fell into free fall, spinning downwards. The crowd both cheered and exhaled as one as the dragon whipped its tail around its body, forming a tornado effect of air, and lunged towards us all. A large plume of wispy smoke erupted from both nostrils; swirling in time with its tail gave a sight not to be forgotten by all present. Smoking trails circled the dragon's body, only dispersing in the frantic turbulence of air after reaching the rear of the creature. With the appearance of a spinning arrow, but much, much broader, the spinning increased, incomprehensible to the mere naked eye, the illusion fascinating to behold.

Then, pushing downwards upon huge wings suddenly having opened, spread wide, its descent, as fast as it began, halted, with only a few feet left to go until it surely would have plummeted onto the very rock we all stood upon. A raucous bellow rose from the crowd and the cheering continued long after Vinn was deposited onto the floor, normally a shaky occurrence in itself as we are taught a lot of things at forest school, but getting off your first dragon isn't easy. This, though, was no normal landing. Vinn, as pale as I have ever seen him, somehow stood.

Nausea overwhelming him, he managed to stand and face the mighty beast that stood there now, although I thought it wouldn't be long until he saw his breakfast again. Kneeling quickly for both support and marking his respect, holding one, still shaking, arm aloft, he waited.

The dragon, moving backwards and forwards slightly, rocking on its hindquarters, hesitated. Suddenly, reaching its immense head forward, it nudged Vinn's hand in acceptance.

As if knowing the effect its glamour was having on the crowd, the dragon gained its full height by stretching its head up, far above all who surveyed it here.

Vinn rose, still shaky, but managed to gain a firmer stance, both dragon and man now nodding to each other, now tied in friendship and battle.

The brilliant dark green of the dragon seemed to show a darker side of the beast, with no highlights to be seen. Normally the dragons I'd seen boasted coloured hues, shimmering into each and every scale, individual sections somehow showing effervescent colours, vibrant, works of art no mere painter could capture. This dragon, though, was different.

Beauty was evident through the darker patterns its scales displayed, initially appeared to be totally one colour, covered in minuscule scales, not one larger than my hand, should I say minuscule, for a dragon's scales anyway. They individually slotted into one another, giving an appearance of armour; a formidable beast indeed. Unusual for such a large beast, too, its talons seemed slimmer; instead of the giant gripping claws these were shaped, curved into sharpened, piercing needles. A fearless look on its face showed all that this was a pure fighting dragon.

Turning to jump onto dragon's rock, it bellowed in defiance, showering everyone with clouds of smoke. People took sudden cover, in case of flame, but the dragon was just showing its potential, its elegance, its immense power, brutish in its size and strength, and with a final guttural roar, leapt once more into the air. No one near could stand under the force this dragon mustered and, after it had gained height, again it roared, in defiance, it seemed, of life itself.

Plunging down back into the cloud-filled abyss, wings encapsulated against its armoured body, it disappeared with its roar still echoing around acceptance ledge, people still picking themselves off the floor, or climbing out from behind log seats from their hiding places.

Vinn vomited, turned to shrug at everyone then collapsed with the shock. That night, as the colony celebrations continued, Vinn was the subject of many a joke, but all agreed we couldn't have fared any better with the spinning.

ELEVEN

Over the next few days colony life seemed to return to relative normality; the general tidying of the colony had progressed well. Large pieces of stone were being brought back home on giant sledges, pulled by both colony masons and warrior priests. already starting to show the initial carving made while trying to remove them from the ground. This labour of love would take many months more of fine carving, to allow them to fit in place of the repaired tree sections in the temple, temporarily placed there.

The wells, too, had been mostly refilled, both by hard labour and the natural water course having time to recoup. Many trips by colony members to Pohalith, the Great Lake, brought back precious water in large earthen vases, sealed with mud caps to prevent leaking. Edges of the wells, too, had been restored, colony masons painstakingly taking time to repair these to look better than before. Hunting parties now occasionally set off, bringing back meat once more, and fruits in great quantities, with the balance of life appearing back to normal. Guards still occupied the edges of colony life, and as White Banner students we had a part to play in this as well.

Gavriel gave out duties to all and alongside experienced warriors we stood guard too, especially at night. Ivan had returned with the masons after sourcing the stone needed and more often than not, he and Gavriel seemed deep in thought, often walking around, surveying different parts of the temple, walking into the forest, or appearing randomly from places not normally trod. Searching, I would have said, maybe for answers to the recent attacks, but more than this, I felt. It seemed sometimes as if Gavriel searched himself more than his surroundings.

Colony life starting to repair, structures improved, balance once again. But still the constant thought of what happened that night. Warrior priests were dispatched to all parts of our lands, still searching for answers, still hopeful that somewhere, somehow a truth would be found, or told.

Senior colony members of great importance travelled to all regions known to the Tracouttie, questions being asked in every colony, only to be answered with similar questions. All colonies from Qeraviel to Banclian had been attacked, members of each colony taken or killed. But no one had seen the catlike figures we'd witnessed that night of our attack. Silver fingerprint marks were common in tales, though, from colony members, somehow marking areas, again to which end no one knew.

Qeraviel was a large expanse of land; our colony had always been here, history stated. It was the founding grounds of our forefathers who formed the Tracouttie colony.

The lands around here, slightly higher than surrounding territories, gave it an advantage. Maybe that's why our colony based itself here. Fertile land helped, edged to the north by the forest of Ewomatlan, even further north reaching into Banclian colony grounds, then into the mountainous wasteland. Few travellers ventured here, due both to the hostility of the ground and barren waste holding little worth or life seen.

Our southern flank was protected by sheer cliff faces from Rai's breaking of the world, impenetrable expanses of broken, spines of rock, sticking out of the earth, some reaching hundreds of feet into the air, a constant reminder of Rai's power, sat here, if we ever needed to remember, with the south-western region home to Pohalith, the Great Lake. Enormous in size, a body of water so large, none had traversed its entirety. Fresh water, luckily, beautifully clean, holding fish of many varieties, Pohalith held a place special to all colonies. Often seen, even the faraway members of the Banclian colony travelled this far to gather its precious resources.

Western regions led to the Ibothiel plain, home of the game herds. But so much more lay here. Recently learned by me whilst travelling, precious stones lay hidden, mined currently and mostly by the outlanders. And further west lay Mortwedge, the newer colony formed by the outlanders.

It was said that before the Tracouttie colony another had made this area its home. Again, history taught us that many centuries ago two large colonies held most of the world we knew today. One was a more peaceful group than the other. Years upon years of fighting weakened both sides. It is said that Rai himself grew up here. Stories of a young man found in the forest one day turned out to be Rai himself, not born to a mere human, it was said, growing to be more powerful, knowledgeable and wise than all around him.

Rai's followers even then always sought a peaceful path but were forced to fight on more than one occasion.

This was also the first time that dragons entered our history. Rai was found talking to a great beast once, seated on the floor as equals, it was taught. And the dragon gave Rai a gift more precious than most could hope for, a dragon's egg. Shenash eventually broke free from that very egg, growing into the most powerful dragon ever known.

Legendary tales from that time speak of how Rai's ability to communicate and fly with Shenash set them in folklore. No names of the colony have ever been recorded as far as I know, but today we refer to the group as Astohar, meaning simply, the old people.

Astohar gained knowledge, and with Rai and Shenash seeking a peaceful but powerful existence, the colony grew strong. Strength and power are dangerous things for everyone concerned. Having both can be an advantage but shows your great value to others who want but don't have. Lessons taught to the Tracouttie from early years show that the great battle that rose from the Astohar time shaped our very world today.

Numerous attacks between the two older colonies continued and continued, decades of fighting, neither side willing to just live and trust together, until Rai's patience wore too thin.

Clouded are the lessons from that early time, but all agree that Rai and Shenash's anger settled the troubles. Where Qeraviel sits today was part of an even larger plain system than we can witness, stretching out for many miles to where it sits now. Several days dragon's flight could be achieved simply by following the tributaries east, it was said.

Ambushed during the night, the two Astohar colonies fought, hundreds losing their lives during this particular battle, so bloody in its lust for power and control that Rai's anger finally spilled over. Pleading for peace, even just a willingness to forget and forgive, Rai tried to gain talks from both sides. But neither wanted peace. Limited knowledge in these times of magic were truly known; detailed documents sometimes hinted at minor powers, gained from study. Allowed to process this forgotten path, few took and travelled, seemingly disregarding its truth. Some colony members were adept at lighting small fires, producing light with mere thought even, but most held the rumour of the magic in disbelief.

Rai, on the other hand, learned all, absorbing the knowledge. Some even said that he wasn't born a man, he was always a god in human form, found as a baby to teach us from the wrongs we set in place.

Riding on the back of Shenash, Rai used magic never before seen as powerful as that night, indeed proving himself no mortal, both dragon and magic overwhelming the Astohar into subjugation. Powerful surges of dragon fire and lightning from Rai's fingertips literally split the very ground, the earth, in two. The eastern side eventually collapsed downwards, splitting the ground between the two warring factions. A huge crevasse, hundreds of metres deep, miles wide, bore witness to the immense power displayed that night.

This indeed showed Rai's powerful nature, and once highlighted never to be hidden again.

Separated forever, the two colonies could no longer fight, each knowing not of what happened to the other. Rai flew away that very night, sending peaceful teachings back with messengers, taking no side, it was said. Shenash's future children became guardians of the very world we lived in. A constant symbol to remember, if ever needed between the two worlds, now split, that a peaceful life must prevail. It was written that the Astohar, after many, many years, eventually withered, disbanding even, years later to once more become fractious colonies wandering the great lands, leaving a few old colony members who chose to remain and document the events of the splitting of the world.

No knowledge had ever been written of the colony whose lands fell that day; they were never to be seen again. Astohar had been broken into two, and so it remained that way.

From these early teachings, the Tracouttie learnt its valuable lessons, praising Rai for the god he always was. Offerings were often given in praise of his greatness, hoping for forgiveness of our mistakes.

Acceptance by Rai held no other equal, and all male colony members must step forward to be either accepted or shunned by our god.

Time sometimes allowed escape from this fact, but no longer could recent events put off the inevitable; my acceptance was close.

꙳

Gavriel had taken the whole section of White Banner students aside one day, reaffirming that we still needed to complete our carvings, making sure we understood still the necessity of our prayers, and to be ready for our own acceptance day. Peshy had been given his day, a mere month away, swiftly followed by my own.

One day, whilst my mind wandered, sitting carving the final scales on my dragon's tail, Gavriel approached. Gently placing himself next to me, slightly startled, I looked up. "Wicker, this last year has been tough on you, tough on all of us, it must be said. Tragedy has struck you more than most, though, and you have managed to continue throughout. Rai has noticed your work, and your time has come to set these bad omens aside and concentrate on your acceptance into Rai's servitude. You will be a strong colony member, an appreciated warrior priest with much to teach. Stay strong and remember you hold a great power within; you're the only one who can defeat your own beliefs."

With these words he got up and wandered off into the forest. As I sat pondering his words, I realised that I had indeed managed to wander through this year, even though it had proven awful for me.

Peshy awoke me early the next day, concern the major emotion he displayed. He hesitated, making sure we were alone before speaking. Gavriel had paid Peshy and his family a visit at their home, late last night. Sitting Peshy down, he started to explain that he had received many tales, objections that Peshy wasn't studying properly for his acceptance, alongside frequent messages about Amia always present within the colony.

Gavriel didn't need to repeat the last piece of his conversation as Peshy already knew people were unhappy about an outlander walking freely within Qeraviel.

Recently, with the fire and the attack, colony members were becoming more openly hostile to the outlanders, even though they knew the attacks had been widespread, effecting all lands, including losses of children, too, in Mortwedge.

Gavriel raised his own concerns regarding the laws and teachings of Rai, leaving little doubt in Peshy's mind where he stood on this matter.

He forbade Peshy to see Amia again, telling him to concentrate on his acceptance day; this was the only option and the right option for the colony and his family.

Peshy's parents had done the rest; Peshy explained to me that for the rest of the evening, his parents had prayed for his forgiveness, reminding him of the colony's needs and his obligation to them. In the end, whether just from tiredness or the constant berating, he agreed to all.

Sitting with me the next morning, he challenged his own thoughts, struggling with his need to support his colony, his family, wanting the best for Rai, but his own wants too; a struggle seemingly impossible to reconcile. Amia was a friend to me, but much more to Peshy. Sometimes life makes choices too hard to accept and Peshy this day sat in turmoil with his options, which were none, it seemed.

Later that day Gavriel himself set off to Mortwedge, a few warrior priests for company. White Banner students had already been assigned duties, assisting the remaining warrior priests, supporting their guard duty. Peshy and I, so close to acceptance, were allowed time to finish our carvings and offerings so we made our way to the forest classroom once more.

Gavriel's path to Mortwedge wasn't a long journey, well-travelled now over the years, but still not a light undertaking. Trust between the two colonies was fragile at the best of times. And recently with the attacks, both held little faith in the meeting of the elders from both colonies. Gavriel's status held him on higher ground, though; his prowess as both a leader and fighter made most other colony elders back down. Outlanders here were no different; once themselves living in Qeraviel, they all knew Gavriel and his potential.

Travelling most of the day, with several small breaks, still allowed Gavriel time to enter the edges of Mortwedge while the sun still lazily hung in the sky that day. A forward party had been sent to inform the outlanders that Gavriel was visiting, and a small committee of higher ranked colony outlanders met Gavriel and his warrior priests soon after entering their territory.

Pleasant enough the meeting, conversation soon switched to colony life and a peaceful ride into Mortwedge was accomplished by all.

After refreshing Gavriel after the day's ride, the outlander elder community arranged food and accommodation for that evening. Accepted with gratitude, if not delight, Gavriel agreed to a meeting the following day. All that night slept with a wonder of tomorrow's discussions, warrior priests on guard around the building they called home that night.

The next morning, early to rise, Gavriel was ready way before the outlander elders and made it clear that the meeting was to be made henceforth. Outlanders, more used to a steadier place in life, rallied to meet the demands of their visitor and somewhat unwelcome guest.

A normally reasonable man, Gavriel seemed more perturbed than normal, it was witnessed. Even sitting in the middle of unfriendly faces, he barked his demands once more of the outlanders, knowing their place in society, especially amongst Qeraviel, once again forbidding their entry to the region, stating the mistrust held between the colonies a driving factor for this. Accusations of the recent attacks, although broached with malice by Gavriel, couldn't have been the outlanders, in truth. Gavriel stated agreement in this matter was not up for discussion and used all his might and power to back this up, with threats of reprisal if again broken. Anger not easily reached, he produced; all company present, it was stated, became uneasy to anger such a man, and agreement was reached.

Gavriel, not wanting to stay in Mortwedge a moment longer, gathered his warrior priests and in defiance of all previous meetings left without a parting word. Mortwedge and Qeraviel had always been separate, two halves of the same whole, but right now a bitterness sat deep within the people of this region. Mortwedge was a large colony now; that said, it remained significantly smaller than ours, numbers steadily growing through becoming fallen, but now outlanders' births probably outweighed the shunned. The ground on which it called home, a somewhat lower elevation too.

Qeraviel to its east, the forest of Ewomatlan guarding its northern territory, with a great view to the sea on its western side a beautiful reminder that even though not a particularly fertile area, beauty was set all around, within easy access to the plains of Ibothiel to allow both colonies good hunting.

The initial elders who based Mortwedge here hadn't moved far from the past, Barbarrow market bordering the north-eastern aspects a place where all colonies eventually met.

Mortwedge was a colony of constant change; one minute having to accept someone they had considered unfriendly just days before, now officially outlanders too, must have been hard for all concerned.

This recent meeting showed a bitterness I couldn't wholly accept with honesty. Amia and the outlanders I knew had helped me search for Acacia, helped try to find the attackers who nearly took my life that night in the forest.

These people were part of our society once, simply turned away for no discretion of their own, a hard truth to learn, a harder truth to accept, now that I knew these people were being accused of things they didn't do.

After Gavriel's return, the whole colony learned of what had occurred in Mortwedge. Most colony members were relieved, it seemed, that Qeraviel had once again become a safer place. Some, though, I must say, especially Peshy and I, became sadder, for we had lost a true friend. Gavriel seemed relentless over the next few weeks, constantly setting harder tasks for the White Banner. Missions were given out to all of us, allowing little time to focus on the upcoming leaps, or anything involving other colony life.

Early starts turned to late nights and the days sped past rapidly now. Within a week Peshy would make his succession into manhood and final preparations were progressing well for him. Outwardly he maintained calm, doing everything asked of him by warrior priests, his parents and Gavriel. Meetings with all in this final time laid heavily on his demands and I, with half a mind on my own day coming soon, was glad the pressure dropped on us all onto poor Peshy.

Internally Peshy still struggled with his thoughts, often talking to me and the other White Banner students regarding his troubled sleep, holding conversations about Amia only with me as we couldn't wholly trust the others not to mention his fears to Gavriel.

Neither of us had seen a glimpse of Amia; whether like us she'd been warned of the consequences of trying to meet us, or whether again like us her colony had been keeping her busy. We'd ventured to Barbarrow on more than one occasion to see if she would be sneaking a visit there, but to no avail. Peshy's mood over this had become darker and questioned his own and Amia's feelings over their friendship on more than one occasion.

Both agreed, though, that one day we'd hopefully catch up with her, telling her that somehow things would be worked out, not knowing how this could be achieved though in reality.

⸺

I was travelling on one such occasion, my own trip to Barbarrow, on a produce pick-up from Ivan. Gavriel had wanted me to replenish inks for the temple, as recent acceptance leaps had seen many students use valuable resources here. Parchment and quills on the list, too, meant I held a list of needs nearly as heavy as the coin Gavriel gave me. Ivan, as always, was the man for this, and already had all I needed waiting, I'd been told. I saw Amia for the first time in weeks, talking to Ivan as I picked my way through the crowds always flocking his stall. Flushed cheeks apart, she didn't appear any different, and part of me wanted to run straight over to her and see how she was. Stopping myself seemed both wrong and right at the same time.

People all around Ivan glanced at her with suspicion and I realised that's why she appeared flushed, anxious even, in the presence of others.

Floating on the wind I heard several comments on the fact she was there, and in embarrassment I stayed out of sight. Turning away from the sight of her awkwardness, I pretended to vanish into the scenery, taking a larger than needed path to the other side of the market, heading away from both the need to help and the thoughts of cowardice I felt.

Amia was feeling uncomfortable and only made the trip to Barbarrow as her mother needed thread to repair worn clothes. Several stalls on the market sold these and most things could either be purchased, sold or traded for in Barbarrow. Some people sold themselves, their skills anyway. Builders, masons, tanners all peddled their wares here or offered work for hire. Food aplenty was the main fare traded though, the smell of freshly baked bread a constant on the edges of the wind, assaulting every sense one had.

Ivan had stopped Amia on her journey past, and reluctantly she'd stopped to talk. Aware of the new hostilities, Ivan didn't give these matters any thought. He liked Amia and treated all who visited him the same way, not seeming to care where one came from. Amia had looked at Ivan with disbelief, the same way I'm sure I did the day Ivan gave me my charm. This day he held a brightly coloured green orb, set again in silver, dangling from an ornate silver chain. Hanging from his fingers, the colours appeared to dance, involuntarily, sparking off each other within the tiny ball they were set.

Greens of nature were somehow captured forever within, a perfect contrast, balanced perfectly, occasionally forming a predatory bird in flight, momentarily showing the magic it obviously held. Amia, whether transfixed by the beauty of the object offered to her or the inability to fathom how one could hold such an object, stood still. Ivan physically hung the fine silver chain around her neck with Amia standing stock still.

Moments passed as she gazed at its beauty, mesmerised by its charm. Nodding his assent to her gift given, Amia couldn't add anything to the moment and fled at great speed hiding, I'm sure, more than tears of gratitude; tears of recent frustration. Someone showing any kind of warmth to an outlander was much needed in these times, especially to this young woman.

Standing still in thought, I wondered how I could remain a friend to Amia, the likelihood being very slim after Gavriel's words. Still pondering, I ventured over to see Ivan.

As always, he held an enraptured crowd around him, this time all focused on a particular tray of small bottles he was showing around, seated into a tiny fur-lined wooden box. The box held approximately a dozen of these little dark green bottles, no bigger than the size of my thumb, stoppered with a tiny rag-clothed cork tied in place with a multi-coloured ribbon, tiny but highly decorated. "A fine bottle indeed," I said, out loud it must have been, as Ivan turned his attention to me. Wafting effortlessly to my side, Ivan started his tricks. Master of sales, I'd seen him practise this magic often whilst sitting talking to him over the years. Sleight of hand second to no one, he produced, then made the tiny box of bottles somehow disappear, only to reappear on his market stall, several feet away. Crowd applause only heightened the trick, once more making the bottles disappear from his stall, back into his hands.

The bottles, we were told, held a very special drink, acquired all the way from the Banclian territory. This was a region seldom travelled to by anyone, its colony members known for being more sophisticated than the other colonies of the region. Higher-priced goods often worked their way to the Barbarrow market, more often than not, by Ivan. Banclian food and drink held a higher regard, regarded as sweeter than anything from within Qeraviel.

High prices could be fetched for goods from Banclian and while crowds massing around us bartered with Ivan for the small glass beautiful bottles, I started to gather the needed items on Gavriel's list. Once much lighter of coin, but far heavier in inks, quills and paper, I slowly headed back to the temple, leaving Ivan with a large smile and a far heavier purse than I think even he anticipated over some small glass bottles.

Banclian territory, although far north from our location, was protected by the mountainous Lerandra slopes. Fertile grounds here, fed by glacial water runs, allowed sweet beets, sugar cane and fresher produce to be grown. At times a colder region than ours, protection from the winds often seen in Qeraviel and Mortwedge, once more allowed crops to survive, with a far greater yield often managed.

Through the forest of Ewomatlan, still several long days' travel, only then brought you into the Banclian territories. So hardy travellers only took this route, seldom at that. These grounds were also more dangerous a route to travel, as the forest of Ewomatlan often held greater numbers of hunting cats, this area known to be their dwelling, with even the Veiled Sinivore witnessed here more than anywhere else.

Night travelling therefore was not advised, and campsites were often surrounded by predatory cats late at night. The stories of their calls were often told to scare the younger children, to warn of dangers of the forest. Banclian colony members were hardy folk, described as tough but with levels of great intelligence. It was known to all the large deposits of books they held, matters of all aspects written about by their elders.

Metallurgy was invented in this region, with two small foundries working there today.

Everyone's weapons came from this area; swords, pikes and all ceremonial metal work originated from Banclian. All metal ore mined from the foot of the Lerandra mountains gave them both great knowledge and wealth. A very powerful ally indeed.

It was more than rumoured that Gavriel was born here, growing up as a young man, learning his skills as a warrior. His knowledge indeed was far greater than all others and early tales of the young Gavriel fighting for peace in this region held many truths. Only after many land disputes had peace finally reigned for all regions, and Gavriel become at peace with himself, devoting his life to Rai, setting up the priesthood in Qeraviel. Many followers of his story, his legend you may say, were the initial priests, swelling into greater numbers over the years with Rai's blessing.

Known throughout the lands of being a tremendous character, both in and out of battle, his reputation only grew with tribal negotiations, always seeking a peaceful answer first, giving him respect and honour, knowing his sword might talk, if groups didn't, became a mighty power indeed.

Further north, beyond the great mountains of Lerandra, sat the wastelands; huge expanses of flat lands, a dry and arid place, few had sought to travel. Maps of this region marked it as an inhospitable place. Holding no water, to travel here was near impossible, so no one had ventured there much. A place to avoid, with little or no resources to collect.

East, very much like in our region sat the scarred land of the breaking of the world, again not fruitful or reachable, pinnacles of rock hewn forth in a mighty reminder of Rai's strength.

As we lay south to the Banclian, their vast lands, although challenged in width, covered many miles, with their western edges meeting the sea.

Mortwedge could traverse coastal paths, working down to the sea from higher land, Banclian could access the sea from beaches, scattered across many points on the western fringes. Fishing again was a scarce commodity with us, having to travel to the Great Lake in Pohalith, but here commonly obtained for food.

These areas were commonly known for the amount of Shaebeas here, often fishing themselves, especially around early autumn, mainly their cub season. A large animal, heavy black- and brown-coated, traversing on all fours, with large claws making the Shaebea a fearsome animal to deal with. That said, mostly if left alone, these immense creatures would leave the area if approached, tending to somehow favour simply moving than confrontation.

Stories told, though, of cornering one. Old hunting parties occasionally removed larger animals if seen travelling the paths nearer colonies. And much appreciation of the Shaebea's heart in battle was written and talked about. A large Shaebea skull was mounted once in the forest classroom for all White Banner students to examine, explaining that the extra thickness to the bone made it near impossible to penetrate without a sturdy pike, and much strength.

I remember the lesson well, and once, whilst sitting in a tree silently, watched a mother Shaebea with its cubs. Praying I sat, hoping it didn't sense my presence; its power and beauty remained within me after that day, and my respect heightened after it left me untouched in that tree.

TWELVE

Before sunrise I'd made my way to Gold Maple, tasked the night before to get another dozen rabbits for Peshy's celebration. So many leaps recently meant hunting most days now, and fires had already been lit to roast the Uppulas caught only yesterday. Even as the first distinct blue tones entered the outgoing night sky, I'd managed to shoot a further seven rabbits, and I knew others from the colony were out hunting too.

Early rising allowed me to not only ponder the coming days' events, but also gave me time to worry more. I forced these feelings away; after Peshy, my day would soon be here, people reminded me every day, it seemed. Truth was, in less than two weeks this year's White Banner students would all have taken their acceptance leaps and be thought of as students no more.

Warriors all together, ready to serve Rai's words whenever needed.

Another two hours passed, and I easily caught all I needed; in fact, the summer grass currently showing new growth all around meant I could have shot more than I required. Rai's bounty, though, is not forsaken, and taking plenty but not too much was our way. Praising Rai for my success, I'd gutted and skinned my catch, just in time to be greeted by a glorious sunny morning, displaying that today was a new day full of hope, a new day for change; Peshy's big day. His acceptance leap had arrived.

Dropping my freshly prepared meat at the large central area of the colony to be cooked, I managed to enjoy the proceedings a little. Peshy I'd glimpsed early on, walking with his parents and Gavriel to the temple. Tradition normally meant that parents walked their children to Rai, accepting them back at dragon's rock as men. Today Peshy even from a distance appeared larger than himself, already dressed in his ceremonial gown, coloured both white and black, showing the transformation from student to warrior had begun.

After being shown to the temple by his parents, Anselm and Indira would help prepare the huge meal always associated with acceptance; that was, until just before the ceremonial walk, when they would stand proudly in acceptance area. Anselm wasn't a warrior priest; he'd been injured as a small child and never gained the rank of, or the permission granted to be, an accepted warrior. Many men of the colony took vows to serve Rai in other ways over the years. After all, other trades and skills were as highly needed. High status sat with the warrior priests, though, and most chose to try and walk that path, Peshy no exception.

After dropping the rabbits off, I hastily made my way home to change as well. As a White Banner student nearing his leap, a student could pick the students and warriors he wanted to escort him along his long walk to acceptance ledge. Peshy hadn't hesitated in asking me, nor I in agreeing, to be part of that walk. I would very soon be returning the favour, after all, even though he would be a warrior then, no longer dressed in white, or, as today, white and black, but in the full black robes of the warrior priest.

Properly washing the already busy day's dirt from my hands, Mother helped me dress too. Not venturing out of the home these days, even Mother was getting ready for Peshy's leap. My brother of sorts, she knew how important this day was for the colony but also for us both. Peshy's parents and my mother has grown up together; this had always formed a close bond. She was there for them as much as me. Putting aside her constant torment, she even managed a smile occasionally, upsetting really as I knew she didn't believe it, but held it anyway.

Dressing in my white tunic, ceremonial belt and shoes, I was ready.

Today I had to assemble with the other White Banners near the temple for Peshy's return.

After initial prayers at the temple with Gavriel, Peshy would have to show he'd finished his carving on the benches, seated in the forest classroom, with a demonstration of his warrior combat skills added into this scenario afterwards.

We'd all been taught how to use the colony's weapons, ever since we'd agreed to be accepted into the White Banner students. Weekly lessons were taught by experienced warrior priests. Funny, we used to think they'd go easy on us at first.

We all learnt quickly that it wasn't the case. Bruises, abrasions and welts all showed our ineptitude, and soon learning to fight became a necessity to protect our hands and faces from the lightning-fast blows from the priests. Over time we all improved; balance as in life gives us strength of character, force and will gives us momentum, learning to control these took time, something we worked on daily in between our other lessons.

The trials asked of us on our acceptance day were never explained by the other students who travelled this path, each holding their day's activities close to their chest. Peshy was a strong fighter, and this was his area of expertise; tenacious and slightly arrogant he always seemed to succeed in trials of this nature. I held no fear over this one of his trials today; mine, though, I constantly wondered upon.

So, making my way to the temple I started to join the other students and warrior priests waiting for the first real sight of Peshy.

Standing outside the temple we set ourselves up in parallel lines along the path which led from the doorway. It was strange that this side of the temple seemed untouched by the recent attack and didn't seem even to show signs of the unholy, unnatural burning flames of that evening. Large areas to each side of the temple showed that an expanse that used to be tree-laden was now barren, giving a well-lit area now where it used to be more subdued.

Standing in lines, with the occasional joke passing between us, we waited.

After what seemed a very long time, Peshy, accompanied by Gavriel, appeared from the forest. Peshy, slightly red, appeared to have been working hard, whereas Gavriel emitted calm, with an inner peace he carried with ease. After a recess at the temple, where words of praise could be heard from where we all stood, the large wooden temple doors opened to show Peshy standing in front of a small group of senior warrior priests, beside Gavriel.

All marching in formation, they started their way to acceptance ledge. A mere nod from me to Peshy I hoped would help, but he couldn't say or do anything now except march in time with all around him. The warrior priests and the White Banner students, including me, made our way too, judging our footfall in time with the smaller group placed slightly behind us. An honour guard, if you will, we paved the way, a long walk through the forest initially, but meandering through the vast areas of the colony too.

Those members of the colony not able to gain a seat at acceptance ledge lined the well-travelled route we now took, several throwing flowers on the path in front of Peshy, marking his steps somehow to the greatness he was about to embark on.

Pride filled me here as I marched with my best friend; even Rogan and Vinn seemed in wonder at the day, despite recently having been through theirs. Eventually making our way through a large part of Qeraviel, we reached our destination. Splitting into smaller groups, the forward party we made up now lined the path into the arena. Peshy had slowed slightly on purpose and now entered the main arena, standing next to Gavriel.

Taking his mark near the front edge of dragon's rock, a simple bow was met with rapturous applause, the crowd standing now cheering loudly. Peshy's parents seated in the front row couldn't have looked on with more pride in their eyes, and I tried to squash the reality of this day's events into a memory to always remember.

Peshy, turning to accept his offering from a senior warrior priest who had carried it for him, now held it up for all to see.

Offerings were as individual as the person making them, but most comprised similar objects.

Pelts, skins and hides gained from hunting showed Rai an ability to hunt well. Ornate carvings, much smaller in size and normally in the shape of simple flowers or birds, represented Rai's beauty, the nature around us always shown to be important in these things. Finally, everyone normally added something held close to the person making the gift, not always seen by the onlookers but placed inside the hide's stitching.

Peshy, I thought, like me, probably wouldn't place the necklace from Ivan inside, which had been our original idea, mine constantly around my neck these days. But a familiar rattling alarmed my senses as he turned to show his offering to all once more. The crowd already taking their seats allowed my senses to realise what that noise I'd heard was.

Peshy had placed the Veiled Sinivore's teeth within his offering.

As if he felt my stare boring into him at that point, he turned to face me. Unable to speak my fear of the bad omen he'd placed, I just shook my head slightly; if he realised, I'm not aware, or he simply chose to ignore it then and there.

Turning away he walked over to acceptance ledge, and whilst the colony members played light music to fill the air with sound, Peshy dropped his offering over the edge. Normally the sounds of the giant beasts below held a silent reverie, but as always with any offering the guttural roars from below were heard that day.

Gavriel stood tall as his speeches carried to everyone present. He told of the young man standing here today, told of his sacrifices to both his family and his colony to be able to make today's leap. Every time Gavriel seemed to succeed in saying similar things about everyone while making it individual to every student. Peshy was a proud young man as he listened, and expectation started to heighten as the speeches drew to a close.

Peshy simply thanked everyone, drawing special thanks to his parents, his fellow students and Gavriel, gestures taken well by the colony, so he hastened to the point of acceptance.

Walking the short distance from the centre of the area, Peshy now stood on the very edge of acceptance ledge. I wondered if he remembered, as I did at that moment, the first time we'd each dared the other to look off the spot he now stood on. Without looking back, not even raising his arms he leapt a giant leap forward, falling into the air, disappearing so fast it was as if he hadn't occupied the scene at all.

Heart beating out of my chest, like all others here I waited. Waited for the sound that normally followed, the beating of the dragon's wings, bringing our warrior back, bringing my best friend back.

A sudden roar, much closer than the others earlier. It was the first noise we all heard, in fact most were startled as it came from out of the sky, seemingly surrounding us. A clear day with excellent visibility, but no sight to be seen. Calmness held, with fear just held at bay suddenly starting to spill over from warrior priests around the arena. I'd heard of this happening before but didn't, couldn't accept that Peshy might not return.

Cries from the crowd grew louder as several warrior priests gazed over the edge of the precipice. All I had rooted me to stay still, the surrounding guard all standing, hoping this wasn't a reality; as the minutes passed, more guttural sounds lifted on the air around us, but that was the only thing returned that day.

Peshy had become one of the fallen.

The party tables still stood in places that evening as the darkness descended, most having been hastily cleared away, colony members hiding at home after hearing the news of the day's events. Some had taken food back home, not wanting it to waste, merely to keep out of the way of the warrior priests who were guarding the route from acceptance ledge to Peshy's home that night.

Peshy didn't return, his parents inconsolable still after several hours had passed, in grief for their son, losing more than flesh and blood this day.

Gavriel had initially taken them to the temple, spoken to them alone and now orders were given to guard them on their way home for the last time.

The march, or shall I say an amble, made its way through the colony's centre back towards the homesteads, members of the colony already shunning their existence, turning away, some shouting comments of hatred, others merely ignoring the events occurring, acting as if this was a normal day, going about their daily chores, blocking out the truth of Peshy not coming home.

Anselm and Indira walked arm in arm, holding each other up it seemed, the proudness earlier displayed withered now, showing only frailty in each of them. Guarded all the way home, never raising their eyes once to look around, they approached and entered their homestead, door closing, hope forgotten.

No lights were lit that night, and as darkness closed over the day, the sounds of crashing and things being moved could be heard long into the early morning.

Separated from Mother and me by a forked path, ours was the closest homestead to theirs, a small coppice of trees marking the boundary path between the two homes. Mother had been turned away that night from trying to visit her friends; we were told to stay away, not allowed to venture close to their home anymore.

Before the sun had risen the next day, a large wooden wagon arrived and several warrior priests loaded belongings onto it, some furniture, but mostly personal belongings it seemed, hastily shoved into wooden crates, covered in blankets and clothes.

Gavriel didn't arrive at all, and knowing the outcome of their destination, never gave any words of comfort, it seemed. As they trudged along behind the slow-moving wagon flanked by warrior priests, they didn't see Mother and I waving. Everyone else in the colony had already forgotten them, for outlanders weren't people in our colony's eyes.

Devastation sat upon me once more. I watched with tears in my eyes as torches were thrown into Peshy's home, the fire soon catching hold of the wooden structure, sending it into a mass of crackling, burning wood and reed, the heat evident from hundreds of feet away, the smoke trailing upwards, spiralling skyward a sign for all, both witnessed in

Qeravial and beyond, marking another fallen, another slight to Rai's good name.

Part of me didn't believe that statement at all, another part wished it wasn't true, and yet another still couldn't understand it.

Warned to stay away, I couldn't, but followed slowly and out of sight of the main group of warriors walking the miles from Qeravial to Mortwedge with Peshy's parents. Little words were spoken on the part of the journey I witnessed, and when they were it was merely to discuss directions between the warriors. No words, no consolation given, no words of sustenance, nothing worth hearing with honesty. Eventually the group snaked its way across the ground into the edge of Mortwedge, grinding to a halt, warrior priests marking their arrival by sounding two large horns, Uppula antlers, hollowed out to make sound. A morose noise, fitting, I felt, in these circumstances.

Hiding myself in a thicket of bushes and gorse shrub, we all waited, unsure at first, until I noticed a smaller band of outlanders gathering together before closing the distance between the two groups. Simple nods seemed to be the only communication here, no words or noises I heard in my hiding spot, and as the warrior priests departed, I got a last look at Peshy's parents as they lagged behind the outlander group who now took them further into Mortwedge. Outlanders now, to start a new life, to try and forget, to forget their son, my best friend.

As I sat in the bush, waiting for the warrior priests to leave so that they would not see me, I spied a silvery glint in the bushes way across from me. Trying to focus on the exact spot I'd noticed, movement caught my eye. Someone was watching me also. Freezing, I tried to minimise my thoughts, my actions, waiting for a second glimpse of who sat there, only to find the person break cover and start heading in my direction. Amia.

A part of me lifted in that moment. Maybe just the fact that I'd not seen her for a long time, or that here stood someone who understood my current woes, either way I didn't get the chance to think for long as Amia rushed at me, breaking through the silence with her sobs of sheer anguish as she hugged me. I hadn't cried over Peshy; I still found it extremely hard after Acacia to show feelings, but Amia had no such misfortune. Her words were truly lost to me as she spoke, indistinguishable amid the tears. I caught the odd word resonating true, that's all.

After an eternity, it felt, Amia looked up. Although saddened beyond words could help, I think being together helped each of us that day. Sitting in that bush we talked for several hours, neither of us complaining of the brambles, or the cramp we both inevitably felt.

We discussed Peshy, how he'd missed Amia, and how he always talked about her. How Amia had tried to come to see us but had been sent away by the warrior priests. I even mentioned the market trip where I'd seen her get her pendant from Ivan. She wore it constantly, she told me, the green within somehow calming her, keeping her safe, she felt.

In fact, darkness had begun to set in when I realised we'd been there most of the day. I'd described Peshy's day for her, and the horrible moment he didn't return, each of us feeling awkward and inept, recalling memories of Peshy without him being there, both, I think, not wanting to believe we'd never see him again, too big a subject to truly think of right here, right now.

Darkness hung over us now like a thick woollen blanket, both agreeing to leave each other's company that night, but promising to talk again soon. Wandering slightly still sticking to darker patches of the forest edges in case anyone was about and would see us, we agreed to meet the next day if no one would miss us. Turning to say goodbye I was relieved to see, if not happiness but hope in Amia's gaze back at me.

We'd each recently lost two friends, and although one could never be replaced by either of us, we'd got another back. Sometimes holding on to what you have makes a small victory worthwhile; this felt better than yesterday. As we walked in separate directions, I'm not sure either of us noticed the charms around our necks glowing slightly.

Not realising how dark it had become, I stumbled more often than walked the many miles home. Trying to maintain my balance, crossing into a section of Ewomatlan forest, northerly bordering the edge of Mortwedge, I continued homeward, suddenly finding myself face first on the floor, cursing my stupidity of falling, wondering what I'd tripped on, not clearly visible with the dimly lit star skies above. Rubbing my legs whilst standing, thankful for no real injury I noticed a large mass, crumpled on the floor, then a thick section of cut log, or trunk, placed very near a pile of smaller logs. I hesitated whether I should look twice, this dark forest holding no fears normally for me, and this being a simple mishap, I turned to carry on.

Whether I then noticed my necklace glowing, or the reflection of red bouncing back from my necklace on the object on the floor, something made me stop in my tracks.

A faint glow only, but something caught my eye. Leaning forward, trying in the darkness to focus on the object, I suddenly realised I was staring into another eye.

Reaction to strange things occurs in many ways and standing in the darkness of an unfamiliar part of this forest gave me limited options right here and now. Suppressing the urge to run away as fast as I could, controlling my breathing, I reached forward. The eye never moved, didn't blink, never closed, but remained staring at me, entering my world with its presence. As my shaking hand got closer, I realised that the red glow from my necklace brightened slightly, throwing a dull but welcome glow over the scene in front of me. The eye belonged to a large Tusked Mortogg, once a huge beast.

Somehow it had wedged itself into the pile of logs placed here, lying on its side, as if it had tried to hide itself. Death hadn't been kind to this animal. The side it had tried so hard to protect was obviously open down its entire right flank; matted black hair showed it had slowly and painfully met its end here, bleeding to death, hiding away from who knows who, or what. The beast's left eye, turned up to face into the forest, still on guard, had been the only giveaway that it was there, except my clumsiness tripping over it. I stood awhile, thinking of what could cause such an injury to something of this size; the laceration had been mighty and deep, no hope for the Mortogg's survival.

But if someone had been hunting the beast, why leave it here? Whilst standing and thinking I heard a small noise in the distance behind me.

Still on edge of the situation, not knowing who was responsible for hunting this animal, I simply stood to the side, making sure I was carefully hidden away to anyone approaching.

The noises I'd heard repeated several times, a rhythmical tapping. Maybe, I thought, just another creature moving through the forest, but whatever made the noise was nearer than before, although not moving at a pace to concern me. I decided to stand my ground. Waiting in these situations often becomes knowledge, so I concentrated on my other senses, sight being of little use right now in the dark.

Crawling, yes, crawling the sound I could hear now; something approached as I said, not at speed, but making its way towards me and the downed Mortogg. Fear started to attack me; whether the smell reached me first or the anticipation of the memory of the last time I felt this way did I couldn't tell you.

Fear unbelievably gripped my every sinew. Not knowing whether to chance my escape, scream in terror or continue to hide, I couldn't tell you what emotion overwhelmed me more, but my body chose to continue to hide. Last time I felt this way was on the night of the attack, frozen in body but active in mind, being dragged through the forest school in Qeraviel.

It took all I had to not vomit in fear right now as I noticed the small hand of the catlike creature enter my vision.

Dragging itself forward using only one arm, only occasionally stopping to rest, it slowly made its way through the undergrowth. In life we have all smelt foul odours, rotten food, fermenting rubbish maybe, but the smell this creature exuded was unlike anything I can describe. Ever-changing, it appeared thick, if a smell can actually have form, substance, clawing at the back of my throat, making me want to cough, not breathe at all.

A smell of death, unnatural to my world, or what I knew of it anyway. The creature, not sensing my hiding place, crawled further forward towards the Mortogg, seemingly focused on the huge beast in front of it. I initially wondered why this catlike creature didn't stand, didn't just walk forward, hidden by the cover of darkness that hid me so well. Then it came to me that this creature was badly injured too. Behind the legs being dragged along was a wide blood trail; not seeing the wound from where I stood, I could make out its severity. Blood loss slowed the catlike creature to a mere stop now, gasping and panting for breath, its efforts focused on getting to the Mortogg.

Rising to my feet, I tried to grasp a smaller cut log for protection, not wanting to feel the numbness and pain I had felt that night, held captive by these creatures again.

Managing to face my fear and finally placing my hand around a suitable piece of wood, I restored my standing position, watching as finally the catlike creature got to its destination, the side of the Mortogg.

Still darkness reigned around me, but as the catlike creature reached upwards, pulling itself into position at the Mortogg's neck, my thoughts strengthened and clarified. I needed this beast. I had to take it to Gavriel and the others, back to Qeraviel.

Fear can be a terrible thing to encounter; it can force your hand to be something you don't want to be or accept your failures in life. Right here at this moment fear gave me something I needed more of: power.

The creature appeared to be draining the very blood from the downed Mortogg, and although not moving more, the catlike creature seemed to be regaining some strength, becoming more fluid in its actions, speed returning. I knew I had limited time to react. I'm not proud of my actions here, I must add, attacking something not knowing or sensing its immediate doom isn't right, isn't fair. But I had no choice, I felt. Stepping forward with sheer panic, raising the wooden club I'd picked up from the forest floor, I struck just as the creature turned its head to notice me for the first time. All the might I had was concentrated on hitting this creature, how many times I do not know, but I continued far longer than needed, I'm sure.

Fear still pulsing through my body, I checked that the creature was indeed dead, and with no signs of movement or life, I sat shaking on the floor. Initial thoughts, of travelling to Qeraviel to fetch help, to seek out Gavriel and the warrior priests to help me get back with this creature of the night, soon turned to reality. Although unworldly, this creature wasn't very big, and I couldn't risk the fact that it might not be here upon my return. Would anyone believe me, anyway? Wrapping thin vines around the creature's wrists and ankles, not knowing entirely why as the creature was no longer alive, I started the journey onwards, dragging the foul beast behind me, a journey that didn't finish until way after the sun had risen the next day. Stopping often to check the creature hadn't awoken, still not confident it was definitely deceased, I slogged homewards.

Breaking through into the forest classroom eventually into the sight of warrior priests on guard there, I explained the night's events. And as someone raced to tell Gavriel, the full enormity of the act I'd committed came to me. I'd managed to capture one of our attackers, or should I have said, murdered one of them.

THIRTEEN

Somehow, I had managed to get used to the smell emanating from this creature I'd dragged most of the night, but standing still, with its body stagnating, brought the queasy feeling back. Warrior priests, gathering closer to view the creature, visibly gagged on the stench. Some hadn't witnessed the catlike beasts before, others remarked on seeing them on the night of the colony's attack, but all agreed, by showing the uncertainty in their eyes, that these creatures weren't from a place we knew of.

Gavriel was running as he broke through the clearing where we waited, out-skirting the forest classroom. His reaction was one of bewilderment, initially, asking me how I'd managed to capture this creature, and where I'd been.

I lied, worried that I might be chastised for following Peshy's parents to Mortwedge, so I said that I'd been walking in Ewomatlan, to try to clear my head, trying to understand Peshy's loss. Whether I convinced Gavriel or he simply wanted further information on this creature I know not, but he believed me. I was honest in the telling of where I'd found the beast, telling the tale of how I think the catlike figure had wounded the Mortogg and the Mortogg had struck back, near-fatally wounding it. I explained I'd heard the commotion and hid, watching the scene play out then took my chance to capture the creature.

Fear at the time clouded my judgement, or temper furthered my hand to not capture but kill the beast. Hanging my head in shame I was unsure I'd crossed a line from which I couldn't return.

Hunting was one thing, to take a creature for food, to give sustenance to many, was needed. But to kill from anger or fear, to kill the unknown, didn't fully sit right within me, even after the attack on me and the thought of these creatures taking and killing Acacia. Killing wasn't right, I knew this, but that hadn't stopped me raining blows down onto this creature until I was sure it was dead.

Gavriel listened to my story and understood my feelings, telling me Rai would understand my plight; praying for assistance and knowledge would help. Gavriel instructed the warrior priests to take the creature to the temple maidens and gestured that he would follow soon. As the warrior priests dragged the beast away, tiredness crept into my body to a level where I could have fallen where I stood.

With a swift arm holding me up, Gavriel held onto me, walking with me as we turned toward home.

Words of faith passed between us, with explanations of what this find might teach us about the creatures, about how we were attacked. Even where they came from might be discovered. My actions last night were not reprimanded, but even glorified, leaving a slightly strange feeling in my thoughts.

It's hard to accept praise from someone whilst feeling guilty also, but I understood Gavriel's thinking, albeit a strange notion currently.

Brief explanations were quickly passed to Mother from Gavriel about my adventures that night, telling her about the creature I left to Gavriel too as I struggled to wash the feeling of grime from my hands.

Scrubbing appeared to make them clean; although they didn't feel it, forever sullied somehow.

A swift drink of clean clear water was all I took before succumbing to the call of my bed; collapsing into the softness, I yielded, hoping for but not expecting a peaceful sleep.

Sleep I did though, mostly unperturbed it seemed, occasionally waking to turn my head away from the light and summer warmth entering my bedroom. Often coming to, listening for noises, not hearing anything but the slight background noises of Mother bustling about the homestead, which reassured me rather than disturbed.

Finally awaking, the summer day's strength vanquished, still quite light, I suddenly remembered I'd promised to meet Amia. This being long before I'd encountered the catlike creature on my return home, knowing I had neither the energy or the chance to make that happen right now, I merely threw on some clothes and searched for Mother and food.

I found her sitting in a chair on the porch, overlooking the ground around our homestead. Like me, forever changed since my sister's death, she appeared thinner, older somehow.

But she smiled glowingly as I appeared, throwing arms around me. We sat simply enjoying the view as the sun said its goodbye to the day over our land. We both ate very well that early evening, for me the first time in as long as I could remember.

The same seemed true for Mother; whether constant worry about me, or just lackadaisical these days, it mattered not, for now in each other's company we sat, talked and remembered, laughing even. Into the night we sat together.

As the bright lights of Rai's past dragons high up in the sky shone down on us, that night we both healed somewhat, which we needed to do more than we realised.

Once more I slept that night, more peacefully than I thought. Being home and comfortable made me realise I'd remained too deep in my thoughts recently. Over the next few days, I tried to remain in that frame of mind, to allow my grief to somehow disappear. So many traumatic events had pulled me in different ways recently, and I had started to forget who I was.

Over these days I returned to hunting, sleeping and just being a normal teenager, although missing my friend, who I had spent all my free time with.

It was unthinkable that I would never see him again, and often I found myself paused in action as I slipped my thoughts into this scenario.

Whilst amid one of these thoughts, trying to skin the rabbits I'd caught that very morning, I noticed the sound of a small pebble hitting the wooden porch near me, jerking me back into reality. I listened as the second pebble landed near my foot. Whoever threw them, if aiming for me, wasn't a very good shot, I thought, as the third caught me square on the head. I'm not sure if the giggling gave her away or the fact that I'd guessed the trajectory of the pebble that time, but either way, rubbing my sore head I wandered into the nearby bushes to meet Amia.

For an hour or so I explained what had happened on my way home from our last meeting. Questions I couldn't really answer I deflected with my ignorance about the creature. I'd been so busy doing nothing recently that I'd not seen Gavriel since, nor had he visited, so I would go see him later to find out more.

I'd fared better than Amia, I think, getting used to Peshy being fallen, something we were taught to do.

Amia fought back tears even when talking about him. Their feelings for each other had been deeper than I realised. We spent more hours sitting in that bush than I care to remember, just talking.

Healing takes time, and time was all we had now. Around midday we left each other, and I headed the short distance home for food. Mother had cooked a simple broth and baked fresh bread, the first I'd seen her make for some time.

The last few days had helped both of us, I think. After sitting and eating, I decided to visit Gavriel for information, wondering exactly what the temple maidens had been doing with that creature, and as I walked towards the temple, contemplating my feelings about where the catlike things had come from, and why they wanted to take us.

No sense could I make from it. Searches had turned up nothing in the past; where did they come from?

~

As I walked around the forest classroom I could hear several White Banner students shouting. Initially concerned, I started to wonder if something was wrong, only to realise that fight training was being held there today. I'd not abandoned my learning, but so close to my own acceptance leap I'd completed most of that which I needed. My carving was complete, the dragon sat so proudly on the bench, placed perfectly fine; I said so myself.

My acceptance gift again was mostly finished, mere tinkering needed, so in my mind it was nearly perfect. Continuing my walk I ventured towards my goal, the temple.

Met by several warrior priests lining the paths around the temple, I wondered what had happened. Rogan being one of them, stopping to speak to my friend he told me that extra guard duty had been handed out since I arrived with the beast. Little had been said to any of them regarding the creature but all were speculating on what had been found, if anything. Orders were to not let anyone in, even members of the colony, whilst Gavriel sought wisdom, but I pleaded with Rogan; I needed to know what was going on.

Speaking with the senior warriors present, one agreed to ask Gavriel if I could speak with him, and trudging off, he agreed to at least check for me. I think being the one who brought the thing back gave me an advantage of cheekiness.

Expecting to be turned away, Gavriel not normally relenting in his orders, I continued speaking with Rogan. Conversation turning to Peshy, but swiftly diverted to my own acceptance leap, Rogan checking I'd completed my carving, and asking if I needed help with anything. Talking with Rogan about training, fighting skills and general lessons, I hadn't noticed Gavriel's approach. Gavriel, placing a hand on my shoulder, gestured for me to follow him, and instead of walking away into the forest, led me straight towards the temple. Slightly amazed, I followed, intrigued to know more, not questioning, simply walking alongside my teacher.

The conversation started as soon as we were out of sight of the surrounding warrior priests. The temple maidens had found some very interesting information, Gavriel told me. The creature's clothes were made from old cloth and skins sewn together, basic really. Black in colour, every part a deception of the eyes, stitched in a way to show contours in the cloth, muscles placed in apparent areas of weaker limbs, clever placement to give strength upon viewing. A leather tail, slightly curved, short in length, placed close to the lower end of the creature's outer jacket, again with a catlike appearance, gave an illusion to the beast. No maps, no clue to where they came from had been gathered though, a worried Gavriel stated.

Small patches of cloth with a writing of sorts had been found, though, and Gavriel produced one for me to study as we continued our walk towards the wing of the temple where I'd stayed myself while my arm mended, after my injuries from the attack.

The cloth I'd been handed was tiny, silvery lines etched deep into the fabric itself. Nonsensical to me, incoherent to my thought patterns. I'd read many books in the temple, written word from our culture and seen several others from the great library within the Banclian territories, but this was like nothing I'd seen before. Gavriel told me that he himself, who'd travelled more than most, had never encountered writing this delicate, this ornate.

I wondered initially if it was even writing. Patterns appeared occasionally on the piece I held and, formed in simple lines, made it indeed seem informative in some way. If only we could read it, who knows what we'd learn.

We arrived at the medical wing, met by several temple maidens. Nodding politely as was the way of their kind, they led Gavriel and me inward towards the inner sanctum. Here in the central, cooler part of the building, lying on a slab of solid stone, was the creature. If I'd forgotten the smell of the creature being so foul, I was soon reminded, more strongly even as the creature now decayed in death, overpowering the room which it occupied.

Cloths dipped in scented oil were being worn by the maidens present and these were soon offered to Gavriel and me.

Gratefully received, I placed the cloth around my face. It did not completely remove the stench but allowed me to actually stay present, not wanting to wretch or run away.

Gavriel said that several large lacerations were found within the body of the creature, asking me if I had inflicted any of these, again asking me to retell my story in minute detail. Explaining my actions again made me feel uneasy, my guilt resurfacing, but looking at the creature now, I felt justified. The large lacerations I felt had been part of the fight this creature had with the Mortogg, fatal to both parties, aided to that end by me.

The temple maidens had opened the creature's body up, looking deep into the depths of the creature, trying to glean any mysteries held here. I was told the catlike creature inside was very similar to us.

All organs were the same, in the same places, just smaller in size. The main differences were on the outside, obvious to all who looked at the beast.

First, its face, strikingly similar to a hunting cat; temple maidens stated that this somehow has been adapted, shaped somehow, forming the shape of a predatory animal. Some teeth had been removed, others shaped to form sharpened points, animalistic in form like the Veiled Sinivore. Whiskers were present but not growing from the body as hair would in humans. These whiskers were placed into the skin, pierced into the very flesh they sat in, held in place by small metal fixings.

Skin texture was rough, course to the touch, mimicking shortened fur, dark, all over the body, coloured to make it seem darker than it naturally was. The temple maidens had cleaned a section of the animal's skin and managed to remove a section of the darker colouring. The skin underneath wasn't light, it was coloured, darker than most I'd seen, but considerably lighter than the creature wanted to appear. Fur notwithstanding, this was skin, the same as ours.

The more I looked at the creature in the daylight the more I saw the manufacturing of it, as if someone had reconstructed the creature from a nightmare. Its arms shorter than ours, tiny in frame, small fingers and an obtuse digit much like our thumb to the side of the creature's hand or, shall I say, paw. Intriguing to all were the ends of each finger. Small bright silver fingertips, lined perfectly in concentric circles. Gavriel here decided I should see something they had found out about these fingers. Although dead, and for some days now, the fingertips still shone brightly as if they had only just been made. Gavriel asked me to watch.

He stepped forward, holding a medium-sized rock. Wondering exactly his intentions I braced myself, waiting to see his next move. Lifting the hand of the creature carefully, gently even, he extended one finger, placing it onto the surface of the rock he held. Asking me to step forward I watched, wondering what exactly was happening. As he removed the finger, sitting in the place it had touched was a perfect silver fingerprint, an exact replica on the rock of the creature's mark.

The toes of the creature held the same marks, capable of leaving the same silver tones too. Strange marks of silver, tiny fingerprints I'd found and others too around the colony, and in other lands also. We now knew where they had come from, if not why, or what they represented.

The creature's legs were considerably longer than the arms, but still smaller in stature than a fully grown colony member. Curved slightly, muscular tones gave them obvious strength in running and leaping. This had been seen on the night of the fire, with these creatures managing great leaps. One of the toes from the right foot was missing, and I was about to ask why when Gavriel explained what had happened.

Ivan had been given the toe. Macabre thoughts ran through my head but I understood that Ivan was taking the toe to other colonies to tell them of the incident, to explain our gruesome find, to see if others knew of the creatures. He'd left earlier that day and would return with news, if any.

I'd been given the experience and knowledge of their finds over this creature only because I'd been the one to capture it. Gavriel asked for my knowledge to be kept discreetly, not wanting the colony members scared of this creature. I agreed but wondered if that was something I could maintain. I knew I would be asked many questions, but chose to agree that until we knew more it was best kept silent.

Leaving the room, the creature, behind us felt a blessing, and breathing once more the fresh air in the temple gardens a blissful thing indeed.

Gavriel informed me that the body would be burnt that evening, as there was no more knowledge to be gained by keeping it.

Drawings of the creature had been made and added to the information gained by the maidens. I declined the invitation to attend; the smell would be awful, multiplied through burning, I felt. So I agreed to continue with my studies, as my acceptance was close. Thanking Gavriel for his time, I wandered off, informed that when Ivan returned, I would be allowed to hear his findings. Although feeling much better in myself, I still wondered where this creature was from, and how many of them existed.

The rest of the day, I skirted questions about seeing the beast, simply telling all I'd only witnessed the creature again while Gavriel asked me more about capturing it. Most were satisfied with my vagueness, others only wanted to hear the story themselves, so that embellishing the facts gave a good tale to tell and hear.

Eventually learning all I had to tell gave the crowds of White Banner students no more real detail than they had already learnt or gathered, thus allowing me time to venture away peacefully and alone, working my way through the forest classroom unseen, back into the forest of Ewomatlan.

Knowing my path must be secret, I followed a meandering course, keeping a bearing in mind, always towards Mortwedge, hopeful I'd find Amia. I held lots of information I needed to tell her. I knew promises made to

Gavriel were important, but the friendship I held now with my only true friend now that Peshy had gone was equally significant. I trusted little these days, but Amia wasn't included in that; I trusted her to keep my secrets.

Cresting a small hill set within the forest I maintained my course towards the outlander colony, eventually reaching the edges of Mortwedge, still with plenty of daylight left, aware in my thoughts that I didn't want to be travelling home in the dark, still unsure of these terrible creatures' whereabouts.

Not exactly sure where Amia lived, I decided to watch from my hiding place. I sat in the tree line, examining the ordinary lives of the outlanders. As if I watched my own colony, things appeared no different. A simple life played out in front of me, with daily tasks being carried out amid the hustle and bustle of a large colony.

I observed an inner sanctum within the colony routine, a place very much like ours where people sat, met or just hung about in each other's company. From my vantage point I could see stalls set up, offering food for sale, similar to the larger stalls I'd witnessed at Barbarrow market, and people congregated around these, taking a break from their busy day at the edges of this busy thoroughfare.

Realising that I was intruding with my intrigue, I made my way further around the colony, towards where I assumed the outlander homesteads would be, eventually finding similar dwellings to ours.

Closer in proximity to each other, the homesteads here were smaller, but equally as homely, I imagined. Mortwedge was indeed smaller but maintained its familiarity to Qeraviel, with several aspects and places hard to differentiate from either. I suppose once settled, outlanders drew on knowledge from their previous existence in Qeraviel, a reality hard to forget, so replicated.

It was then that I realised I'd been staring into the homestead of Anselm and Indira, Peshy's parents. Guilt and pleasure at the same time is a strange sensation, but both I felt right now; pleased to see their familiar faces, guilt to be seated here, hiding when all I wanted to do was run to them, to see they were all right, to hear their voices once more. To do so would be both dangerous and stupid; Gavriel's warnings had been clear to all, and I shouldn't be here. So with great regret I moved on, glad to see them both safe, although their sadness was reflected in my own thoughts.

Further along the track I followed I rounded several outlanders chopping wood. Their noise allowed me faster travel as they sang songs together; speeding up meant I scanned more territory faster, a thankful relief from the thoughts of Peshy's parents. It was Yamilla who allowed me to find Amia. She'd rounded a corner at speed, obviously doing a chore for her parents, carrying an armful of vegetables.

Trying not to break cover, I was allowed to follow her progress home, until I sat close enough to confirm that I had indeed found Amia's homestead.

Unsure of Amia's presence there, I sat, waiting. It wasn't long before Amia approached. Somehow sensing I was there, unsure of how I remained still, she moved into the trees on my right, working her way unseen to my location.

Tales of the day I recalled, explaining my encounter with Gavriel and what we'd learnt about the creatures. Amia listened with curiosity but with nothing to add. Apart from the silver fingerprints she'd never seen the creatures before and was shocked even by my telling of their description, unbelieving, but knowing I didn't lie. Gavriel had already sent word to all the colonies, including the outlanders' leaders, regarding our finding the creature, and warning all of the danger. Amia had heard the conversations, and everyone was vigilant to the threat they potentially faced.

Amia told me that she'd recently spent time with Anselm and Indira, telling them of her feelings for Peshy. I think that sharing this information helped both deal with their feelings. Amia stated that the outlanders had made them both welcome, settling them in to their new surroundings. I wished I could have visited them, and Amia promised to give them Mother's and my best wishes. Sitting talking about Peshy I wondered what exactly had happened to Amia's brother, Trian. Explaining that day seemed to once more open sad memories for Amia, but she wanted to tell me anyway, somehow relishing in the memory of him in that moment. Trian, like me, had reached his name day; once seventeen he'd walked the path I knew so well, and finally reached his acceptance leap.

Amia told stories of how Trian was obsessed with dragons, wanting so badly to become a warrior priest, to be lifted high above the ground, paired to a dragon. Much like Peshy, though, after his acceptance gift was offered and he leapt from acceptance ledge he didn't return. Amia had been small then, and honestly her memories had mostly been gained from her parents, retelling stories of her brother, I noticed. I never knew her family, as I myself was a small child, no recollection of the leaps back then, consumed with my toys and following Mother.

Trian had been the only son in their family and after Amia, Yamilla had been born, a true outlander as she was born in Mortwedge, never knowing life in Qeraviel.

Two families, with the exact same dreams and visions, living separate lives, mere miles apart; funny how life suddenly changes everything. Anselm and Indira were witnesses to that fact right now.

Parting with a hug, we agreed to meet soon, and I promised that, as soon as I heard anything from Ivan's travels, I would tell Amia. Working my long path homewards in darkening skies, I wandered off, thankfully, this time unseen and with no adventure to tell. Entering the forest classroom eventually back in Qeraviel, I started to make my way through the main colony to my homestead. It was then I saw several warrior priests running towards the temple grounds. Hastily I followed, wondering what the hurry was for.

Soon catching up with Vinn and running as fast as I could, we turned to see a large group of both White Banner students and warrior priests assembled all around the front of the temple. Gavriel stood, furious, near the centre, remonstrating, arms wildly being pointed in all directions, as warriors and students dispersed in the ways he pointed. Vinn and I arrived, skidding to a stop, staying nearer the rear of the group already present.

Gavriel was sending parties out together, searching for something, I gathered, from the words I could make out in between the chaos of noise surrounding me. Locking eyes with me, Gavriel walked towards me. Suddenly worried I'd been spotted in Mortwedge, colour filled my face; I could feel the heat sweeping across my entire body as he swiftly approached, asking but telling at the same time. Gavriel beckoned me nearer, asking if I'd returned to the temple after I'd left with him earlier. Honestly, I told him I hadn't as I'd been busy with the trip to Amia's all day. That's when he told me what had happened; the creature's body had gone missing from the temple.

More sinister was the fact that three temple maidens were missing and another had been found dead in the gardens near the great temple walls. We searched far into the night that evening, covering many miles, to no avail. It seemed that recently all I did was search for missing people, and success rates were useless. Nothing found, not a clue, even, of the path they took, no footprints, nothing. Had the temple maidens taken the corpse, or had something or someone taken it and the maidens? Speculation spread all night, spoken lightly as we searched. Whatever had happened, whoever was behind this, again held the upper hand, none of us knowing how they could easily enter our colony again unseen.

Too many funerals had been seen by our colony over the last few months. Random attacks, commonplace now, were once unheard of. Colony members sought shelter, not roaming in safety as once before, congregating in groups when travelling. Life was changing, but no one knew why it was happening. People turned to our leader for answers, only to be told he had none. Darkness filled our daily lives, sadness surrounded us. It was another day of sorrow for the colony as we buried another temple maiden in the temple ruin grounds, and as we stood in respect for another soul lost, no one expected what would happen next.

FOURTEEN

Dragons.

Suddenly, overhead a sudden disturbance, the noise deafeningly loud, in an instant. The feeling ran through my body, shaking me to my core. The rumbling they produced within their throats, alongside the noise of the ripping wind nearly overpowered my being. Shadows passed over the group of us, showing immense creatures flying above. Compared to the whole group of us, each dragon's silhouette easily covered the entirety of our small assembly, standing or now kneeling, making all present shield our ears from the noise, and eyes from the wind thrown upon us. Circling just above the treetops, if a sudden surprise was needed, they achieved their goal.

Even Gavriel seemed stunned by the appearance of these magnificent beings. Dragons were often seen from the edge of acceptance ledge, then returning our warriors to us after they leapt, paired forever in case of future battles. But rarely were they seen flying randomly over the colony like this. The group, though small in comparison, tried to huddle together, wondering what caused this unexpected visit. I hoped indeed this was a friendly visitation, truthfully not knowing exactly what to do if it wasn't.

The three dragons slowed their flight, dropping heavily into an available clearing within the forest, as close as they could get to the temple where we stood. Gavriel appeared flustered at the sudden arrival, but stoically stood still, awaiting I'm not sure what exactly.

Three dragons all within our forest was amazing enough, but suddenly a rumbling deep-toned voice cracked the subtle serenity gained for a moment after the torrent of the storm winds created by the beating wings of these majestic forces of nature. A voice of sheer wisdom breached my defences, loud, forceful but somehow still captivating. Not violent but demanding. Making all listen, unavoidably, unable to ignore the words produced. It occurred to me then that this voice came from the nearest dragon to me and without thinking the group and I walked slowly towards its source. Barely fitting into the clearing it occupied, we approached with caution. We were friends with these beautiful beings, unsure currently, though, if relying on that was a wise move. Dragons come in all shapes and sizes. I'd seen several in the past, with many colours witnessed, including, as this dragon was, a deep crimson red.

Dragons either side of this large creation started to crash their way through the trees surrounding them, uprooting even the larger specimens with an ease alarming and wonderful in equal measure.

Destruction surrounded us, as both outer dragons made space for themselves to reach the larger red beast in the centre of the area where we stood. Birds took flight, branches split, trees felled in all directions, the noise soon ceasing as they gained the ground they wanted to hold.

The voice returned, rearing its head far above the trees surrounding it, sunlight hitting its crimson face, beauty and power being the same. Light, bouncing off every edge, showed muscular tones to all parts of its very being. Huge in stature, the largest dragon I'd witnessed in my life so far, it spoke.

"Tracouttie you are, dragon are we, together a force of good, natural in existence, paired now in defence of our worlds, always protecting, good over evil will always prevail." The dragon's words, silky smooth, penetrated my very soul; agreeing seemed the only option, even if I didn't feel it was my right to do so, a minuscule part of this world compared to the stunning beauty sitting in front of me. Dragons produce glamour – I'd known this from a young age – helping them subjugate others to their will, often for reasons unknown to mere humans. Dragons needed us too. Knowing this but not succumbing to it are two very different things indeed. And as we, the group of helpless humans, stood in the presence of these mighty beasts, even Gavriel seemed occupied with the glory of this meeting. The dragon continued, "My name is Cenabus in your language. With me stand Raorge and Flanhlin. We came to assist you in your search for knowledge. Ivan from amongst you is a friend to dragons – he called for us, and in respect to him and your plight we came. Ivan shall return tonight after travelling far, seeking things you don't yet see or know. Ivan's call for assistance, help you sorely need, comes at a cost. Ancient knowledge gives you power; this we will help you with, but assistance has to travel our way too. A problem we face, maybe from the same source. After teaching you to help yourselves, we need you to assist us too." Whilst we all stood in awe of the dragon's speech, Gavriel bolstered his courage and stepped forward. "I, Gavriel, give my word to assist you in whatever you need. Rai's wishes and thoughts be with you and us always, whatever we have is yours. How can we help?"

This time Raorge spoke, lighter in tone, but incredibly powerful still. A pure white dragon, stark upon gaze, as standing in the sunlight gave the dragon pure strength of form. Smaller than Cenabus, but still higher than all the trees in the forest. The voice pounded every sense within me, holding my train of thought completely, overloading my consciousness with thoughts of love towards the most beautiful creations ever witnessed in Rai's world.

Raorge spoke, telling us that after Ivan returned, we'd need to prepare for a long journey. Flanhlin hadn't spoken; an air of mystery seemed to permeate from this creature, equal in size to Raorge but muscular beyond imagination, looking as if it had been honed from solid rock. Darker grey, blending into light grey, even white, this dragon appeared different from all the dragons I'd seen.

Normally one colour, if not toned differently, this design bore more than one colour, making me wonder if Flanhlin was older, or just unique. This silent dragon gave me concern; they had landed here in the forest as friends, telling us they were here to help, but Flanhlin seemed to be wary, even perturbed, to be here, never speaking, never flinching, watching all, eyes piercing every nuance of my being. Awkwardly I stood listening, aware that Flanhlin never once took his vision off me.

The dragons would return to accompany us tomorrow to a place beyond the Lerandra mountain range, Raorge stated. A place the dragons called Horchlock, deep within the wastelands, not on any map we knew.

So many questions obviously sprang through our minds but before any could be asked, Flanhlin started to stretch his wings. The next few moments were utter chaos as we all tried to hold place in our world.

Three dragons jumping at ease from the ground into the air, spreading their wings and taking flight, would have been an amazing thing to witness, but reality left us clinging to the debris left lying around from their entrance merely to survive. Several cuts and bruises needed treatment after their departure, mishaps and hazards from dealing with such powerful forces, I supposed.

Stunned, frightened a little, the group of us made our way the short distance back to the temple, unsure of what the message given to us truthfully meant, all agreeing to meet back here later. Hopefully Ivan could tell us more.

Several hours later, we sat in the forest classroom, wasting time, questioning each other about the dragons and what they meant. We were simply talking about the days experiences when we were interrupted by a small group of warrior priests, beckoning us over, telling the news we wanted to hear. Ivan had returned and was waiting with Gavriel at Rai's temple. Finding it hard not to run all the way, the White Banner students, including me, made haste to find out more. Making ground into the temple gardens, rounding towards the temple we saw Gavriel and Ivan seated on a small wooden bench. With few words exchanged and darkening skies above we settled, sitting on the ground near them, approximately forty warriors and students mixed, all waiting. I don't think I'd ever seen Ivan's expression so serious, giving more tension to my already stressed thoughts.

Ivan spoke of his journey. While attempting travel to the other colonies, Ivan happened upon a problem. Ivan stated that after spending a night in Mortwedge, showing them the creature's toe, talking long into the evening about the seriousness, the danger of these creatures, he'd slept, waking early for his long journey towards the colony lands of the Banclian. He'd nearly made it completely through the forest of Ewomatlan when he'd been attacked. Ivan was an adept storyteller and even I sat enthralled as he wove the story into place.

Ivan had been sitting in his cart, numbing the journey's time away singing songs to himself when an arrow embedded itself into the side of his mule. Several more arrows were fired into his old wagon and his mule was hit by a dozen more projectiles too, killing the beast eventually, painfully slow its torture. Ivan ran for the trees, scarcer now as he approached the northern edges of the great forest.

Uninjured, but still an old man on his own, he visually searched for the onslaught, Ivan continued after a pause, as he recalled looking at his downed and deceased friend. It had pulled his wagon for many years, and although only a beast of burden, they had spent many a year together, bonding with stories told over the miles. Reality came back to Ivan as he sat telling his tale, and a haunting expression took over his features as he continued. Twenty or more catlike creatures ghosted their way from the forest around him, appearing from out of nowhere, Ivan told us.

Not one of them seemed interested in looking to see where he'd gone but were consumed with searching his belongings on the wagon, throwing things to the side, meticulously sifting through all his boxes and bags, taking trifling things, unimportant, Ivan thought, probing there for something. Ivan explained he thought they searched for the toe, but he'd hidden that in his pocket for safe keeping on the long journey ahead.

His eyes glazed now when he described the creatures draining his mule of blood, each taking their turn, drinking from the beast's neck. Horror sat in each of us as we imagined the scene, reminding me of the creature I'd killed crawling towards the Mortogg. A part of me wondered if I been near my end the night I was captured, too, but a thought not worth thinking of for too long.

Desperate to move, Ivan had sat far too long for his old bones that night, but fear and anger in equal measure kept his hand, so he remained still and patient, waiting until he could see no creatures left around him, managing slowly to get back into Mortwedge the next morning, with nothing except the toe in his pocket, and a weary heart.

Ivan explained something then, something I think none of us knew, maybe with the exception of Gavriel, but even he seemed taken aback somewhat.

Ivan told us that he had a small dwelling on the outskirts of the Mortwedge colony. It must have always been there; I'd never thought of Ivan anywhere else but travelling on his old wagon, but he obviously needed a home. If the realisation hadn't ever been thought of before now, he explained further. He'd built his small homestead, contained within a small grove of ancient trees, many years ago. Ivan told of his need for somewhere to work and store the many treasures he made, with the added bonus of a safe place to stay over the harsh winters years ago, still occasionally seen today.

Ivan never mentioned why he choose to live near Mortwedge and not within Qeraviel, but most sat listening, enraptured still in his prowess of storytelling. Ivan struggled home after the forest attack that morning, and initially slept.

Sleep, however, was a hard commodity to find. Disturbed trying to see sense in the brutality of the assault, and grabbing only a few essentials upon waking, he'd made his long journey on foot to Qeraviel, seeking help and guidance from Gavriel. It was on this journey Ivan came across a fortunate occurrence.

Deciding that morning not to follow the normal passage between Mortwedge and Qeraviel but choosing to avoid the route through Barbarrow near the great forest, currently holding his cart and downed friend, instead he took a slightly lengthier path across the plains of Ibothiel. A large open expanse, true, with great temperatures this time of year, but clear views all around, something Ivan needed now. After the attack had left him on foot he was vulnerable, something an old wise man could do without, but which had to be overcome.

So, setting out on his chosen path, he carefully threaded his way across the plains to Qeraviel. Life sometimes seems to dictate your choices. Whether it had played its hand that day we will never know, but if Ivan hadn't decided on that path that day, who knows if we'd be standing on the edge of this adventure now. Ivan said he was suddenly plunged into shadow, similar to that of the great dragons flying over us merely hours before in the forest. Circling above him was a giant beast, a beautiful golden-yellow dragon, brighter than any forest flower he'd ever witnessed, and Ivan spoke of the sheer beauty he felt staring up at the creature, one he'd had the pleasure to meet before. Slowly it circled downwards and Ivan told of his delight that the dragon landed a hundred metres or so away in front of him. Bowing in acknowledgement, both creatures, dragon and human, met on the plains that day with a smile and a friendly nod.

The dragon, slim in build, had often seen Ivan travelling across the lands with his cart and they had once before met, sharing time and food one long night while Ivan had been travelling along the gulf of Anathena's coastline. Ivan recalled their meeting with great fondness and reminisced with the dragon, sharing stories again that night, waiting for the high winds to disperse, allowing both to continue on their journeys.

Grogkin was a very intelligent dragon, seeking knowledge from all lands, often flying farther than all other dragons just to witness the beauty of the territories it surveyed and dominated over. Grogkin had wondered why Ivan, alone, was walking across the plains. It seemed simple inquisitiveness had chanced this meeting, but fortune favoured all this day.

The dragon had been drinking all morning at the Great Lake of Pohalith, both water and views absorbed to appease the dragon's inquisitorial mind. Its returning flight to roost had allowed him to encounter Ivan. Now face to face, Ivan told his tale to his old friend.

Ivan told Grogkin of the attack, who listened to every word about the creatures and the outcome of the recent meeting with them, and why now he made his way to Qeraviel on foot, after the slaughter of his mule. It seemed

Grogkin had his own tale to tell, too, and dragon and Ivan sat that day after making their way to an outcrop of rocks out of the day's full-strength sun, more for Ivan's relief than Grogkin's.

Grogkin wove a similar experience which the dragons had faced regularly over the last year. Several of the dragons' precious eggs had been taken, which in itself was a very dangerous thing to do.

To steal a dragon's egg was doubly stupid, for not only were they hard to reach, but to enrage a dragon was normally the end of you. In addition, angering Rai would be calamitous at best, it was said, as dragons were the most powerful creatures living in this world, Rai's deities placed here to protect his world. The eggs, rare, were only laid once every two years, placed on nests hundreds of metres high, set into the caverns of their roosts, special breeding platforms hewn from the very rock by the dragon's own fire, made centuries before. Shenash himself hatched and was born from this ledge, a place of safety to allow the many years it took for the eggs to hatch, seated directly in the sunlight just above the cloud base we could see from acceptance ledge. A great honourable place, unknown to humans, its location kept secret from all except those who used it. Guarded by their own, a bold act indeed to attempt theft from here, but theft had been accomplished more than once.

Grogkin continued, saying that once a creature had been found trying to make its way across a ledge towards the breeding grounds, a swift and painful end had been its reward that day, burning as it fell, never to be seen again.

Briseth, Grogkin called them, a long-lost colony thought to be extinct, their existence not talked about these days, with little now known of their whereabouts or beliefs. A strange-looking race, seeing as they chose to adapt their looks into a cat-type beast. A magical race, holding powers rarely seen or used in today's world. Maybe the enemy in both stories, Grogkin and Ivan now pondered.

Grogkin and Ivan that night stayed in each other's company, the dragon even hunting Uppula for them to feast on, of which Ivan cooked his share on a fire, prepared right there on the plains where they sat. Morning saw both curled up asleep where they'd been talking long into the night, eventually talking giving way to tiredness. A delay to Ivan's plan but a better, more fruitful one couldn't have been imagined by him. Retelling his story to us now as we sat perched in front of him, a glimmer of hope had emerged from that chance meeting of friends. Agreeing to continue to Qeraviel, Ivan would speak to Gavriel, telling him all he'd learnt from Grogkin, and asking him for help to solve both problems surrounding the Briseth.

Grogkin agreed to fly straight to the roosting grounds, telling the human's story to the guardian dragons there, arranging to meet again at Qeraviel as soon as tales were told.

Ivan spoke of his conversations that night with Grogkin. Far beyond land we knew, deep into the wastelands, sat a place dragons knew of: Horchlock. Buried deep within a cave here were secrets of knowledge the dragon explained to Ivan. Ancient magics practised here long ago, powerful spells woven to hide its true power. Dragons held this place secret, not wanting its source to fall into the wrong hands, for once opened, its power could be destructive; the original source of Rai's wrath in the splitting of the world.

Here knowledge would be given back to humans, here our destiny would change forever. Only a select group would be permitted to enter these sacred grounds, and we all turned to Gavriel now, hoping we would be chosen.

Gavriel spoke here about the visit from the three dragons earlier that day to Ivan, speaking of their request for help, and promising assistance too. So here we all sat on the eve of discovery, humans and dragons fighting together again for the greater good. Ivan sat on the wooden bench now, all eyes focused on him as he seemed to lighten in mood. Finally, hopefully, the Tracouttie would know why these attacks were happening, and if these Briseth were truly responsible.

The crowd that was already seated outside the temple the next morning had probably doubled in size in comparison to yesterday's group, who'd listened to Ivan long into the evening. Excited voices, barely making themselves audible to all present. Gavriel stood silently, reasoning, considering, I'm sure, who was going to be part of this adventure. Longing to be a part of it, I positioned myself eventually close to the front of the group. Sitting down, I waited, trying to compose my thoughts, knowing soon the dragons would return.

To describe the ensuing chaos of the dragons' return would simply be repeating myself, as you surely can imagine the same carnage replayed itself into our lives; trees uprooted, sent flying through the air like kindling, was indeed a sight to be seen, second only that dusky morning to the arrival of, this time, five dragons.

Eventually the dispersed group of Tracouttie all managed to get back together and as we stood in awe once more, the dragons forced their way towards us through the now highly damaged forest.

Cenabus, Raorge, Flanhlin, and two new dragons stood before us; another red dragon, much smaller than Cenabus, stood centrally to their group with another, smaller, dragon, this time a deep purple colour. Cenabus spoke first again, introducing Carthian and Drathlo. Drathlo stepped forward at this point and the most beautiful voice ever to grace my ears flowed around us.

Obviously female, Drathlo's much more tender but still mightily powerful tones seemed to make every one of us relax; somehow her voice soothed our anxieties. If this was glamour, no other could surely have matched her in this display: stunningly bright red, even in the low light that morning, sensual, somehow, compared to the other dragons standing here, smaller, slighter, but please don't think that she was not a powerful beast. Respect was obviously paramount when dealing with dragons and she commanded our respect totally here.

Drathlo introduced herself as the last in the bloodline of Shenash. With an audible gasp I couldn't believe who talked to us – a relative of the great Rai's dragon, Shenash. As she addressed us, humbly I knelt, at the same time as Gavriel; others soon followed our lead.

Drathlo spoke openly about the struggles faced by her race. As Grogkin had told Ivan, she explained about the missing dragons' eggs.

She said that recently more had gone missing and the dragons couldn't explain how or why; even if they had known who had done this terrible thing they couldn't say where from or where they had gone.

Emotion ran high in her voice, but her calmness extracted fear. She even appeared to be held in awe by the other dragons present, and I wondered if she indeed was their queen or leader.

Breaking the sudden silence after her speech, Cenabus once more took the lead, explaining the journey ahead in more detail.

Each of the dragons would take two Tracouttie with them, on their backs, on a vast flight over our lands into uncharted territory for us, to a place called Horchlock.

This place was a few days' flight from here, deep into the wastelands beyond Lerandra. Explaining that more details would be told to us on the way, Cenabus promised safe travel. We would need to travel light and fast, and most Tracouttie present seemed more than slightly daunted at the thought of sudden long distance dragon flight. Gavriel had to pick ten colony members to face this arduous journey. Placing himself first, Ivan second, left eight places remaining. Several warrior priests, bowing gracefully to both Gavriel and Drathlo, stepped forward, offering their souls in the protection of Tracouttie and dragon alike. Drathlo seemed to approve, as a low grumbling reverberated around the forest, something akin to an Oravore's cub purring when around its mother. Gavriel soon made his selection, picking experienced warrior priests one and all, and soon nine of the finest warriors Tracouttie held stood in place. Ivan with them making the ten selected for this mission.

"Halt!"

The word, so loud, so unexpected, crashed through the scene; I nearly fell over. Brash, coarse in nature, violence in a place of discussion. Flanhlin barged forward. Even Drathlo moved, such was his muscular dominance amongst them, it felt. Raising his front left leg, he pointed a razor-sharp talon straight toward my direction. Have you ever felt alone in a crowd? I hadn't before this day. Suddenly, an expanse of space appeared around me where none had been before. I stood stock still as one of the largest dragons I'd seen leant its head forward to within a few feet of my face, stopped and stared.

Lowering its voice, but still painfully loud, Flanhlin spoke once more, asking my name.

Shakily I spoke my name: 'Wicker' never seemed a weak name to me, but aloud, now in otherwise silence it lost all meaning. Flanhlin once more spoke. "Wicker must come with us," turning as he made this decision, looking straight at Gavriel. Both I and Gavriel tried to explain that I was not yet a warrior priest, but we seemed to speak words not considered by the dragons. Flanhlin dismissed these words with a puff of his cheeks, evidence of heat and tendrils of smoke stopping all words we spoke in an instant.

"The one called Wicker shall travel with us," Flanhlin said, not looking for approval from us or his own kind, apparently, and with desperation I looked at Gavriel. Looking back, he nodded. Ivan, on the other hand, behind him smiled a deep smile, somehow pleased I'd been chosen. Moving over to the group of now eight warrior priests, myself and Ivan, I felt slightly ashamed, but mostly excited and intrigued about our journey and wondering why I needed to be there.

The next hour seemed to drag slowly as water and bare essentials were gathered for us. Gavriel spoke alone with several of the dragons present but mostly with Drathlo, as a result of which, when we were all ready, his looks towards me were less troubled.

Warriors were placed alongside their travel companions when eventually we were all ready, and if I hadn't already guessed I was placed next to Flanhlin. Fear and trepidation mixed with uncertainty filled every part of me, but climbing up into the giant dragon's back, I soon replaced that with the thought of flying aboard this magnificent creature. Flanhlin told us how to hold onto his smaller scales, ridging either side of his back, advising we use cloth around our hands to protect them from the sharper scaled edges.

Everyone seemed so small on top of their guest that day, and somehow all managed to hold place as one by one these great creatures launched into the air above the forest.

Circling until all were airborne, with powerful wingbeats Flanhlin easily flew as if we weren't there. And with Drathlo the last to join us in the sky, holding Ivan and Gavriel, we all made our way north, climbing steadily higher towards the mountain range of Lerandra and beyond into the unknown.

FIFTEEN

If I ever thought flying on the back of a powerful dragon such as Flanhlin was going to be easy I soon removed that idea from my brain. I sat forward legs draped either side of his wing joints. They barely reached to his sides, such was the ginormous girth of this creature. Behind me sat Rogan, his first adventure too, now he'd become a full warrior priest, both of us holding on, painful sometimes to remain seated as Flanhlin turned suddenly without warning. Sometimes I think he turned just to see if we could hold on, as there was no obvious reason to change course. As if reading my mind, Flanhlin spoke. A dragon of few words, I realised, and the words he used, sharp and to the point.

"Air current." Rogan and I looked at each other briefly at these words, realising that the dragon moved freely; more often than not gliding along in the air current, thus saving himself from having to beat his huge wings all the time. The trouble was that the altitude needed to fly like this was fine for the dragons, but for us not so good.

Realising I was shivering despite having a thick coat wrapped around me for protection, my grip was starting to fail, my hands giving way to the cold temperature and the firm grip they tried to keep. Rogan, one arm wrapped around me, the other holding tight to a scale, shivered in time with me. We'd been flying for a few hours now; after leaving Qeraviel we'd gained height continuously by circling over the great cliffs east of our colony. The breaking of the world allowed the air to rise here, sending initially warmer air high, pushing us upwards following its path.

Viewing Qeraviel from a vantage point I couldn't have imagined in my wildest dreams, the whole colony lands sat below us, easily hidden by my outstretched hand, if I'd been brave enough to hold out a hand in front of me, that is. Trees seemed like tiny pieces of brush, homesteads near impossible to view from this high up. Looking behind me in the distance to the south I could just make out the glistening of Pohalith, the Great Lake. Sunbeams bouncing off its surface reflected skywards, making an image again beautiful and unexpected.

The forest of Ewomatlan stretched out in front of us after leaving Qeraviel, and like a dark green patchwork snake, weaving west to east, formed a giant land barrier, looking like a solid wall below. From here I could make out the undulation to the ground, never realising exactly how much higher Qeraviel was compared to the forest and beyond.

It was here, just after clearing the forest below, that Flanhlin started to descend, following Drathlo, who now took the lead in our procession.

"We land now," Flanhlin spoke briefly, and both Rogan and I thanked Rai. The ground beneath our feet again would be a pleasant thing, if only giving us time to stretch and warm ourselves for the next part of our journey.

Drathlo landed first. She carried Gavriel and Ivan, each seemingly engaged in conversation with the other. Cenabus landed next, carrying both Brock and Larch, followed by Raorge and Carthian together; they held Danj, Fenn, Krist and Jorge between them. We were the last to land and I held my breath, waiting for an impact that never came, although crashing somewhat heavily to the ground, graceful wing beats slowed us down enough to stop the force reaching us where we sat.

Sliding carefully off Flanhlin, I greeted the rest of our party as much as I could without shivering openly and showing my pleasure to be on the ground once more. Huddling together on a bright summer's day seems crazy but all here were freezing cold, and Gavriel instructed a few of us to search for firewood, whilst others searched for a place to rest.

Drathlo remained with us while the other four dragons dispersed one by one back into the air. While we sat on the very edges of the Banclian territory, Drathlo stated that the other dragons would return after hunting. Tonight we would stay here, and in the morning continue on our way. The thought of having a few hours on solid ground, allowing us to warm up and regroup, was indeed a pleasant thought, and our own small hunting party moved out to find sustenance. I returned not long after holding two rabbits, which I added to the generous pile of fare already placed near a steadily building fire.

Drathlo refused all food we offered that night, simply saying she would hunt soon after we had settled. So as a group we warmed ourselves, fed and relaxed, recalling things we'd seen travelling on the back of dragons, unrelenting happiness resounding back and forth between us. Drathlo, Gavriel and Ivan sat in discussion further away from the rest of us, with occasional glances our way, checking the group stayed together.

Drathlo indeed did leave for a short time but soon returned after sating her appetite for the evening on Uppula. Sitting here, darkness fell around us, and most fell into an untroubled sleep. No guards were placed that night as Drathlo promised no harm would befall us with her presence. As I lay looking up towards the tiny bright spots of light in the distance above, I couldn't believe the fortune I'd been given that day.

For the first day in a long time I smiled to myself with happiness. If only Acacia and Peshy could have seen this day, it would have been perfect. Footsteps coming towards me made me shift my focus, as Ivan approached me. Smiling his normal broad grin, he settled next to me.

Our meetings in the past often gave way to debates about some meaningless errand, or local gossip, but today we sat in a completely different place. Ivan stared straight at me, and I asked him if he was all right, after the attack. This was the first time I'd really been able to sit with him for a long time and into the night we talked about Peshy leaving, and the loss of his mule. Simple conversations sometimes give us the most solace, this being true when talking to a friend. And this night we sat together, helping each other a great deal.

Ivan explained to me that that night, while he'd been travelling on Drathlo, she'd told him more of their plight. Dragons' eggs were indeed precious, but more than this was the fact Drathlo's eggs had been taken too. Ancient bloodlines within the dragon legacy were rarer still, Drathlo only capable of laying a single egg every two years. This was the second of her eggs to be stolen, weakening her position, weakening the dragons' heritage further. Shenash's bloodline ran through her veins, the most powerful dragon ever to exist, his memories, his future sat with her alone. Her eggs, her unborn dragon hatchlings, were the future leaders.

She needed to protect them and couldn't. Setting this information aside, other dragons' eggs were taken, too. Dragons are powerful, capable of rending worlds apart if needed, but intelligence kept them above most other species. This is where dragons and humans are alike, able to find independent thought, stopping them from always taking, always destroying, realising more than this must exist to remain true to oneself, even if the cost is sometimes detrimental. That's why now, right here, working together to find a solution that solved our problems, was better than destroying worlds to secure our futures.

Finding out how someone or something took the eggs would have to be important to the Tracouttie now. Our guardians were being taken, something neither of us could let happen. Looking at Drathlo talking to Gavriel in the distance my mind wandered slightly from Ivan's talking. As I watched, I could feel my necklace slowly vibrate under my tunic, giving a mild reddish light to my clothes. If I noticed Drathlo staring back at me it wasn't immediately, but Ivan's voice soon cut through my reverie, allowing me to stare straight into Drathlo's eyes. A mild nod of her head, beckoning me over, surprised me but before I realised it, I was halfway towards her, walking in a daze, straight to the queen of the dragons.

Stopping short of Drathlo I looked on in amazement. Bowing low, showing respect, I hesitated. 'Hello' seemed stupid but at the same time, what else can you say to a queen who has just beckoned you? If a dragon could indeed smile, she did so now.

"Wicker." She uttered my name, apparently ruminating the sound over and over in her thoughts. "So, a young man, not yet a warrior priest, stands with us. Can you explain why Flanhlin asked for you to be here?" A question I'd asked myself on our journey too many times, without reaching an answer. But now being asked the very same question by a huge dragon standing in front of me it seemed more important to search for that very thing. "I know not, my queen," I bowed once more, hoping my sincerity would mute the displeasure I was sure to receive for the answer I gave.

Instead, a chuckle emanated from Drathlo, soft, low but subtle. "No one knows," Drathlo continued, "not even Flanhlin. He is a powerful dragon, head of our fighting force. Flanhlin may be the most dangerous dragon ever to fly this world's course," Drathlo voiced. "But he alone doesn't make an army. Together we are revered, he is my mate, my companion, my strength. But to him I am his everything, he watches, he waits, he sees things others do not, he is an ancient creation, his bloodlines run as old as mine. If he sees something in you then we must, too. Have no doubt, young Wicker, your being here is no mistake. Let's see what luck you have within you, shall we?"

Awestruck, I stood still, it was Gavriel moving next to me

that made me snap back into my reality. As I turned to leave it was then that Drathlo motioned me to stop.

"That necklace, where did you get it?" Drathlo asked. My hands were already placed around it; as more often was the case I held it, unaware I did so.

"Ivan made it for me, your highness," I offered, pointing towards him as if she didn't know of whom I spoke. Smiling, she nodded back. "Maybe that's why you are here," she said. "Dragon stone, I believe, an altogether ancient magic, one forgotten page in history. It was said that those who could control dragon stone held high regard in life, especially with dragons. Can you control it?"

Another question I couldn't give an answer to; a mere shrug reached my shoulders but all I could give, as the light from my necklace burned brightly as we talked. Drathlo peered nearer as I held out the now-glowing red necklace in front of me, explaining I had received it many months ago and my friend, Peshy, had received a blue one at the same time.

Drathlo asked about my dreams; had I ever witnessed anything extraordinary in them?

I spoke candidly about my previous dragon dreams, warning me of danger, about my escape from the Briseth the night in the forest and all I knew the necklace had done for me.

Gavriel looked on as I explained my story to Drathlo, probably wondering why I hadn't told him, but standing here now wasn't the time to hide the truth so all I told was accurate. I told how Peshy had become fallen, and how I couldn't believe it so. Drathlo seemed intrigued but she didn't waver on Peshy's downfall. I suppose that loss was greater to me than most, so I moved on, telling her how the charm glowed most interested her, and she asked a simple task of me here. Drathlo asked if I could concentrate tonight, to think only of the charm, to sleep holding it. "Seek out dreams, Wicker, tell me what you see. Let's see if you indeed hold ancient magic in yourself, magic that could help us all." I agreed, truthfully I would try, and making my way over to my sleeping blanket laid out on the floor, I settled in for a sleep I wasn't prepared for.

At first, as hard as I tried sleep seemed to elude me, but just as I thought the process of trying stupid, I found myself once more flying on Flanhlin's back. This time I sat alone and if Flanhlin knew I was there he didn't acknowledge the fact. I felt no cold this time, no wind rush as before; I sat still on his back, merely enjoying the ride, a small tick in comparison to the lumbering hulk below me. My dream showed me the true colours of Flanhlin; his darker greys, punctuated with lighter hues, not only defined his muscular form but showed his armour off to the full. Truly I think I could have speared him anywhere on his body with the sharpest spear ever made and he wouldn't have noticed. Bouncing off would have been the only repercussion of the event if I'd wanted to do it. Nothing is beyond perfect, nothing unbeatable in combat, we were taught in our lessons, but sitting here astride Flanhlin I would wager more money than I have ever owned to say he was both. After Drathlo told me he was the most powerful and potentially dangerous dragon she knew, I now held him in higher regard than I did before and that was already high. This creature held my gaze, my thoughts, my entity; then I noticed my necklace charm emanating its glow once more. It was then that Flanhlin spoke to me. "Wicker," he said, "don't you wonder why I chose you? Don't you see the power you hold? You cannot control your destiny if you don't realise the path you choose. Remember the lessons you are about to learn, forget you're simply human; you are much more than you will ever realise."

With a sudden inversion, Flanhlin dropped from the sky, causing me to fall, spinning uncontrollably downwards. Still no wind affected me, but the knowledge of falling perturbed me greatly. Even in my dream, could I be hurt? Killed? I knew not the answer, something I was fed up with saying recently.

So many things I needed to know, and somewhere along this path I trod I knew answers lay, so, holding my charm aloft, I visualised my blanket, my place where I slept, no fear, no sorrow, only that. I awoke suddenly, lying exactly where I'd pictured, the glow of the fire's embers still evident, crackling with dissent. Deep breaths in and out calmed my now awake being, and in the near distance, Drathlo slept, curled tail protecting her face from view.

I sat up, looking around me; had my dream been real or just that, a dream?

As I lay back on my blanket to finally rest, it was then that I noticed Flanhlin circling high above. A glimpse of his lighter colours projected against the lightening sky above, guarding all below; no better protector could anyone have so, turning over, I grabbed peace while it existed in my world.

Morning came too suddenly but I awoke rested, more than I imagined. Lifting myself from my blanket, I made my way over to the still-resting Drathlo. Opening one eye at my approach she raised herself slowly to her full height. As I said earlier, she was slight in build but still towered over me as a full-sized dragon obviously would. Nodding to one another, I told her of my dreams as she'd asked. I wondered in truth if they were real, and asked this of her, and a wise look crossed her face. "Wicker, you are indeed an ancient soul," Drathlo said. "No mere human can traverse into the dream state with dragon stone, many have tried and failed. You have managed something incredible with no teaching and no concept of your actions. With training and knowledge you will become a very powerful ally to all your friends. I hope I may include myself in that list," bowing her head low to me as she spoke. Surreal moments in my life were rare but this held first place, a queen dragon calling me a friend filled me with both wonder and possibilities. Perhaps she was right; I might hold more power than I knew.

"Grogkin has sent word that he has arrived at the heart of the Banclian territory. He's explained that we shall be arriving soon, hopefully late tonight we shall arrive in their colony. The Banclian will make space for all of us, and accept all as guests, helping us in our quest." Drathlo spoke to me as if I held sway now, something very new and strange to me, but I told Gavriel and Ivan of her words, as soon as she finished our conversation. *How had Grogkin managed this task without being here?* I wondered silently to myself; if others thought the same no one mentioned it, none of us knowing at this time the answer to another riddle.

Dragons soon arrived above us, but this time as space allowed it they landed further away, walking the short distance to where we camped. Flanhlin nodded this time, either used to being in our company or at least accepting the need for us being there, and even he seemed rested, full of energy for the coming day's events. We ate quickly that morning, with provisions that had been stored in our backpacks, and soon we were all climbing back into our positions between the dragons' wings on their backs.

Holding on for our lives had become second nature to me after travelling a day already on Flanhlin, but the surprise of taking off still shook everyone. Suddenly lifting into the air, powering upward on huge wing strokes with only a small handhold seemed foolhardy, but we all managed to arrive safely back in the skies above.

Still in the same pairs as before, we settled in for another day's long flight, and looking down over the vastness of the Banclian territory in front of us, we knew more memories never to be forgotten would be gathered that day.

As we flew slightly lower this time the chilled winds were more bearable, although we were still wrapped in heavy coats, as we'd learnt this a necessity. Large beasts below scampered, running as if their lives depended on their speed, trying to get away from the shadows hurtling over them at speeds they could never have managed if indeed the dragons wanted them. It was hard to make out the shapes below of some of the things running, mostly small herds of Uppula, who'd ventured far from the plains through Ewomatlan forest into fresher grassland ahead.

The Banclian territory covered a huge landmass, visibly larger than Qeraviel from this viewpoint. The area we flew over now was mostly lush vibrant grassland, still showing pools of fresh water lurking amid the thicker sections, holding firm in their size even as we sat in the middle of summer, territory visited many times by Gavriel, but never had I ventured this far north. Realisation of my novice status amidst the Tracouttie here both troubled and excited me.

Trying my best to focus on the conversation I'd had with Drathlo and its meaning, I hoped I would see my usefulness in this task set out in front of us.

Subtle changes in Flanhlin's wingbeats brought my attention away from the view all around us. I noticed we were deliberately losing height. Flanhlin dropped more sedately than before, and we found ourselves spiralling slowly towards the ground. Drathlo again had taken the lead and even from this far up I knew we were still a long way from the Banclian homeland centre, near the base of the Lerandra mountain range.

Below us, sitting near a large pool of water, was Grogkin, basking in the sun, obviously waiting for us.

Aiming for a large plain section of land, all the dragons easily made landfall and dropping from Flanhlin's back it was good to get an earlier than expected break. All six dragons now met each other with a strange crowing, grumbling noise, Flanhlin chorusing the noise louder than the rest. Grogkin beckoned the whole group of us over and told of his meeting with the leaders of the Banclian. Grogkin described exact details of our resting place within the Banclian homestead.

The leaders were concerned that, if several dragons were seen within the territory, it might cause panic amid their people. Grogkin had agreed and plans were made for a camp just west of the main Banclian township. Instructed to fly low from the west, preferably after darkness had started to fall, Grogkin agreed the plans.

Shelter, provisions and tools had been agreed also, things needed for the next part of the journey. A day had also been set aside for us, the humans, to purchase warmer clothes; the mountains and beyond, even in the summer months, grew colder at night, and if we thought it was cold before, this time we were warned it was going to be treacherously bitter at the altitude we would soon be flying at.

Drathlo agreed the plans were suitable and said we should relax for a while here, allowing natural conveniences to be made, gaining sustenance for the journey ahead of us.

Resting merely for a few hours, soon we were ready to continue. This time Ivan chose to ride along with Grogkin, both friends together, allowing Drathlo the ease of only having to carry Gavriel. It was nice to think that Grogkin now joined us; a group of five dragons was easily the most visible powerful thing around here, but six was even better. Still not ready for the takeoff, we all managed to leave the ground without mishap, and soon all six dragons flew in formation further north towards the Lerandra mountain range. The white peaked tops of the highest ridges were now visible far off in the distance, occasionally showing themselves between the haze and cloud cover at that height.

Before long, only hours in reality, where on horseback or in wagon trains this journey would have taken weeks, we approached land where the odd wooden building had been erected. Grogkin had taken point now and with the rest of us following his lead, turned north-west, ready to locate the base to the west that the Banclian had promised us. Darkness had well and truly taken over the sky and flying now seemed as though we danced between the twinkling lights themselves, on dragons' backs, in between dragons' souls. Everything here belonged to these amazing creatures, and no conversations were needed as the Tracouttie were led on this magical escapade. That beautiful night flying into that Banclian camp will stay with me forever.

A large expanse had been set aside for us, and honestly even though big there was only just room for six dragons, and us within it. Several colony members greeted our arrival, even if wary of why we were here. Grogkin had spoken to the leaders of Banclian only about our visit and we were told to hold our tongues if asked why we were here. Gavriel was taken to see their great leaders; even with dragons present, his reputation proceeded him, he was revered all over our lands and was treated as such everywhere, but especially here in Banclian. Drathlo agreed to stay with us and the rest of the dragons, to reduce the worry and confusion in the midst of the township. And we all settled down early for sleep whilst we could. Pallets had been arranged for we humans, with large areas swathed in freshly cut straw for our dragon friends. We occupied the outer edges, leaving the greater space within the centre for Drathlo and her large family. Flanhlin once more appeared to not rest, watching everything, and everyone. With a legendary dragon guarding over us, I once more slept better than I had for months. Morning appeared and before the light truly filled the sky, the dragons flew off. Keeping low to the west, they needed to hunt and rest further as the next part of the journey was going to be particularly tough on all of us, and they needed lots of food, far more than could be provided by our current hosts. Gavriel had returned in the night, something I'd not been aware of, sleeping as I did, but he had returned with both coin and instructions given to him by Drathlo and Corinaska, current leader of the Banclian. Our tasks today were to buy much warmer clothes and Gavriel had been told where to search for these.

The township we were in now was the biggest by far in all the lands on our side of the divided world. Banclian was a powerful colony, highly intellectual, with many a year devoted to learning the knowledge of elders, passing this on to the young colony members. Known for producing the finest fabrics, the best ornate goods, with a honed ability for metallurgy; the finest weapons known in the region to be manufactured were from Banclian hands. Strange then that with this knowledge their colony was not known to produce great warriors; either training seemed benign to them, or they simply had no need for a large army. The region had maintained peace for many years now. Qeraviel lacked certain resources, but we were known for our fighting force; maybe that's why Banclian and Qeraviel were good colony neighbours, each knowing the other's strengths and helping each other in times of hardship. Peace had reigned for many centuries, it was said, and each viewed the other with peace, if not sometimes envy of the other's knowledge. Goods often travelled between the two large colonies and Ivan normally travelled here several times a year, selling Banclian goods at Barbarrow. Highly sought after, these items brought Ivan a steady living, if not an obviously elaborate one.

The township was completely different from Qeraviel; most buildings here were made from stone, ornamented with wooden beams for added strength. Qeraviel still used mainly wooden structures; only our temple buildings were built from stone, a far harder product for us to gather, having to source it from miles away. Digging and dragging it back took many hours of precious colony time, therefore only our special buildings took its need, its security, its finish.

Here, though, a ready supply was brought from the Lerandra mountains close by, mining teams working constantly, for the precious stone demand always high.

As a group we walked together here, although not for safety as we blended in with the Banclian, albeit our clothes less refined. Traders from all over old Astohar walked here, peddlers, such as Ivan, mixed along the same streets as did wealthy individuals. Outlanders ventured this way occasionally, again accepted as anyone was, so long as peaceful intentions reigned.

Following Gavriel's instructions we made our way through the bustling inner markets that thronged every walkway. The smell of food cooking on every corner, mixed with exotic spices, awoke every sense I had, making me feel hungry even though not long ago I'd broken my fast back at our camp. Sweetened goods were offered as we walked and several warrior priests succumbed to the temptation, eating or drinking as we walked along. Eventually we came to a halt next to a large older-style wooden building in an obviously older part of the township. Ivan pushed the small green door and our troop entered one by one, not thinking we'd all fit. I hesitated near the back but pushed on, not wanted to be left outside by myself.

Inside, darkness hid the true size of this dwelling which was larger than it seemed. Shelf upon shelf held folded fabrics, woven garments of all colours and thicknesses, Dank and more than dusty, the smell intoxicating for all the wrong reasons. I'd been handed more coin than I'd seen in my lifetime and told to get thick woolen trousers, outer garments to repel cold weather, water and anything thrown at it if possible. Two elderly men frequented this shop; it looked as though they lived here as well, as two chairs, threadbare, sat next to each other on the other side of the wooden counter where they stood. Cups on a table with remnants of food lingered there too. If they ever left this place, it wasn't for long; from talking to them it appeared they spoke at the same time, so probably they stayed in each other's company always.

Glylib and Troyne, painted over their heads, gave us their names, and for the next few hours, this place became a hive of activity, more than even they were used to; ten people, all getting changed, trying on trousers, shoes, shirts, anything warm, caused mayhem here.

Glylib threw gloves and hats around to us all, wondering why in the height of summer we wanted to purchase such goods. Troyne seemed more than happy to think about the coin needed for such quantities of clothes, and individually made a list for all of us to see and agree to as we filed out one by one holding more stuff than I'd ever owned before. Vacant of coin but happy to be outside once more, we made our way more slowly this time toward camp. A strange sight we must have made, walking in the bright sunshine, holding armfuls of thick, dark winter clothing. But made our way through the crowds we did, resting here and there, giving our tired arms the respite they needed. Eventually we returned to camp, thankful for that adventure to be over at least.

For the rest of that day I honestly tried my best to rest, thoughts always returning to the next flight, the next section of our trip. The dragons weren't there but had left us mingling around a huge campsite. Members of the Banclian colony brought food aplenty, and things I'd never tried before intrigued my palate. With warrior priests sleeping on their pallets around me, I sat contemplating our next move.

It was a clear night once more, twinkling spots of light above me as the dragons returned, Drathlo entering the grounds followed by the others. Following the same pattern, we all strode up wearing our new clothes, bulky, cumbersome and feeling extremely hot we waited as the dragons lowered themselves enough for us to gain our places again on their backs.

Drathlo had instructed us that this time we would fly east after leaving the township, keeping the Lerandra mountain range to our left for a while. The lower part of the peaks, still hundreds of metres above us, were located near the breaking of the world. This section would be easier to traverse with us aboard, so accepting their knowledge we lifted into the dark skies above. Watching the fires burning in the Banclian territory become small specks of orange light behind us, we rose higher and higher, far away from humankind, into the unknown.

SIXTEEN

I sat as still as I could, thankful indeed that I had purchased thicker clothes; the wind ripped past and being night time the temperature was even lower than before. This far north it was always cooler, even in these hazy summer months. Our convoy of giant flying dragons meandered forward as planned, the Lerandra mountains dwarfing even our mighty hosts to our left as we flew parallel to them, gaining ground toward the edge of the breaking world. I'd have said we'd been flying for a good four hours when I started to notice the jagged edges of the cliff protruding from the floor beneath us in the near distance.

Flanhlin turned his head slightly, highlights of the small lights high above capturing the silver placed within his eyes as he spoke to Rogan and me. "Soon we climb. Hold tight and lean forward, move as I do, move as I turn, follow my direction, and don't fall off."

The last he added with a slight smile and as I looked at Rogan, I think neither of us needed telling of the consequences of falling from this height, only to be increased from here on in.

Holding as tight as I could with thick gloves covering my already cold hands, we started to turn towards the north again, Flanhlin following close behind all the other dragons in front of us. It was evident the extra beats Flanhlin had to make, powering forward, upward, but easily managed for a beast of this size and strength to achieve. Stretched out in front of us, Drathlo led the way upwards, and from this far back in the darkness I could just make out the odd colour of wings moving in the distance. Raorge, followed by Cenabus, gained ground easily right behind Drathlo; slightly further back towards us was Carthian, his deep colour purple showing brightly even in this light, flying in tandem next to Grogkin.

These dragons were definitely exchanging thoughts or words, as often each faced the other, even while flying nearly straight upward at this point. Grogkin even seemed to be encouraging the smaller purple dragon onwards, his large yellow wings beating in perfect time, rhythmical, even hypnotic to watch, I found, sitting behind them both.

Flanhlin, the most powerful dragon among our group, always seemed to take the rear position, watching all, confirming everyone's safety. It was reassuring that he was here and that I sat upon him, if I could even think about being safe, barely holding onto a dragon's scales, vertically flying over a mountain, in the dark.

If I thought the hours previously has been cold, been hard to hold on for, I realised I'd been foolish, as this was the hardest thing I'd ever tried to do in my life. Rogan barely held his place behind me too, desperately trying not to cramp up as we continually leant forward, changing position as Flanhlin turned slightly here and there to manoeuvre around mountainous ledges, outcrops and occasionally larger clumps of brush growing from the mountainside.

The heights we now climbed, though, soon made these things less of an obstacle, although the temperature now threatened to loosen even the strongest grip I held. My fingers, now mostly numb, somehow stayed true, to this day I know not how, but eventually the dark wall in front of us we'd been staring at for hours gradually become lighter as we neared the very top peaks.

I'd seen the peaks only a couple of times in my life; rarely they showed themselves even on the clearest days but in the past I'd witnessed the snow-capped ridges from the higher ground within Qeraviel. I'd been told the snow stayed always, never left the coldness there, not relinquishing the grip it held on this place. I now knew the bitterness it brought to this region and wondered again if I could hold on as long as it had. I hoped the answer was yes as we gained speed in the thinner air here. Earlier I'd placed a cloth around my face to protect from the coldest wind I'd faced; it was covered in ice crystals now. I couldn't remove my hand to free the restriction I felt; breathing rapidly, trying to gain my breath, became harder and harder too. And just as I felt I could hold on no longer, a sudden huge gust of wind nearly unseated both me and Rogan.

Breaching like a fish jumping out of the water in the Great Lake Pohalith, we crested the top of Lerandra, dropping now like a stone over the other side. The sudden change in direction was both satisfying to allow our backs a change of position, and terrifying due to lack of strength and ability to continue to hold on. After only a few minutes of this speed I couldn't hold on any longer and shouting to Flanhlin, I pleaded for rest. Knowing we couldn't stop in mid-flight I'm not entirely sure to what ends I pleaded, but hearing our cries for help, Flanhlin opened his wings and slowed our rapid descent. Unable to concentrate on anything apart from the pain in all my joints, especially my fingers, I couldn't say here how the others fared, but I knew Rogan and I struggled.

Flanhlin couldn't maintain the level of power he now displayed, gravity at this height pulling him dangerously close to the mountainside, ever downwards too. A combination of drops and sudden expansion of his wings allowed both parties respite, each knowing if he didn't achieve it we would all perish here and now.

The violent actions having to be taken just to survive brought mixed emotions flooding in, fear, panic, worry for Flanhlin's strength even, which, together with a sickness I couldn't shake, eventually forced me to turn as best as I could, vomiting my stomach contents over myself, Rogan and Flanhlin. Rogan, too, couldn't hold onto his stomach either; barely holding our grip on life, we plummeted downwards.

The journey down to the wastelands, although shorter, taxed me more than I realised, and finally, as Flanhlin levelled out, I think I lost consciousness for a while, awaking to find I still gripped tightly onto the scale I'd held for so long.

Eventually, lowering slowly, the ground rose to greet us and never have I seen a more beautiful thing. A barren, dark grey patch of earth, burned, scorched and normally uninhabitable, but still, it sat still in time and as we landed with a huge thump, I fell from Flanhlin's back, unable to take any more. Lying on that still-warm clod, head spinning, covered in my own vomit, I smiled before once more losing my existence to unconsciousness, only awaking to water thrown over me from Gavriel, whose first words were, "You were sick all over Flanhlin! Maybe not the best thing to have done, young Wicker," as he smiled and walked off. *Time to apologise to the most powerful dragon I knew*, I thought.

As a group we all made it back to the ground, although unfortunately we'd not all made it without incident. Vomiting on Flanhlin now seemed a lesser problem, albeit one I still needed to be forgiven for. Carthian remained lying on the ground as one by one we all merged into a larger group, checking we were alright. I hadn't earlier realised that Carthian was, in dragon terms, a youngling. Dragons aged differently to humans; a dragon of Carthian's years was still considered barely old enough for such adventures, although in human years he was the equivalent of around eighty years old. As he lay on the dry earth ragged breaths were all he managed to achieve. The humans and dragons gathered around him.

His bright purple scales seemed so much duller now, and even trying to raise his head from the floor was more than he could manage. Little could we do; as we watched him we could feel the energy and heat being released with such force from his body. Sadness welled up in all of us as we realised we sat in this barren place, with very little to help our new friend.

Drathlo quickly summoned the other dragons present and before long both Grogkin and Flanhlin took once more to the skies above, seemingly heading straight back up whence we came. Before long even their bright colours in the brightening sky above could not be picked out from this far away.

We emptied several of our scarce water bottles over Carthian's head, but still he remained lifeless, only his heavy breathing letting us know he still survived. The heat emanating from him was ridiculously high now and the other dragons gave him shade from the rapidly increasing sunshine of that morning by covering him with their outstretched wings, which I used also to get out of the already burning heat of the early day.

The wastelands seemed exactly that to me, a large wasted land, burnt dry by constant high temperatures, an arid expanse of flat, featureless ground. For miles and miles, it appeared flat, or reasonably so, anyway, with the occasional raised section, blurry, looked at through the heat haze in the distance.

Gavriel was talking to Drathlo about what our next moves would be when he was interrupted by shouts from several warrior priests about the return of the dragons above. Yellow could be easily picked out as Grogkin grew larger, getting closer, with the larger shape of Flanhlin close behind, his white and grey not so easily distinguished in the bright sky. As they dropped nearer, we could see they carried something, and soon we realised it to be large pieces of snow cap. Drathlo had instructed them to get these and they managed to tear large pieces each to carry back. Holding a steady pace, they soon dropped back next to us, holding huge chunks of still-frozen ice and snow in their talons. As a group we all started to pack as much as we could of this precious cool life-saving ice around Carthian, making sure we nearly covered his entire head. Still sheltered under wings providing shade, I simply sat next to Carthian, hoping the ice wouldn't melt any faster than it was doing, praying to Rai that this plan worked and made him feel better.

An eternity seemed to pass sitting there, all present but silent, waiting for something to change, a sign from Carthian that meant he was improving, but nothing. As the sun's last rays closed behind us that day, with a signal fire burning bright for light, I'd started to give up hope. All eyes still firmly rested on Carthian until I fell into a deep sleep, still leaning on him to let him know that he wasn't alone, as if he needed that. It was sometime in the night that I was awoken by a movement from Carthian, not large, but enough to wake me, and as I lifted my head, I saw he'd done the same. With a weak smile forced onto his face he stared back at me. He was not back to himself yet, but he'd made it, he'd be all right with time.

Drathlo had overseen the next day's tasks, Gavriel, too, giving us small missions to undertake. Carthian, although now awake, obviously wasn't well; time would be needed for him to improve and so as a group we had to stay where we were for now.

Raorge took a solo flight for more ice, both for Carthian and all of us to use as water. This was a dangerous thing to do, with little rest and no food, something we all appreciated. The warrior priests and I gathered firewood; it got as cold in the night as the days were hot. We also looked for hunting opportunities, finding none here was easily done. No tracks, no signs of life existing here except us, gave the wasteland another reason to be named as such.

As we sat exactly where we'd landed the third night came upon us. Carthian had improved remarkably, able now to fully stand and even walk small distances; flight, though, would take a lot longer and as a group we were all called upon by Drathlo to gather near a large fire we'd built. "Carthian can't make the next stage of our journey," Drathlo said.

This was something I think we'd all been wondering. He had, after all, just been brought back from possible death. Carthian lowered his head. If dragons could seem shameful he looked now as if he thought less of himself, a rare thing for a dragon to show, let alone feel.

Drathlo went on speaking, "Carthian will stay here. He will continue his recovery while we travel onward to Horchlock. It will be tough to leave him behind but if we are to succeed in our task we must move. The heat will only start to affect us more if we hesitate here and weaken us all in the process. Don't forget that after we gain what we seek in Horchlock, we must get back, back over Lerandra's peaks once more." The thought of that sent a shiver not only through me but every human standing there, I wagered. The dragons themselves seemed daunted slightly too; the journey here had not been uneventful, Carthian was evidence of that. Just as Gavriel stepped forward to agree that leaving Carthian here would be a loss to the group but a justified one, Fenn and Jorge stepped forward. Fenn led with his thoughts, saying them for all to hear. Backed by Jorge they agreed that if Carthian was staying then they would stay too.

They had started this journey on his back and they wanted to help him while he remained here, leaving eight of us to move on, to find the magic the dragons spoke of. If Gavriel had second thoughts about the idea, he didn't voice his concerns, and Drathlo and the other dragons seemed humbled by the solidarity both Fenn and Jorge showed to Carthian. We'd spent a lot of time with these dragons, talking into the early hours most nights, and even our small gestures had helped Carthian survive those first nights here. We were a team now, and mutual grumbling from all the dragons vibrated the very air around us.

I think even after rubbing my vomit off Flanhlin's scales with dry dirt, with more apologies than I'd ever made in my entire life, I'd finally grown to be trusted by him, even if it was by necessity. Plans were made for the morning to move forward, onward to Horchlock.

Fenn, Jorge and Carthian would stay here at camp, allowing more recovery time, with the bonus that we now could lessen the load on the other dragons, leaving the heavier clothes and equipment we'd brought here with them for the return flight. Feeling positive for the morning, we rested while we could. Carthian, I think, felt rejuvenated now that he had company staying with him while he waited for our return. Mornings here seemed to start earlier than expected; the heat rose suddenly as soon as the sun's first rays penetrated the morning mist, burning all beneath.

Already set from the night before, we ate a meagre meal of simple dry biscuits which we'd bought at the markets in Banclian. Tough but surprisingly nourishing, I couldn't complain of my lot even if I had wanted to, remembering that the dragons had nothing; no game herds here to satisfy their hunger. I hoped that Horchlock might provide more chance for them to hunt but felt reluctant to bring it up. I didn't want to remind them that they weren't eating, as part of me was hoping they continued to have the strength to get us all home. So once more climbing onto Flanhlin, grabbing my accustomed handhold, I sat waiting. A wave to those left behind, promising our return as soon as we could to bring more supplies, we took off into the morning's heat. Keeping low, merely a hundred metres off the ground in some places, allowed the dragons to keep an excellent viewpoint of our direction, maintaining energy too, by not flying too high.

As always so far in our journeys, Drathlo took the lead. This time Flanhlin remained close by her side, with Grogkin, Raorge and Cenabus keeping to the rear of the group, flying this time more closely together. I wondered if this was to make sure all were all right and asked Flanhlin as best as I could over the noise of the wind. Even flying this low down the noises were very loud and eventually he understood my questions, answering that this land was still greatly unknown, even to the dragons. Being closer together made for a larger body in case of sudden attack; we can defend better or attack much quicker this way, Flanhlin smiled. I wondered to myself that if there was anything here, surely it wouldn't want to, or be able to attack a group of dragons? Thankfully the question never needing answering as Drathlo veered slightly more to the west, and in the hazy distance I could just make out the growing shape of a small line of trees, a line of straight sticks seemingly pointing up from the haze of the ground. A sight more beautiful than I'd seen in a long time, apart, that is, from the group of dragons, amongst which I sat.

Horchlock was indeed a strange place that I couldn't have imagined would exist. Sitting within a clump of trees, in the middle of a huge barren wasteland, were several wooden huts; ramshackle, beaten things, barely holding up from the constant heat poured onto them every day. But here they sat, a reminder to all of us that sometimes survival is a state of mind. These basic huts surrounded something even rarer here, something in all the miles flown over this dry land we'd not seen anywhere else: water.

Our group had flown over the trees initially, the dragons concerned, making sure we were safe to land here, showing Horchlock in its entirety. Small in capacity compared to colonies back home, but sitting here in this vast expanse of land, its qualities shone brighter than any precious ornament I'd ever seen or held. Trees encompassed the water nearly in a complete circle, only managing several feet high, standing in just two or three rows in places. This couldn't be called a forest, but lines of trees purposely planted, I was sure, many years ago. The water was coloured heavily from the surrounding earth leaching into the edges of the pool, but a large area nonetheless; I'd guess at thirty metres around the circumference would have covered the size, fed from an underground spring, the dragons told us. They'd used this small lake for many centuries travelling the world and named the area after the dragon who'd found it originally, Horchlock.

So land we did, and walked the short way to the tree line. Shade is a marvellous thing and we all rushed for the cover of it, all humans, that is. The dragons much preferred the heat; warming their bodies helped their muscles use the strength they obviously held within. No dragon would race to the shelter of shade to gain mercy away from the sun's relentless heat. Standing under the trees took minutes before several rushed to the water's edge to quench their thirst. Raorge had already taken his spot near the water's edge, talons gripping the earth as he consumed hundreds of gallons of water. Each took their turn, and eventually, sitting again under the trees' shade, everyone present had spent time drinking and cooling off in this wonderful place.

Ivan and Gavriel had even had time to wander around the small wooden huts placed here, long since abandoned by whoever manufactured their existence. Nothing of value was found, not that that was what we looked for, nothing in fact of any use to our party, only basic furniture carved from pieces of wood, now broken and left behind. We all remarked, wondering who'd once lived here, whose home this was. No wonder they lived just here in this place: the water was such a valuable commodity that no other place for miles could have sustained life.

Even if the life they had here would have been tremendously difficult to survive and endure, someone had, long enough to build shelters and plant trees, a tough colony of people indeed, we all agreed. Food was a current problem for us, as even rationing the supplies we'd brought with us, we all remained hungry. The dragons must have been more so, as they hadn't hunted or eaten since leaving Banclian at least four days previously. The dragons all seemed fine though, not mentioning hunger once, unlike us, who occasionally complained at the lack of game here to hunt. Drathlo motioned for us all to listen, as we sat motionless between the trees after grabbing rest and water in abundance. She'd just been talking with Gavriel, Ivan too, and now it seemed the plan was set. Rested and ready to challenge our next goal, we all listened intently.

Within walking distance from where Horchlock sat in this world Drathlo spoke about the magic's hiding place. Grabbing small tools we'd stored in our packs, we started moving as a group, following the mighty red dragon's path across the dirt stretched out in front of us. Less than ten minutes' walk found us standing next to an abandoned mine entrance, expertly hidden, only found by Drathlo's exact knowledge of this place. We could have searched this whole area looking for such a find, perhaps only by chance discovering it, but here we stood, eight humans and five dragons, all looking into the darkness below us. A shaft black to view into, with warm air currents somehow swirling from the void, permitting thought to wonder if the space below was larger than the small space it appeared to be. Dropping a chunk of hardened dirt to check depth, Gavriel waited as we did for the noise to confirm the bottom. Several looks passed between us when no such noise arrived; it was either a huge cavernous expanse, or the bottom of this place was somehow not solid, something we'd not expected.

The twine we'd brought with us had been woven from tree vines back in Qeraviel. It had been made to a considerable length and all now hoped this was long enough as we tied the end around Grogkin's front leg and lowered the end into the space below. Drathlo explained that many centuries ago, this place had been important for humans. Many travelled to this exact place to seek knowledge held here by a mystical colony. After many trials and many wars fought over this place, Rai considered this place too powerful, rendering it to dust, Shenash by his side. The people moved on, never returning, but the knowledge they held stayed. Records of their wisdom sat below us, guarded, hidden even by the earth they sat in; long forgotten by humans, protected by dragons.

This place held a magic most powerful; indeed, waking it again risked problems, wars even, but sometimes knowledge forgotten must be revisited to save the future. We carried nothing to provide light, so dropping into the void was precarious indeed; slowly inching down the rope, Rogan took first place. I followed behind and it took a fair while for my eyes to adjust to the darkness after being in the sunshine above. We'd agreed to go in twos down the rope for safety, added to the knowledge that the rope we'd brought couldn't be fully trusted with more weight. Lowered slowly, rope wrapped around my left foot, holding tight, I allowed time for my vision to return.

Only a few metres below the ground brought an amazing relief from the heat; adjusted vision now allowed Rogan and me an extended view of the place we now hung in, swaying slightly on the rope we held onto. The space below was sectioned, with several larger caverns to all sides, carved, it seemed, by hand. Several walk-ways intercepted below us too, branching off in all directions. Realising that the depth wasn't as great as we thought, the rope easily reached the bottom of the cavern and carefully we both eased our way to the ground. The stone Gavriel dropped hadn't made noise as we'd expected, due to the fact that even here the ground held dampness, soft to stand upon, firm enough not to sink into, though. With a call up to those above us, the warrior priests started their journey down to meet Rogan and me, and soon all eight of us stood in the only circle of pooled sunlight reaching down from above. Breaking into twos again we made our way into individual caverns either side of the central space we occupied.

Drathlo told us that the knowledge we sought was in written form; these books were very old, very rare, and as far as she knew sat hidden here still, so search we did. Smaller caves were located off the larger caverns and it became difficult to see due to the darkness back in these areas. Also, although not massive, the area kept you turning back on yourself; several times I found myself thinking I'd found a new cave only to realise I'd stood there before. Lots of the smaller caves still held artefacts from people living there, clothes remained as well, and often I felt a strange sensation, as if I searched someone's home. Eventually a shout echoed around this place as Brock had found something. Searching now for Brock, Rogan and I soon found the smaller cave he and Larch now stood in. Fumbling around in the darkness Brock had discovered a large wooden chest, still sealed by a metal clasp, heavy, far too heavy for us to lift but containing something, surely, from the weight.

Gavriel and Ivan eventually rounded into the cave, while I moved slightly nearer the entrance to allow them a clearer view of Brock's find.

Ivan fiddled with the clasp, which moments before had baffled us, but he seemed to understand its workings and with an audible click it fell to the floor. Opening the chest with a sigh, the contents revealed themselves to the onlookers. From my standpoint I couldn't see within but knew from the excited comments that we'd found what we'd come all this way for. Passing the books between us all to carry, I was given a large, obviously old, heavy book, covered in dust, sealed too with a metal clasp. So slowly we made our way back to the central cavern, back to the rope we hoped remained in place for us.

Rounding a corner together, we walked straight into a group of people kneeling in front of us, lined up, ranked together even waiting, in silence. Gavriel drew his sword faster than anyone else here, holding it aloft in readiness for an attack, but none came. These people knelt, eyes forward, no movement from any, just kneeling, perfectly still. It was only when challenged by Gavriel that the person kneeling at the front rose up; bowing to all of us in turn he introduced himself and the group together as Jabbnor colony members.

If Gavriel knew of this colony he had never mentioned it; the dragons also believed this area to be devoid of human life, so to find a colony underground held surprises for all, I think. They stared at us too, maybe in disbelief that another group of people had ventured this far into their lands. Their numbers here reached several dozen as far as I could make out in the darkness. Thin individuals, hardened to their conditions, but apparently not a fighting group. They had small children here, women too; we'd walked into their lives, their homes, uninvited and all they did was kneel. These people understood hardship like few others and had already worked out that our lesser numbers still held a power they didn't have, fortitude and resilience. And dragons.

SEVENTEEN

Ameek, mild race, the Jabbnor continued to speak openly. Their existence was one of pure hardship, struggling along their path through life as they knew no other. We all sat now, listening to each group take turns in speaking, asking questions of one another, not in a harsh way but in an inquisitive manner. Gavriel told of Qeraviel, the warm days, the wet days, the expanse of space there. He mentioned the land surrounding ours, the other colonies and the food and water easily reached, offering all here a place with us if they so desired, a place to live freely, with less struggle. Asking someone you have just met to leave their homelands and move hundreds of miles away, might seem foolish but after only a few days in this tundra we knew the life they lived, and could provide a much easier one for them to exist in.

They had very basic rations here, but willingly shared all they had with us. Although extremely hungry, I couldn't force myself to take more than the tiniest morsel, understanding that to them this meagre offering was a huge amount of their survival rations. As a group, we all did the same, and asked if they would return with us to the surface, where we had some food for them to take back. The Jabbnor existed on a day-to-day basis and staying underground kept them out of the glaring heat, which was a necessity. They wanted to come with us, but terror stopped them from entering the central cavern where we'd initially descended. Dragons, curious as to where we had got to, were trying to look into the space. People of the Jabbnor hadn't seen dragons on the ground before, only mentioning they'd spied them flying overhead occasionally. Realising that these creatures were powerful they'd stayed hidden, in case of being found out and eaten. A sensible idea if you didn't know what you were dealing with.

Dragons were immense creatures, powerful beyond belief; even knowing the ones overhead still filled every sense I had with awe, my trust for our companions having grown over the time spent with them. But had I not known these beautiful beasts, I, too would have hidden in fear.

Rogan, Brock and I climbed back up the rope, carrying the books tightly tucked into our clothes, to be greeted with a low grumbling noise by our friends. Drathlo commented on our time below ground, and truth was we had spent longer there than even we imagined as the skies overhead lacked both light and heat now. Explaining of our finds, both book and people, Drathlo promised to meet with the leader of the Jabbnor, Drathlo promising safety whilst with us. Spare food was gathered if we had such a thing, but after seeing all they had our offerings appeared much needed, something the dragons too remarked on.

A few Jabbnor colony members climbed up but not by our rope, showing Gavriel and the others below a secret set of steps carved into the earth leading upwards. Removing a section of wood showed the entrance only a few metres away from where we stood now. Ravenous mouths soon ate all we'd given, both here and below, where the food had been taken, and with water replenished from the small lake, we sat once more leaning against the trees; now with new friends, five large dragons listening, looking over the trees' limited canopy.

The Jabbnor asked how we'd arrived at this place and Gavriel, alongside Drathlo, explained our journey, and the importance of finding these books. The Jabbnor knew of their existence but none of them could read, so simply left them in the wooden chest they'd been found in. These were a simple people, living a very simple life, and the warrior priests and I appreciated their honesty in that. The Jabbnor asked if we knew the paths still further west from here, asking if we'd ever travelled over the great sea. Their people originally came from the coastal shores of the gulf of Anathena, travelling further inland around Lerandra mountain range.

Small boats had carried the original settlers around the coastal rocks and managed to safely bring them to these shores. Promises made back then that the land had been rich in both resources and discoveries had initially been accurate but soon the breaking of the world had changed all the hope found here. The weather soon changed, withering crops, changing landscape from lush scenery to what we saw now. Hope had been lost and most returned to the fishing colonies west of the Banclian territories all those years ago. However, some remained, trying to reclaim the glory they'd found here, staking claim to this land, forever hopeful the rains would return but they never did. By then the boats had long since vanished and trying to walk back over Lerandra impossible. So they had stayed, with generation after generation toiling here, surviving alone until we arrived in their world.

Drathlo had already discussed with her dragons the possibility of returning a different way. From the information supplied by the Jabbnor it seemed as though a new much safer route could be used. Even if it took slightly longer, as least the dragons now, with much less energy, could manage with us aboard. Flanhlin started to make his way to the clearer ground ready for take-off; when I asked if I could join him, he nodded consent and, once more sitting in my familiar place, launched into the air with an ease I still couldn't believe of a creature of this size. Banking sharply west as he rose on the rapidly cooling wind, we headed for somewhere neither of us knew, but understood that if we were all to get back home we needed to find.

Failing light hindered our view but directionally we were exactly where we needed to be, eventually travelling once more with the Lerandra mountain range to our left, the western region of this land open in front of us. The ground remained level except for the odd ridge and broken section, lifted by the sun barely feet into the air. This place was barren and Flanhlin wondered how anything could live in such a world.

It was during this time that I asked Flanhlin why he'd chosen me, why he'd insisted I travel with the group. Hesitating, he remarked on my charm once more.

"Dragon stone doesn't show its true colours to everyone," he told me. "To unlock its power, you must first hold an inner truth that even you might not know you have. Only a person truly a master of their own destiny, someone prepared to seek knowledge and power but not to betray the answers you find of it, can work dragon stone. Your god, Rai, held such a stance; Shenash gave him a dragon stone, made from his own blood and saliva, as he was the most powerful dragon ever to have lived in his time," Flanhlin said.

"Dragon stone has a memory. It's placed there by its creator, each as individual as the dragon itself who made it. The stones hold a power which is known by us to be called on whenever the holder of the stone calls upon it. But no ordinary person can call a dragon to do its work for him, the stone requires payment. The stones take energy back, even memories, it is said, in payment, adding to the experiences it already holds within itself, never too much to drain the holder completely, but eventually the stone and holder become one, a rare being indeed, complete in the knowledge that both now hold a place in history, a breed of thing not seen these days. Not seen until I saw you for the first time, Wicker," Flanhlin spoke.

Not fully understanding his words we climbed slightly higher to gain better views in the darkening sky. "You are not merely a human anymore, Wicker, you hold a dragon stone, but more than this you have awoken it. It has started to work for you, to save you in your time of need. Now you must practise, to learn how to control the great power you now possess. You will one day need the power, I'm sure, you will grow to become more powerful than even I, I feel.

"Dragon stone isn't made very often, and when it is it's normally by a dragon of great age, even passing from this world onto the next, it's been told. Every dragon is capable of making a stone, but only one stone can ever be made by each dragon. The stone holds memories placed within, thoughts, ideas, strengths, things only known to the maker, eventually passed over to the holder. Something normally made for an individual from another. A rare gift indeed. The fact you hold such a stone is an honour, but to be able to use such a stone is impressive."

With those words resounding in my head, ahead of us we saw in the distance the gulf of Anathena and as we drew nearer the great body of water. Flanhlin nodded his giant head left. "Look," he said, and turning, we looked at a huge break within the rock wall; the very foundation stone of Lerandra opened up here. A ginormous opening, far larger than Flanhlin, appeared and showed the way back to our lands, only a few hundred metres above the ground, far easier to manage than climbing the heights we'd reached just getting here. It might take longer to get back, especially if Carthian hadn't fully recovered, but it had to be worth a try. Marking the location in my mind, we turned once more back towards our group left in Horchlock. Thoughts of Flanhlin's words still echoed in my head, and under my shirt I could already feel the dragon stone glowing away, understanding its own hidden power; if only I had the same knowledge.

On the way back, we flew mostly in silence. I pondered Flanhlin's words, wondering if they were real. How could a simple colony boy gain powers this mighty dragon said existed. And why me?

This was something I still wondered about as we reached the waving arms of our party, still sitting around the trees at Horchlock. Night time now well and truly upon us, we sat and told everyone of our find. Grogkin was the first to offer the long flight back to Carthian to tell him the better news that he didn't have to fly once more over Lerandra. He volunteered to stay behind, to bring Fenn and Jorge home too, making sure Carthian returned to his normal self. We all knew that they needed to rest here and recoup for a while; even if just the water helped them, it must be done. Grogkin set off straight away, and as little planning was needed for him to achieve this goal, off he went. Gavriel decided we wouldn't need the clothes we'd left behind so told the Jabbnor where they were, so that if they needed them, they could decide if the long trek there would be worth it. The limited equipment we'd brought with us wouldn't be needed either, so a gift of these also seemed an obvious thing for the Jabbnor to receive.

Agreeing to set off at once, while the strong summer sun wasn't beating down on us, we said our goodbyes for now. The Jabbnor had shown us a way back home, far greater than they could manage on foot, but on the backs of dragons easily accomplished. Gavriel promised to send word to the fisherman colony Jabbnor originated from, asking for help, even aid to be sent, food being a priority. Those wanting to return he was sure would still be welcome, something the Jabbnor must think about together. Gavriel promised to do everything he could, vowing to return again soon with the help he promised.

Offering peace and goodwill we climbed onto the backs of our dragon friends, one by one leaping into the air, leaving this barren place behind us. It was with a twinge of regret that we left our new friends behind, knowing the suffering they experienced every day, but we had to return, as our journey here was for reasons that still remained. Our thoughts now returned to Qeraviel, hoping no future attacks had taken place whilst we'd been away.

The journey to the huge hole we'd found in Lerandra mountain range was straightforward, all of us making the journey unencumbered. Approaching with the mountain range still to our left as we flew, the dark skies made easy viewing of the hole near impossible. Questioning my landmarks, I considered we'd not reached it yet or even passed by in the darkness. Flanhlin reassured me, though, by saying he knew we were right. It was just harder to see in this light, or lack of it. Several navigational turns eventually meant Flanhlin had both guaranteed its placement, as well as allowing the other dragons to see for themselves the space they were about to fly through. Honestly it appeared we were flying into a wall of solid rock as we turned for the final time, making our way straight towards the side of Lerandra.

Flanhlin's eyesight was far superior to mine, subtly manoeuvring his huge bulk effortlessly between the rock forms jutting out here and there. Passing through this vent in the face of the mountain was easily accomplished for a dragon of his skill and intellect. The others, too, Drathlo close behind Flanhlin, managed the task with no problems, soon all the party passing through, back into our world, flying once more over trees, grassland, flowing water and lakes, such a change from the world we'd lived in merely moments ago. Before long, it seemed, the dragons circled for landing. They'd not eaten for several days and, dropping us off to camp here for the rest of the night, took their leave from us to go and hunt, something I was sure they desperately needed. As for us, it didn't take long to catch, kill and prepare a dozen rabbits to satisfy our want too. Watching them slowly roast over a roaring fire we'd made, thoughts turned to hopefully seeing Fenn, Jorge and Carthian back this side of the mountain very soon.

While dinner cooked, Gavriel and Ivan started to study the three large tomes we'd recovered from that chest in Horchlock, all closed with a neat silver clasp of unique quality, covered in a skin of some unknown animal.

Gavriel was looking strangely at the text within, not able to read the runes, symbols and writing placed there. "Dragonash," Ivan muttered to himself, an ancient language spoken only by dragons, occasionally taught to humans, it was foretold.

Rumour said that Rai himself learnt Dragonash, communicating only this way with Shenash. No other could listen in to their conversation this way, except another dragon, that was.

The books dusty, heavy and cumbersome, were passed around for all to look at. We held several large books, scrolls, too, from which we often read; these were kept within the great temple of Rai. The ones we held now were different, though; an energy seemed to pulsate from the one I held, making me look around to see if anyone else noticed it. Ivan staring straight at me, quizzically frowning, stood and quickly approached my spot around the fire. "It calls to you, doesn't it, Wicker?" he enquired.

Without realising, I'd opened the book, my necklace glowing slightly, giving the page I'd turned to a homely red glow. The pages, after many years placed within this book, took on a yellow tinge, now mixed with the red, forming differential shades, patterns to the page, tricks to the eye who viewed it. The words Ivan said were Dragonash, but as I looked the words swirled on the page. Runes moving, forming new arrangements, a magic I couldn't comprehend flowed onto the pages before me. Before long, Ivan and I still staring at the wonder I held in my hands, letters, phrases and words started to appear that each of us could read.

Changing continuously as we read further down the page, Dragonash became readable; sentences, paragraphs, the entire page now sat there for all to read, under the red glow of my necklace. If the light moved or obscured certain words they remained unreadable; Dragonash remained under normal light, only the power held within my charm, the dragon stone itself, gave another secret to us that night. Gavriel must have seen the expressions on our faces, soon joining us to stare at the pages transformed in front of us, asking to hold the stone and book closer, if he might. Reluctantly I handed him both; after all; he was our leader, my mentor.

The light disappeared as soon as I placed my charm within his hand, only showing itself again once back in my possession. Clearly this stone was attached to me, or me to the stone, but already a sense of belonging to it held me in its grasp. I needed to know more and maybe by reading these books I could unlock the power that this stone showed me. Ivan promised to help me and for most of rest of the night we read as much as we could. Gavriel occasionally asked, seated next to us, to repeat passageways we'd read, so that, reading aloud to the warrior priests Ivan and I took turns revealing the secrets of the books we'd travelled so far to find.

The dragons soon returned. Drathlo was surprised by how I'd managed to start reading the books we'd found. Dragonash, she informed us, was indeed an ancient language, not understood by humans; dragons' first language of many they'd learnt over the years placed on this earth. Drathlo commented after showing her the books that we should concentrate our efforts on the smaller book of the three we'd gathered. This book held the knowledge needed now, the ability to learn to control forces around us, bend them to our will; a powerful magic lay in these words, Drathlo said, a magic we'd need to spend our time learning, and once learnt, take caution using. Drathlo asked how I'd managed to read such runes without a dragon's help.

As I explained again about the dragon stone's guidance she simply nodded. "A most powerful dragon must have made that stone, young Wicker," she said. "You will learn many things from it, and you must teach it, too. Together you shall become indeed a force to be reckoned with, a friend and an ally to all dragons, I hope?" inquisitively looking at me. I hoped she was right. I told her there had been another stone, very similar to mine, blue in colour; my best friend held it, Peshy. He'd fallen and was lost now. Drathlo enquired if he'd been able to use its power, if I'd seen him use the stone like I had. I hadn't, and said as much, but if Peshy had seen its light, he'd never spoken of it. Ivan had given us the treasure, manufacturing, moulding it into the necklace charm I wore today. Ivan spoke now to Drathlo alone, perhaps telling her where he'd gained such a gift. They seemed similar to the stones and gems I'd seen Ivan and the outlanders digging for in the great Ibothiel plains. These, though, shone brighter, held more sustenance in life. Alive, they seemed alive, if a stone can be as such. Walking away I stopped and hesitated, remembering another stone existed, this time green: Amia's. Turning to tell, something stopped me, a fear it might be taken from her. Maybe, just maybe, for me to know its importance could be shielded. I'd wait and speak to her first, when I had a chance.

Gavriel asked Drathlo if the dragons themselves could use this magic the books contained. Drathlo only said that all dragons hold magic within them. Some try, some fail to reach it, some can use very powerful magic. However, this held a special place in time; old magic was dangerous to both the holder and the target. Dragons don't deal in things they can't control, Drathlo said, turning away from the subject for now.

Gavriel asked a favour of Drathlo now. He asked if he could fulfil the promise that he'd made to the Jabbnor, seeking Drathlo's permission to leave for their homesteads along the coast of Anathena. He would have to search for days, maybe, to find them, but he'd promised, and must do all he could to help those who had helped us and who continued to help Carthian.

Drathlo agreed and Cenabus stepped forward to take Gavriel to try and find from where the Jabbnor originated. Leaving tonight was paramount as they knew not how long it would take, so they prepared themselves to leave straight away. This allowed us to continue with tomorrow's first light back towards Qeraviel.

With Cenabus taking Gavriel away, and Carthian, Grogkin, Fenn and Jorge still in Horchlock, our party was much smaller than when we'd started.

Drathlo, Flanhlin and Raorge remained, a towering presence over all of us still. Ivan, Brock, Larch, Krist, Danj,

Rogan and I had been together from the start, and all longed to be home. Flying the next morning had to be managed slightly differently from how we'd been used to, as now, with Cenabus away with Gavriel, we had an extra body to fly back home.

Flanhlin was the obvious choice, as his sheer size, even compared to the other dragons, was enormous. Rogan, Brock and I easily fitted onto his back, and if he minded Flanhlin didn't comment; the only comment made was not to vomit on him again. A glint in his eye, as he made it, showed that even Flanhlin now had lightened his manner towards us. Bonded, our group had become; for a young colony man this was something I never imagined could happen but was so glad it had.

Flying over familiar ground, south-east towards Qeraviel, we once more crossed the Banclian territories, before long reaching the forest of Ewomatlan, this time taking a more southerly direction, straight towards the Ibothiel plains. The dragons still needed more food, Flanhlin telling us that another night would be spent on the ground before reaching Qeraviel, for them to hunt the great herds of this plain. A single night located on the northern edge of Ibothiel allowed all of us time to relax, eat and learn more about the books we now carried. And before long another day rose, with us on the wing, heading home to Qeraviel.

EIGHTEEN

Confusion reigned as we landed back in Qeraviel; colony members rushed away homewards as the dragons made space as best they could upon landing. Warrior priests rushed towards us, I think it was because of our return, but the look of relief upon seeing us made me think that they initially weren't sure. After explaining that the rest of our party was hopefully safe, elsewhere, we clambered off our hosts. Once more the dragons stated they would return later as they had their own needs to attend to, and bidding them farewell for now, I waved as they once more caused chaos flying away from Qeraviel.

Walking the paths of home felt amazing.

We'd only been gone around ten days, but it seemed we'd travelled a lifetime away and back. Reality meant that in my short life, I'd seen and learnt more in these days than most others.

Warrior priests confirmed that all had been well since we'd left and asked if we'd been successful. The next few hours were given over to explaining all our findings, our journey and what we'd found. All listened to the tale with wide eyes and thoughts of both envy and some gladness that they'd not had to fly over Lerandra's heights. Ivan took the books, saying he'd stay with them at the temple. This was the safest place for them, we all thought, so off he went, flanked by several warrior priests as his escort. I, on other hand, made my way home. Mother would be waiting, and although I was glad to be on solid earth, unmoving as I walked, I'd forgotten how slow it was to walk everywhere.

Mother and I spent that evening talking about all the places I'd been to, the people I'd met. Here I sat, a young man, telling my mother about the world, her world; places she'd never visited, people she'd never met. I explained the new colony we'd found, the Jabbnor, too. She listened in wonder as I talked and soon night time was once more upon us. We ate a simple home-cooked meal, but it was one of the best I'd had in weeks.

Soon tiredness encroached upon me. Sloping off to bed mumbling apologies I walked with the sudden understanding of my mother's last words, snapping me back to reality. It was my seventeenth name day in just three days' time. I'd completely forgotten, with our trip to Horchlock. I'd have to ask Gavriel on his return if that meant my acceptance leap would still be then, or whether, due to the books we'd found, I'd be given more time. Now with a head full of worries I continued to my bed.

Amia was in my dreams that night. I woke to find that I needed desperately to talk to her as she also held a dragon stone, something I needed to tell her the significance of. I needed to tell her the importance mine held, wondering if she'd noticed anything strange happening with her stone. Ivan must know she held it as well; another thing I needed to sort out in my head, why he'd given away such things. Mother fussed all morning, and it was hard for me to dismiss her attentions, having been away from home recently. So much work still needed to be done, though; I had vowed to Gavriel before he'd left that Ivan and I would spend all our time researching the books. Drathlo had told us to concentrate on the smaller book of the three, so that's where our current attention lay. Deciphering dragon runes was my job for the next few days, at least.

I made my way to the temple. Ivan was already there when I arrived, studying the books where he sat, turning the pages over and over, as I approached. "The pages are indeed a strange material," he said, not looking up, his deliberations unwavering. Sliding the book towards me, smiling as always, he asked, "Shall we start?"

The pages were indeed a strange material, thick to touch but light in weight, coloured each one, sometimes changing as you viewed them. Runes were placed here in apparent ink, although it was no ink I'd encountered before. We often practised writing, copying great passages from the temple books kept in the archives. Gavriel always wanted us to educate ourselves on these works, learning both patience and skill in writing with the thirst for knowledge. The parchment and ink we used were always brought from Barbarrow, travelling the distance from the Banclian territory where it was made by craftsmen there.

These books were made completely differently. Whoever made these books wove magic into every page. This writing was not for everyone to read; knowledge contained here was special, not intended for human eyes at all. Without the dragon stone's light changing the runes into our language, the contents within would remain hidden.

Dragons' knowledge, dragons' law was indeed intriguing; spoken in rhyme, more often than not. Ivan and I spent many hours working out the magical runes from in between dragon verse. Pages upon pages of song lay here, betwixt powerful incantations. Ivan held the dragon stone above himself as he continued to read aloud the verse transfigured on the page. I repeated the spells over and over again, concentrating particularly on the sound. Even after many attempts we only managed to make small steps forward. I'd managed, accidentally at first, to move one of the books with my words, lifting the book high into the air above us, floating, held magically in place hovering near the ceiling.

With practice, eventually both Ivan and I managed to have dozens of items held in place above us, frozen in time. Small vases, several pieces of fruit, quills and a bottle of ink, all perfectly still in mid-air, incredibly balanced, impossible to believe, but here they were. It was much further into the day's learning when we discovered how to unfreeze them, attempt after attempt eventually allowing the right phrases to send all of the items crashing down. The bottle of ink shattering brought warrior priests running to investigate the noise, only to find Ivan and I laughing at our discovery.

Magic had always been present in our land. Ivan himself held a power, I knew. Without him on the night of the great fire, the temple, if not the entire colony, would have burned. Ivan's strength in these matters was far greater than I could have imagined, and I was thankful he allowed me into this world a little further.

The book we worked with held many secrets, and as earlier said, this book apparently held magic relating to defence.

Lifting, moving items, holding force, learning to manage things around oneself, were all this book's intentions for the reader. Runes embossed on the front of the book spelt out the word protection, in our language. The other books held similar runes on their covers. Much larger books these two, one translated to read strike, the other conceal.

Working late into the night, every night, the next three days were all spent within temple walls, Ivan and I both learning skills unnatural and sometimes unsettling to us. Even after a short time we became adept at holding things in the air around us, managing to stop things thrown at us and move large objects with ease. It had become second nature already to hold a barrier around me, a force field of energy, balanced perfectly within my surroundings.

Each day, the book challenged us. Phrases, if not spoken correctly, didn't work, but the challenge, actually, was more with us and our limited knowledge of the dragon language, than the book itself. We agreed the next day to practise more of the things we'd learnt, giving us time to absorb the facts before moving on to the next book the following day. Pleased with progress I'd decided it was time to try and meet up with Amia, so early the next day I set off on the journey to Mortwedge. Grabbing a work horse to save time, I saddled up and rode out of Qeraviel as the early morning sun rose once more to greet me.

Faster on horseback, much slower than dragon flight, I made my way into Mortwedge. Securing my horse in a grass-laden field not too far from where Amia lived, I walked the short distance left to her homestead. Deciding that caution was no longer needed I knocked on her door directly. Gavriel had warned me several weeks ago not to be seen any more in Mortwedge; these days, though, more pressing, more important matters were evident.

Amia answered with a shocked look on her face which was swiftly replaced by a smile nearly as bright and as large as that morning's sun. Quickly joining me outside, we made our way to the shelter of a thicket of small trees. Sitting in the shade, backs leaning against a larger tree, the next hour was taken up with trying to answer all Amia's questions about my recent journey. Wonder stayed with me of the experience; flying on Flanhlin I don't think I'd ever get bored of talking about, and Amia seemed to join in the delight I held in it. Amia seemed amazed that we'd managed to survive the flight over the Lerandra mountain range, and her expressions changed as I described the hardships we'd faced in the wastelands, too. It was only when I mentioned my charm, and its dragon origins, that Amia became even more interested.

Explaining, I tried to inform her how important these stones were. My red stone was the only thing capable of translating the runes, to allow us to read them. Peshy's blue stone, too, and bringing him up again I knew caused each of us pain. Amia clasped her stone tightly within her hand as I spoke. Like me, I think it was something she did automatically now, not always consciously, that we held on as much as we did. And as I spoke about the potential of her charm, we saw the red glow emanating from mine mix with the green glow from hers.

Dragon stone, a magical, beautiful object, more powerful than even we could know, holding memories within from millennia past. Wisdom placed inside, sealed forever, only venturing forward if the stone felt the holder worthy. The fact that both Amia and I held such treasure left us amazed. The fact that Ivan gave them to us still left us in awe and we wondered if Ivan really knew what he'd held before giving them to us.

I couldn't ask Amia to lend me her charm; it would have been the same if someone had asked me for mine, something unachievable, unreasonable to ask. But I longed to know if Amia's stone would change the runes too. Would her stone be as powerful as mine? So many questions. Amia agreed to travel back to Qeraviel to see if her stone worked the same way as mine. Maybe we could both speak with Ivan, too, maybe he'd speak more about his knowledge of the stones.

The journey back, even on horseback, took longer with both Amia and I travelling. Soon, though, we entered Qeraviel. Colony members gave us some strange looks to see us riding on the horse, but soon we approached the forest classroom where I knew Ivan had been practising. If he was surprised that I'd arrived with Amia he hid it well, simply nodding in her direction.

Amia's stone glowed brightly here, a green glow giving extra life to the forest. She held the stone at arm's length; it somehow grew, life all around us hesitating. We stood there waiting for something to happen. Ivan reached into his backpack, removing the book we'd been working from. He asked Amia to step forward. The light shone onto the pages, and as soon as it fell upon the runes they shifted. This time, though, instead of forming spells or enchantments they spelt out something else. Drawings appeared, lines, map-like in structure. It appeared that each stone awoke new discoveries in each book. Ivan pondered this and spoke openly about how he'd discovered these stones, just as we were about to ask him.

Whilst out in the Ibothiel plains digging, many years before, Ivan came across a battered wooden box wrapped in oiled animal hide, cracked now, dried mostly from being buried deep within the earth. Ivan had been digging there after being told that the area in which he searched contained the shiny gemstones he required for his charms and trinkets. Hours had passed and he'd gained a good amount of the small coloured gems but hunger for more drove him onward, he said.

After digging this strange package out of the ground he sat back, pondering its placement here, but having no name or markers on the wrapping he decided it had been here for some time and took it back with him to his home. Unwrapping it, Ivan found four coloured gemstones within, much larger and brighter than the small, scavenged pieces he'd found that day. These were different, he said; holding them, turning them to the light, images appeared deep-set into the stones themselves.

Ivan explained that for many months dreams followed him, telling him that these stones were no normal treasure and showing him the details needed to turn them into beautiful charm bracelets. Immaculate, intricate pieces of art, the finest he'd ever made, the skills learnt from producing these four necklaces he took forward onto his regular trinkets, and soon became known as a fine craftsman, his work sought-after by all within our lands.

Ivan hid away the bracelets, never once thinking of selling them for profit, although each would have demanded a fair sum from anyone. Years passed and occasionally Ivan said dreams would return to him asking him to watch out for the true holders of these pieces to arrive.

"Wicker, you were the first person the stones told me about. I saw you in my dreams, holding the red stone. Peshy next, then Amia. I had no choice. The stones told me who to give themselves to," Ivan said. "You mentioned there were four stones?" asked Amia.

Ivan seemed disturbed but continued, "Yes, a bright yellow stone, perhaps the brightest one of them all. One morning I couldn't sense it anymore and it had simply vanished, gone without trace. There was no evidence it had been stolen, the dried, once oil-soaked hide the only thing remaining. I searched for many hours," Ivan said, "but never found that stone. I never felt its presence again."

While Ivan spoke, both Amia's dragon stone and mine glowed brightly, casting their colours over the trees surrounding us. They gave the impression that they heard everything Ivan said, listening with contentment alongside Amia and me, remembering his words, holding onto memories somehow, pleased they had been found and made into such beautiful objects. Being given to us was something they themselves wanted; if a stone can want.

Everyone standing here, though, knew these were no simple stones.

Sitting in a circle on the forest floor the three of us spent the next few hours looking at the books. Ivan and I were fascinated by the way Amia's dragon stone changed the book we'd been working with days before. The green light from the stone changed the runes completely, forming not words but an ancient map. At first glance it appeared to be of a land foreign to us, although as time passed, we all realised it was Qeraviel, but not as we knew it.

The map showed a time many hundreds of years before the split in our world, both sides evidently together, stretching out to form a large land mass. Lines woven into the paper included elevation height, water formations, with several now non-existent mountain ranges, one making Lerandra look tiny, such was its height. Green light shone on the pages, each moving, swirling with movement of the stone, uncovering more and more land with each page turned. I couldn't help myself from being captivated by Amia's stone; smaller than mine, but only just, it still held like mine a swirl to its centre. As Amia held it high above our heads so that we could all view the book's changes, I often found myself staring deep within the stone's centre.

Similar to mine although green, a dragon rode the storm set within, appearing then disappearing at its own will. Fascinated at the wonder of all this magic we sat consumed by the knowledge we held, but as yet didn't fully understand, only to have our reverie broken by the return of the real dragons overhead.

I assured Amia not to be scared as Ivan, Amia and I broke cover from the forest classroom into the scene once more of chaos as the dragons landed. By now to say I was used to this display wasn't entirely true, but it didn't surprise me half as much as it did the colony members and Amia, who had never witnessed a fully grown dragon this close.

Leaves still cascaded down as everyone around tried to settle back into normality, if normality could be claimed, amidst awestruck people and several large dragons.

Gavriel climbed down from the back of Grogkin, having been successful in both finding and asking help from the colony of Jabbnor for their forsaken people in the wastelands. Carthian, too, sat here once more, looking sleeker, but just as powerful as when I first laid eyes on him. The sun glistening off his purple scales gave him a presence larger than the others, even though his actual size belied this. Cenabus sat centrally, magnificent in size and power, nodding in acknowledgement as we approached them. Raorge, turning, also dipping his head in hello as we drew nearer. If Gavriel was bothered about Amia's presence, he didn't show it; instead, a huge smile lighted his face as he saw us walking towards him. Full of stories, he seemed different from the leader and teacher I'd known all my life. Suddenly excited somehow, to be both home and have information he'd not been able to share on his travels, he lurched forward, shaking Ivan's hands as well as mine.

Asking quickly how our studies of the books had progressed, we stood, dragons on every side, talking randomly about magic. The dragons towering over us listened too. Somehow, suddenly our efforts seemed both awkward and minuscule standing here amongst giants, knowledge they had once known now hidden, as far as we knew.

Warrior priests brought forth food and drink for Gavriel, alongside a dozen or more Uppula carcasses, a small snack for four large dragons, but mighty work for our colony members, nonetheless.

Appreciating the gesture, the dragons made very light work of dispatching the pile of meat, with everyone watching in both awe and concern at how easily they devoured such a large amount of food so quickly. Cenabus spoke, his booming voice still overpowering our colony. Everyone must have heard his voice, even at the other side of our lands.

Drathlo and Flanhlin had stayed behind to prepare for the warrior priests who would now return with the dragons, sent to help guard the dragons' eggs on their nest site. Luckily no new theft of eggs had been reported, and both dragons and warrior priests were grateful for this.

Cenabus continued, this time turning to stare at me and slightly lowering his voice, "Flanhlin sends his good wishes to Wicker, and both Drathlo and Flanhlin will return to see you leap on your acceptance day, to show further gratitude for our newfound friendship." All eyes turned to me.

I thanked Cenabus and asked him to please pass on my thanks to Drathlo and Flanhlin and that I would be honoured to see them again. No dragon had ever been there before to witness an acceptance leap, only seen bringing back our warriors.

To have the queen of the dragons watching my ceremony would be a great honour. This had been bestowed on me, one that brought the reality of my leap closer and, more importantly, squarely into my thoughts. This was the time when Gavriel stepped forward and exclaimed to the colony members standing around us, with the dragons listening, "In two days' time, Wicker will take his acceptance leap. Prepare the colony, gather food for not only us, but our dragon guests. We have much to do." As the colony cheered and dragons roared, I stood stock still. Reality had well and truly reached for me this day.

NINETEEN

The morning I'd dreamed of so many times had finally arrived. Today would be my acceptance.

Still darkness clung on, holding its place above me, unrelenting, not wanting to succumb to the morning's sunrise. Recently so much work had been placed upon my shoulders that I'd even relaxed about this day, but it crashed into my thoughts now as I sat on the edge of my bed. I'd managed to grab a few hours' rest, and nervous anxiety sat awkwardly on my shoulder right now. So much time had been spent reading the magic books, training, trying to learn the knowledge needed to help the colony within their powerful words. Early mornings, late evenings, sometimes all night. I'd started something that only I could finish, and Ivan and I had yearned for more knowledge once we'd started.

Today, though, I needed to push all thoughts of the magic aside. Today was my day. After a simple wash, I entered the living quarters of the homestead. Mother met me as I entered, a smile already beaming on her face. I wasn't sure whether she placed it there to hide her own anxiety, but she was pleased also that this day had finally come. The expectations were on us now. Finally, soon we could move forward; it was as though our lives revolved around the looming acceptance day, but no more, after today.

Breakfast was brief. I had to get dressed and quickly make my way to the temple this morning; with the knowledge of a day full of celebration later, more food than I could possible eat would be thrust at me anyway. Promising to see Mother later, a quick hug and kiss on the cheek was all we had as I bundled myself out of the door.

I was greeted by Rogan, who stood there already fully adorned in his warrior priest ceremonial dress. Smiling just as hugely as Mother had, he held out his hand in greeting, soon pulling me into his grasp for a hug too. Rogan and I had always been friends, but after the loss of Peshy, with the added trip to Horchlock, and the training we'd put ourselves through since our return, we'd grown closer. I was glad my friend was with me as we took the steps towards Rai's temple, still under the cover of darkness.

Conversation was minimal. Rogan himself had completed this day only this year, so he understood how I was feeling. We mentioned the weather, commented on the next stage of events, just passing walking time together really, but I appreciated it nevertheless. Soon arriving at the temple, Rogan said his goodbyes, promising to see me later for the ceremony.

Rogan was the first on the list of warrior priests and students I'd asked for on my walk to acceptance ledge; he'd agreed with delight and I knew he'd be there for me.

With a final wave, turning I walked the stone path up to the temple door. With one loud knock, the solid wooden doors creaked slightly as they opened wide to allow me to enter. Trepidation made me hesitate slightly but a will to succeed pushed me forward, onward, to today's first task.

Inside the temple Gavriel stood alone. Expressions can hide a multitude of feelings, I have found, sometimes showing you the full range of someone's emotions, but today Gavriel seemed to hold neither emotion nor feeling. He stood silently, bowed to me then beckoned me forward, further into the temple.

My acceptance offering had been placed on a large table, deep inside the temple. Surrounded by candlelight we walked to where it had been placed. Gavriel stood to my right side and asked me about its construction, its meaning, its purpose, and asked me to explain my work.

Have you ever been told to do a task? Something you know will take a lot of your time, something especially time-consuming, something at first you might not want to do? The more you take time, more you pursue the idea, the less the thing becomes laborious, more special. That's where I sat with my acceptance. It had become a labour of love for me. Initially stuck for ideas, I had simply collected animal skins from hunting, preparing them, storing them, waiting for an idea. As I collected the skins, I'd shown patience, thoughts running through my head of the structure needed to place them all together.

Rai had taught us that patience in hunting allows us to prevail. The different animal skins I'd stitched together showed skill in the hunting of these different animals, but also the beauty in combining all Rai's creatures together.

Within the patchwork of the skins I'd placed different objects, seen through small openings just big enough to allow viewing, but not too large to allow items placed inside to fall out and be lost. Inside I'd placed a small carved dragon, similar to the larger creation I'd carved on the tree benches in the classroom and several stones, all marked in different ways, which I'd collected from all parts of the world I knew. Stones I'd gathered from as far as the wastelands, trying to show diversity in my thoughts, travelling with Rai's blessing, allowing me always to return. Finally, placed inside were small glistening glass orbs purchased from Barbarrow's market, made by craftsmen in the Banclian territory, beautiful once turned to capture light placed on them. My offering complete, I hoped both Rai and dragon would see the time I'd spent making it, as well as lessons learnt from its construction showing my commitment to our colony.

Truthfully it was a small, fur-lined, stitched-together box, containing things I'd found or bought. But it was far more than that.

It showed that if you have something to achieve, something to learn, you must tackle it with all you have, search for the thing that makes you proud, find yourself in your work, and always hope for acceptance in that field. This small gift showed in the small things placed inside it that I'd travelled, I'd learnt, I'd grown, I'd matured. I don't think anyone can give more than themselves, and I was in this offering.

Gavriel bowed, beckoning me to follow once again. This time we walked slowly through the temple into the garden complex in between the temple and the temple maidens' building. Here we sat watching the sunrise in silence. Contemplation time, Gavriel stated, and while we sat welcoming the new day into existence, Gavriel just watched me. After an hour of sitting still, Gavriel stood. Pleased to move again I followed him, this time walking more briskly towards the forest classroom. It was still very dark here; early sunlight unable to penetrate the depths of the forest, we walked over to the bench where I'd placed my carving.

The circular tree benches, all carved in time, spiralled outwards, forming seats for all to sit and learn Rai's teachings, read to us over the years by Gavriel himself. My bench already had several completed carvings; now mine, too, sat proudly completed.

A full-length dragon draped itself across the rear of the bench, each mark placed precisely, correctly even, in its making. Years of work it had taken, and more hours than I could tell you I had sat here. A dragon had to be my design; long before I'd even seen a dragon I'd known which carving to choose. Now, not only knowing several dragons but having ridden upon one, this design seemed even more realistic to me, each scale, every talon placed with care. One of Rai's most beautiful deities, placed here for all to see, forever. A symbol of power, strength, knowledge, something that all should reach for, seldom accomplished by most, but hopefully something to prove my worth to Rai.

Gavriel spent a long time staring at the carving. I knew he'd watched all White Banner students while carving their pieces, but he seemed to view this today as if it was the first time he'd seen this bench; a fact I knew wasn't true. He observed today with a judge's eye, a teacher's look, a mentor's glance. Today was different in lots of ways, a fact dawning on my thoughts.

Next was the part of the day I'd dreaded for a while; although students kept their trials of the day normally to themselves, occasionally someone spoke of the fighting trial.

As we walked over to the arena only entered for fight training, I remembered conversations about the beating some had received here. White Banner students often became training partners for warrior priests, allowing practice, showing tactical skills, and more recently we'd trained heavily here working on the magic power we'd just learnt about. Stationed around the arena in racks stood staves, wooden swords, pikes and all manner of training weapons. As we centred in the circle where we now stood, I wondered which to rush for when Gavriel gave his instructions.

Smiling, Gavriel sat down.

"With recent events, Wicker, I have no doubt you have become very adept at training," he said. "Fighting skills have been learnt over many terms within this forest," I know, he continued. "However, more pressing matters you have been tasked with, so let's see how that is coming along." Still smiling, he motioned for me to sit opposite him, and placing myself down into the soft sand there I wondered how strong I had become in the magic I'd learnt. Moving objects had been a rapid, easier skill I'd picked up, so I showed Gavriel the ease with which I could move some of the training weapons from their stands to where we sat. This not only looked impressive, but also showed that I'd progressed from the small stones we all moved these days with incantations running through our minds. Gavriel asked for more, though, himself moving the weapons back to their stands from whence they came just as easily as I had.

"Use the power you hold within you, Wicker. If in trouble, can you defend yourself at a moment's notice?" he asked. He whirled suddenly up from the floor, twisting himself completely, momentarily seeming inhuman as he launched to where I sat. I felt the glow of my necklace always these days, somehow there, resonating within me, with moments like this far stronger a bond between it and me.

Bright red light burst forth from the charm and the forest canopy above glowed with dappled sunlight, enhanced by a raging red light. Time itself gave way to the light's presence and Gavriel, although I knew was moving quickly, now appeared to be travelling at a snail's pace. Before I could honestly think about an incantation, I was repeating one in my head, words already forming into sentences, sentences forming phrases, repeating to give it an actual structure to grow, and before I realised it, Gavriel was held firm, frozen in place in midair, feeling as if trapped within the red glow itself, his expression told by his eyes, which were the only part of himself he could appear to move.

He didn't speak, and without pain he simply remained motionless, stopped in his tracks whilst in his attack.

The incantation was a basic one, somehow applied without conscious thought, quickly. The charm held in my necklace, once more being at one with me, stopping harm, stopped fear, growing stronger. The charm and I had an understanding, as if we both grew together, nothing surely could harm us now.

After several circumferences of Gavriel and muttering another incantation, the light diminished, faded all around us. Gavriel fell harder than we expected and as I rushed over to him to help him up, we laughed out loud. "Training has indeed increased your fighting skills, young Wicker," Gavriel said, rubbing his leg as he stood. "I must learn that one," he commented as we walked back towards the temple.

"I have watched you grow from a small child, Wicker. I have taught you many things over the years, but every day you continue to teach me as well." Gavriel and I walked and talked. "You have overcome many things, Wicker, and today you stand in the presence of Rai, ready to become a warrior priest, to serve your god, your people, your life in the best way a young man possibly can. I believe you are ready. How do you feel?"

A strange question. If someone asks you how you feel, how do you normally respond? A quick reply, a happenstance gesture, maybe. Standing there in front of Gavriel, right here and now, I honestly felt ready, scared but ready. I had learnt so much, he was right, with so much more to learn, I thought. I had barely touched the surface of magic recently found. Growing up, I knew I'd always wanted to be a warrior priest, and the day was finally here. A huge part of me felt disappointed that my father, my sister and my best friend wouldn't see the day, though. So, with a humble heart, I told Gavriel these feelings. "Another reason to know you are truly ready, Wicker," he smiled, and we continued to the temple.

꙳

If I'd worried about the fighting earlier, I'd have swapped it back again for the next part of the day. Full warrior ceremonial dress was complicated. Gavriel, after walking me back to the temple, now left to get prepared himself, leaving me with several temple maidens, scrubbing my hair, skin, until I thought I'd never been so clean. Layer upon layer of cloth, tightly wrapped around me, bound down with laced cord, held everything in place so tightly that I wondered if

I'd be able to walk to acceptance ledge after they'd finished. Ceremonial shoes were laced just as tightly with a full headdress too, eventually finding me standing in front of a mirror staring at a stranger.

This was hopefully the last time I would wear full white clothing; after becoming a warrior priest, the colour would change to white and black, showing acceptance, showing rank amidst the colony. I was glad to be finished, also glad I'd not had to complete this look alone, as I wouldn't have even been able to bend as low as my feet in all these clothes. Before long Gavriel arrived, dressed also ceremoniously, and once more we walked together from the temple; waiting outside were a group of friends, my warrior priest escort. With music already playing we started the journey towards acceptance ledge. Warrior priests ranked on either side of me, very little was said, a proud moment for me and my friends too; no words were needed.

Welcoming another warrior priest into the ranks gave all here a moment to hold their heads up high, and as we walked, large numbers of colony members greeted us, waved, occasionally throwing flowers in our path, celebrating another great day for our colony.

With each step we took we seemed to gain more followers walking behind our ever-growing group. I was not sure if they turned out especially for me or for the dragons who promised to be at my acceptance leap, something never seen before. The distance from the temple to my acceptance was a long walk, taking twice as long today due to the slow speed at which I had to walk in these clothes, fast movements being impossible, time, though, which allowed me to soak up the atmosphere.

Soon, after rounding a final bend in the path, I saw, sitting upright, proud as ever, my friends Drathlo and Flanhlin, two of the mightiest dragons ever seen, who waited near the front of the arena next to acceptance ledge. As I grew closer I could hear the music playing louder, musicians hidden now behind them, the chatter of dozens of people interspersed with the notes of the sound being played. Bowing as low as I could physically go, I showed respect to my dragon friends, thanking them for coming as they said they would.

Rumbling, their approval of my thanks vibrated the ground I stood on, a familiar experience to me now, knowing it to be a pleasant thing. Flanhlin, leaning forward, his head low to the ground, spoke briefly to ask my health, and that he would stay and watch the ceremony, speaking to me afterwards. Drathlo lowered her head, too, graceful and elegant, proving her queenly status. Walking now next to Gavriel I entered the acceptance area. People gasped as Drathlo and Flanhlin raised their wings fully open, aloft, in unison, making it look as though I'd walked through two huge living dragon doors, closing behind me the outside world, leaving only the people inside the arena to bask in the sheer beauty of the dragons. Glamour tingled in the air, with shouts of amazement rising up from the crowd occasionally.

Making my way to the centre of the arena, I had my first chance to stop, to take in my surroundings. I'd sat in this arena many times, been part of other White students' ceremonies, but today felt special, felt perfect, my time. Spotting Mother sitting next to Ivan on the front row, I simply bowed low again, my respect for her unparalleled.

Sensing the love from her looking back at me I turned to await Gavriel's instructions.

I've cried over many things in life; listening to Gavriel speak now made me very close to crying again. Gavriel always spoke about his students at this time, normally celebrating their journey from a child growing up in the colony to now, listing their achievements, talking of their strengths. Gavriel did all this and more. "Wicker," he said, "has grown from a young boy into a man. This past year alone he's faced more turmoil than most see in their lifetime, has continued to grow and become a stronger person for it. Wicker loves and cares deeply for all his family and friends, and serves his colony like no other does, even better than I," he added. "Wicker learns new skills daily to protect us all, a mighty warrior already, tough and resilient, knowing humility, kindness and knowledge which will lead him to a better world. Missing family and friends would be proud of the man standing here today, so I ask all present to stand and give thanks to Wicker."

I think a tear may have fallen as the crowd, as one, rose to clap and cheer, and with the roaring of the dragons accompanying the cheering I hastened my steps to the edge of acceptance ledge to hide this. A single final glance back to Mother was all I took, then I threw my acceptance gift forward from shaking hands, watching it drop away, soon to disappear into the swollen white clouds billowing hundreds of metres below me. As soon as its sight had left me, I stepped forward, plummeting downwards far quicker than I was expecting.

Trying to stay upright was impossible; falling at this speed I found it hard to maintain vision properly, the wind rushing so fast, making water stream from my eyes. The thick clothes I wore saved my body now, helping me overcome the efforts of the wind to rip them from me, in the process keeping me warmer too. I hadn't realised the coldness of the wind here and was thankful now that the temple maidens had placed so many layers on me. My mind temporarily took me backwards, remembering flying on the back of Flanhlin over Lerandra mountain range, the coldness similar but hopefully not that prolonged. Entering the clouds that seconds before were hundreds of metres away, I tumbled head over feet, spinning, trying to reach out for something, anything.

Occasional glimpses of colours, so varied, from green, red, yellow, every colour you could think of span past. Noises too, aside from the ripping noise of the air current passing my face; screeching, rumbling, scratching even.

With limited visibility within the cloud base, I couldn't tell how high I was, how far I'd travelled, or even how long I'd been falling. All I could tell was that I was still falling and I prayed to Rai to save me.

Sudden blackness, not from my vision but a large, blurred mass, approaching through the cloud, shaped smaller than I'd thought a dragon could be. As my eyes reached for the shape, the outlined edges of what approached, I was sent spiralling sideways as another black shape hit me from behind. I was sent spinning again, this time struggling to catch my breath, such was the force of the impact I'd just received. A terrible noise filled every sense; if you could imagine seeing noise, it seemed I did right now, loud, abrupt, painful even, making me raise both my hands to cover my ears, and eyes. Still falling I tried again to see anything around me.

This time the impact made me spin back the other way; another black shape had collided hard into me. If I noticed the bleeding then I can't remember, but the pain started to increase, making me notice that something wasn't right with my left leg.

Just as I started to panic, wondering how much further I could fall this way, a third impact took me from above, forcing me downwards this time. Noticing that I somehow now was travelling slower but still downward, I managed to open my eyes fully. Grasped upside down, I realised I hung from a black sentient being, very similar to a dragon but much, much smaller. Sharp, black talons pierced my left leg completely; it held me tight in its grasp, emanating a foul odour, screaming as it flew, as if the creature itself was in pain. As I tried to struggle the creature stared straight at me. Instant nausea, a feeling of uneasiness encroached every pore of my body. The creature swung me from side to side, spiralling ever downwards. Panic took hold of me completely now and, trying to reach for my necklace buried within my ceremonial dress, I shook, trying to release its grip on me.

A sudden whip from its tail caught me around the back of my head and the last thing I recall was losing consciousness. As the darkness took over me once more, I realised I'd been caught, but not by the dragon I'd hoped it would be.

On waking I found myself in a crudely fashioned wooden crate. Trying to move my legs caused severe pain, and I cried out, unable to stop myself. The crate being moved, carried on I knew not what. Hardly any light entered the small gaps in between the wooden slats, and what there was didn't highlight anything of importance. Nausea still overwhelmed me, my head was spinning, swellings all over my body already appearing as I checked, trying to find out where exactly the pain came from. My left leg was my biggest problem; I was unable to move it without an excruciating pain shooting up my entire body, and even then, movement was limited when I tried. A large wound had obviously pierced straight through the leg from the creature's talons that had held me; dark sticky blood, not fully dried, caked my clothes, and I knew it was a severe injury.

Wave upon wave of strange, foreign sensations covered my very being. Unable to shift comfortably either physically or mentally, I felt trapped both literally and metaphorically. I couldn't think properly, somehow unable to function here and now. I'd obviously been beaten but had no recollection of events after falling and being grabbed by that black creature. The thoughts of the day mixed, I wondered what had happened, what was going to happen to me. Eventually the crate I dwelt in crashed down onto the floor, making me scream again in pain, as the action rocked the entire wooden frame of the cage. A foul-smelling liquid, mud-like in its consistency entered through the wooden slats on the bottom of the cage, the floor obviously heavily trodden, soaked with water, or what I hoped was water.

Uncomfortable, nauseous, confused and in pain, I started to shout for help, unsure if that was the best thing to do, but currently my only option. The water thrown at me was just as foul-smelling as the floor's liquid, and was accompanied by laughter I was sure, but no speech, no help to be gathered here. Shaking with an uncontrollable force willing itself onto me I again tried to turn; the surge of pain once more blotted my senses to almost a level I couldn't contain. Turning back to my original position, barely able to restrain the fear I held, tears fell once more.

I think I slept for a while, or maybe dropping into unconsciousness again was probably the real outcome. I awoke, still cramped within my wooden cage, pain and nausea my only companions, staring once more out of the slats, trying to see, trying anything to find out where I was. Placed above me and all around were several other crates, some piled high on top of each other, some individually away from others. I wondered if it was now nighttime as the darkness here seemed to permeate everywhere, into everything, but at last my eyes were starting to adjust to the lower light levels.

It was then, whilst staring forward towards another wooden crate, that I looked straight into the eyes of my best friend, Peshy. He stared blankly back towards me. A sudden rush, exhilaration to see someone I'd lost, thought dead. Calling his name, louder and louder, again and again. Giving no response, he turned away from the front of the crate he occupied, and I questioned my own mind as to what I saw; was it really him?

Suddenly my world went from despair, to hope, and seeing Peshy once more, back to losing all hope.

Realisation broke within me as to what had happened. Rai had forsaken me, I'd failed. I'd fallen.